OPERATION
IN
PROGRESS

S.H.A.D.O.

TECHNICAL OPERATIONS MANUAL

Chris Thompson
& Andrew Clements   Writers

Chris Thompson   Illustrations

Christina Logan
Graham Bleathman   Additional
                     illustrations

ANDERSON
ENTERTAINMENT

CONTENTS

From the desk of:
COMMANDER EDWARD STRAKER

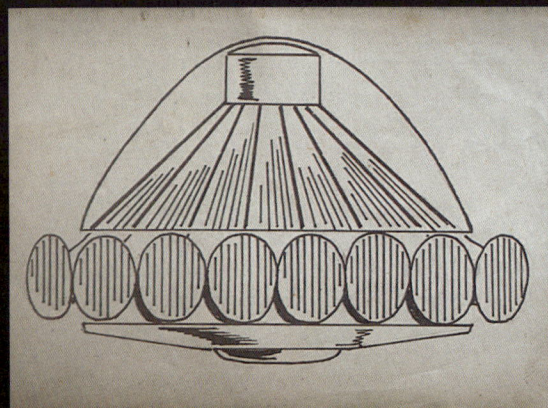

S H A D O

SUPREME HEADQUARTERS . . . . . .

ALIEN DEFENCE ORGANISATION . . .

F O R E W O R D . . . .

If you are holding this book in your hands then it means that your life, as you know it, is over. You have undergone the most rigorous physical and psychological training, you have studied to some of the highest academic standards, and you have proven your dedication and commitment to the preservation of human life. All these tests and trials have allowed you to gain access to the book you are holding, the history and details of the largest and most secretive operation mankind has ever undertaken.

This book contains a full breakdown of SHADO, from our secret bases on the Earth and the Moon, the equipment we use, essential personnel, and everything we currently know about the alien threat at your clearance level. In the wrong hands it would almost certainly compromise the entire organisation. As such, when not being read, it should remain in the destructor case it has been issued in.

Ultimately, we recognise that you are sacrificing the option for you to lead a normal life, a sacrifice that no-one will ever hear about. That is the point of SHADO – because of us, the average everyday citizen of the world will be able to lead their lives, never having to fear their loved ones being taken or know how close they've come to annihilation. But know that I, and the operatives around you, acknowledge the sacrifices you have made to get this far, and that you have the respect and support of the entire organisation.

WELCOME TO SHADO.

COMMANDER EDWARD STRAKER . . . . . .

THE BIRTH OF SHADO

For thousands of years, there had been stories of visitors from the stars, lights in the sky and people vanishing into thin air, but it wasn't until the end of the Second World War that the governments of the world started to realise that there may be more to those old stories than originally thought. As our own technology developed, encounters with Unidentified Flying Objects would not only increase but could now be recorded and documented. From 1952, film, photos and eyewitness testimony started to be gathered and collated by the US Air Force under the aegis of 'Project Blue Book', alongside similar programmes underway worldwide.

By 1970, a definitive pattern had started to emerge. People were going missing in increasing numbers, while suspected sightings of UFOs had drastically risen. However, without hard evidence to connect the two, it was difficult for any form of defence programme to be taken forward. This all changed one night in England when Royal Navy officer Peter Carlin survived the abduction of his sister with a clear photographic negative of the alien craft undeveloped in his camera.

Once passed on to the US Air Force, General James Henderson and Colonel Edward Straker immediately began to reach out to key governments to gather international support for their proposed response. However, after landing in England and en route to meet the British Prime Minister, their motorcade was attacked by an unidentified aircraft. The incident left the British Minister of Defence dead and General Henderson in a critical condition, while providing the final piece of the puzzle that the USAF needed to convince the world of the UFO threat. The aliens WERE real, they WERE aducting our people and they WOULD use extreme force to protect their agenda.

A few weeks later, at a top secret international summit, a unanimous vote was passed to take the first steps to creating an international defence agency to protect the Earth. Supreme Headquarters Alien Defence Organisation – SHADO – was born.

EARLY YEARS

It was decided that SHADO would operate in complete secrecy and have total autonomy over matters of Earth defence. The attack on Henderson's motorcade had made it clear that the aliens were watching developments on Earth and were willing to take pre-emptive action. As such, SHADO's earliest operations were largely low-key intelligence gathering – researching the ongoing sightings and abductions, tracking UFO flight patterns as they ingressed and egressed the Solar System, and investigating the aftermath of attacks.

During the organisation's first decade in operation, potential recruits were approached from all walks of life and rigorously vetted, undergoing physical testing in some of the harshest conditions. Only the top percentage were considered for the next stage: extreme psychological testing. And only after passing this stage would the true purpose of their recruitment be revealed.

As the years went on, SHADO's order of battle was being designed and tested. These included a corps of armoured land vehicles that could be quickly and discreetly deployed at an incident site; a fleet of aircraft-carrying submarines to intercept and bring down alien craft within Earth's atmosphere; and finally, the first indefinitely-manned base on the surface of the Moon, which would act as a screen intended to bar aliens' access to the Earth.

SHADO's development into a
fully-functional organisation did
not come easy, even within the
envisaged ten-year timeframe.
The new operatives were working
18-hour days, seven days a week,
to prepare the sprawling network
of bases, test and evaluate the new
vehicles and craft, and refine the
new technologies needed to run
the organisation. All the while,
the number of abductees rose
unopposed. The aliens were clearly
aware of what humanity was
planning and made various attempts
to undermine SHADO's development
through direct attacks on personnel
and bases. They seemingly didn't take
humanity's attempt at resistance too
seriously, either through lack of
information or possibly hubris.

By 1980, it was finally time to fight
back. It was on the day that SHADO
finally put its defences into motion
that they were able to down a UFO
and capture an alien alive. While
the creature did not last long in our
atmosphere, it gave us our greatest
glimpse at whom we were fighting.
The creature was nearly human
but sterile, with signs of genetic
degradation. Its lungs were full of
a breathing liquid from prolonged
space travel which had stained its skin
green. Its organs were a mismatch
of multiple transplants, some human,
but crucially the heart was a direct
tissue match to Leila Carlin.

While SHADO's resistance certainly couldn't have come as a shock to the aliens, it is clear that they have been forced to rethink their strategy. UFOs now arrive in greater numbers, and direct actions against SHADO's operation have steadily risen. Over the past few years, our understanding of the aliens has slowly expanded as every encounter gives us a greater insight into their motives and capabilities.

At time of writing, SHADO's main goal is to hold the line. With little evidence to the contrary, it seems Earth is their main source of body parts, and every UFO SHADO stops from returning to the alien planet sets their species one step closer to extinction. While this is most certainly a long game, it will be far from an easy fight as the aliens will most certainly take increasingly desperate measures before they admit defeat. We must be prepared for this war to get worse before it gets better, and that is where you come in.

DEPARTMENT:
SHADO HQ

1

HARLINGTON -STRAKER STUDIOS

Harlington-Straker Studios is a modest film studio located in Wessex, just south-west of London. As the cover for the most expensive international military operation in history, no expense was spared in creating the facsimile of an average workaday filming studio with all the necessary facilities, but one deliberately designed to remain overshadowed by major studios while remaining outside the pockets of low-budget clients. This keeps HS Studios from drawing unnecessary attention while providing an effective cover – as far as the general public is concerned, HS Studios is just a series of offices and soundstages where average movies are made.

A small number of the staff at HS Studios are aware of the subterranean complex below, with many of the guards, porters and set builders actually serving as undercover SHADO security who provide additional protection for the facility.

This elaborate cover offers many benefits. It allows unusual deliveries and operations to be easily explained away as film props or bespoke equipment, while analysts have concluded that positioning SHADO's head of operations near a metropolitan area provides a measure of safety from alien attacks.

STUDIO HEAD

Commander Straker serves as the public face of the studio, attending the occasional press junket and sometimes hosting studio tours to offer plausible deniability as to his actual role. Much of the film work by HS Studios is conducted by the company's 'other' partner, 'Harlington', a manufactured identity used to disguise a small team of analysts who endeavour to choose those movies that best help to maintain SHADO's cover.

Much of the command staff serve dual roles between SHADO and the studio, with Colonels Foster and Lake acting as producers and Colonel Freeman serving as part of the studio's acting repertoire. Many of their movie responsibilities are delegated to their personal secretaries, with the Colonels stepping in from time to time to help enforce their cover.

The majority of HS Studios' employees are (fortunately) unaware of what goes on beneath them, and remain free to conduct the day-to-day activities expected of a busy film studio.

INTERIOR

Unlike the elaborate studio 80 feet above, SHADO HQ is a much more spartan affair, made up of five levels of offices, research laboratories and a large scale vehicle hangar. At the top of the base lies SHADO control, from which the entire organisation is run; every monitoring station, training site, airfield, seaport and Moonbase reports to this station. Upon exiting the elevator or stairs from above, an orderly will confirm your identity before allowing you to pass or escorting you to where you need to go.

A Control room

B Security hub

C Restaurant

D Medical centre

E Lounge

F Reception and induction

G Psychoanalytic department

H Computer room

I ID check

J Garage

LEVEL A
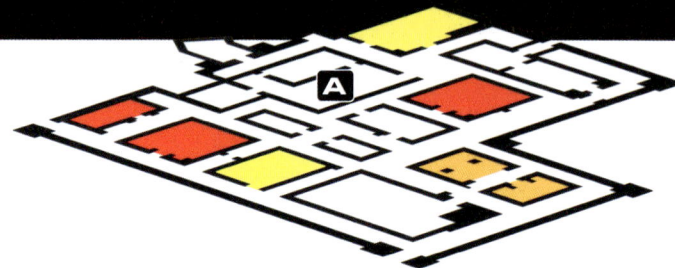

LEVEL B
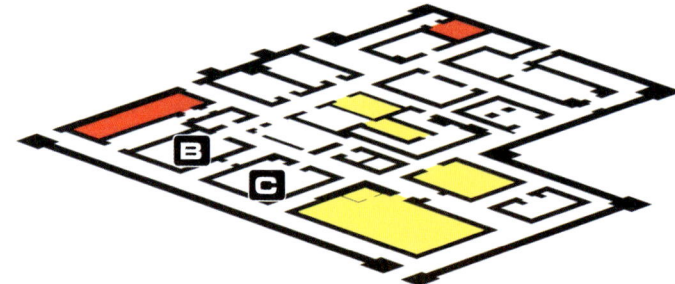

LEVEL C
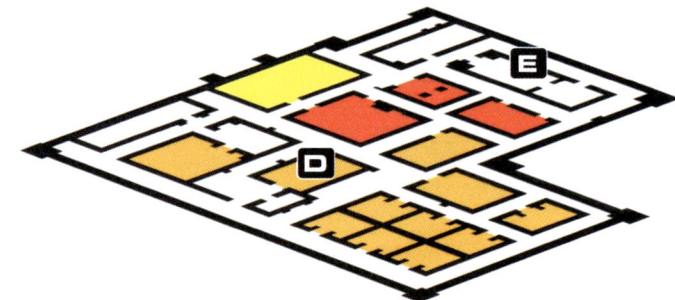

LEVEL D
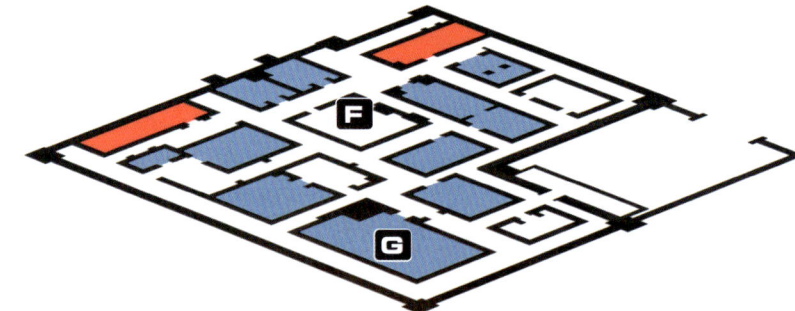

LEVEL E
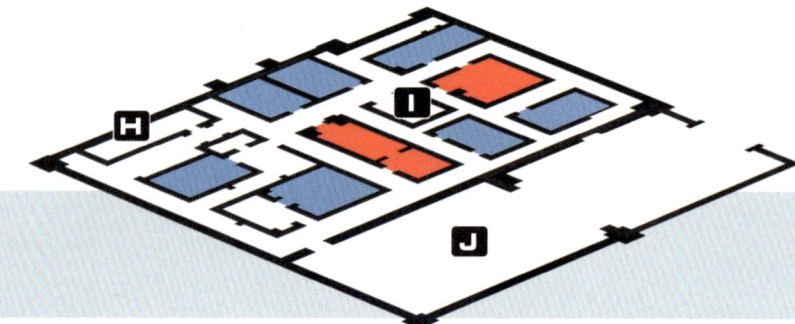

TRAINING AREAS

Given the extremely high risks involved during direct encounters with the aliens, SHADO operatives are trained to the highest level of combat excellence, whether in the air, land space or sea. Simulators and shooting ranges are used daily to prevent skills fading.

LABORATORY SPACES

Every known or speculative alien sighting ever recorded has been stored within the vaults of SHADO Headquarters. This enables constant research into the strategy and tactics of past incursions, allowing for the ongoing development of countermeasures by analysts. UFO wreckage as well as damaged SHADO equipment are all brought back here for study.

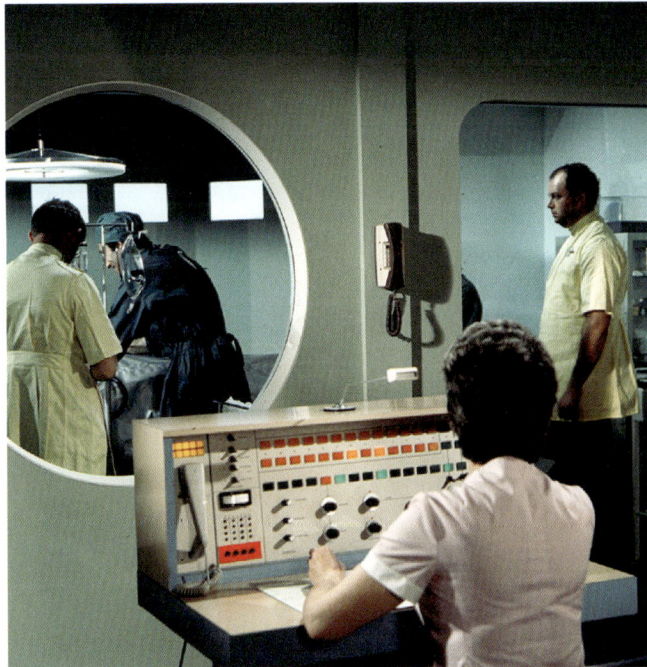

MEDICAL CENTRE

This section's primary function is to assess the health and well-being of all SHADO operatives, providing frequent physical and mental check-ups of all staff. However, the Medical Centre is in constant readiness to receive aliens, alive or dead, for examination. As knowledge of their physiology increases, the medical section can be adapted to accommodate them.

CONFERENCE AND HEARING SUITES

While most administrative meetings are held off site to protect the location of the base, conferences are sometimes undertaken at HQ; these include after-action debriefings and, when necessary, court-martials. There are also facilities for the temporary holding of civilians that may need to give testimony before being given memory-loss drugs.

SHADO CONTROL

Located at the top of the base (but beneath HS Studios), SHADO Control is the nerve centre of the organisation. All information from external sources is collated here, providing the Commander with a constant up-to-the-minute situation report. This fluid global picture allows for quick, direct responses to any developing situation.

The room is split into two separate areas: a raised area housing the main computer system, maintained and operated by a team of expert computer technicians, under the supervision of Colonel Lake; and the lower section, which acts as a communications hub, with stations relaying information and instructions to SHADO forces.

In theory, this control room should be able to survive even the most devastating alien attack; however, in the event that SHADO Control is rendered inoperable, command and control automatically shifts to Moonbase, or, in the upcoming months, SHADO's new LA operation.

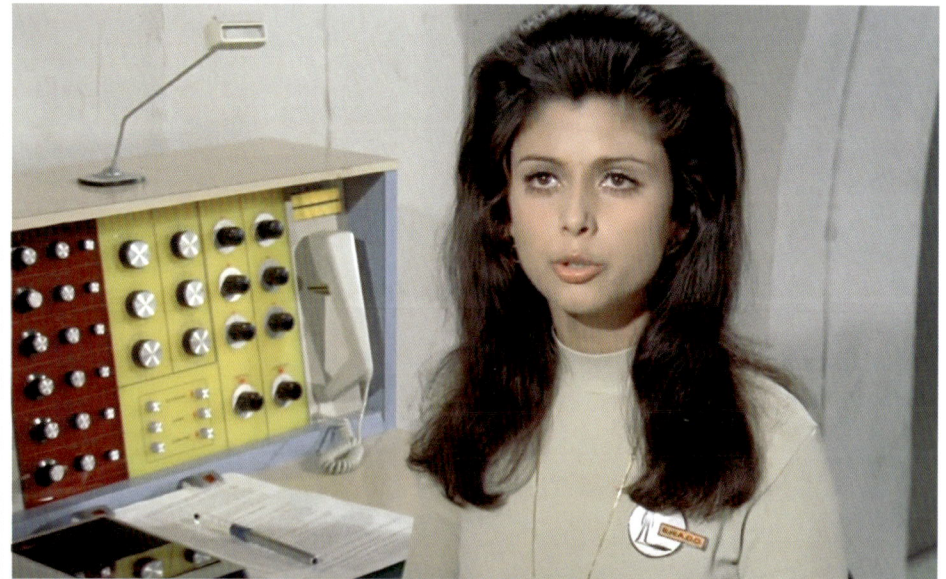

CONTROLLER'S DESK

While overall command of SHADO is in the hands of the Commanders and Colonels, the organisation's day-to-day operations are in the hands of the duty officer at the controller's desk. The current lead controller is Lieutenant Ford, who has been with SHADO since its inception.

COMMUNICATIONS OFFICERS

Below the controller, a team of communications officers pass on reports and information to be programmed onto the master computer.

VIP RECONFIGURATION

In certain instances, the room can be moderately reconfigured to accommodate VIPs, usually members of the International Space Commission or foreign security dignitaries who may wish to see how their investment in SHADO is being spent.

MAPS AND CHARTS

The centre of the room can be quickly reconfigured with tables and charts in order to allow the Commander to oversee and direct operations. A comprehensive library of maps is held on site, and key locations can be brought up to the control room within minutes of determining a UFO's designated landing site.

A **X1 COMPUTER BANKS**
Used for coordinating information between SHADO stations and interpreting data from SHADO's satellite network.

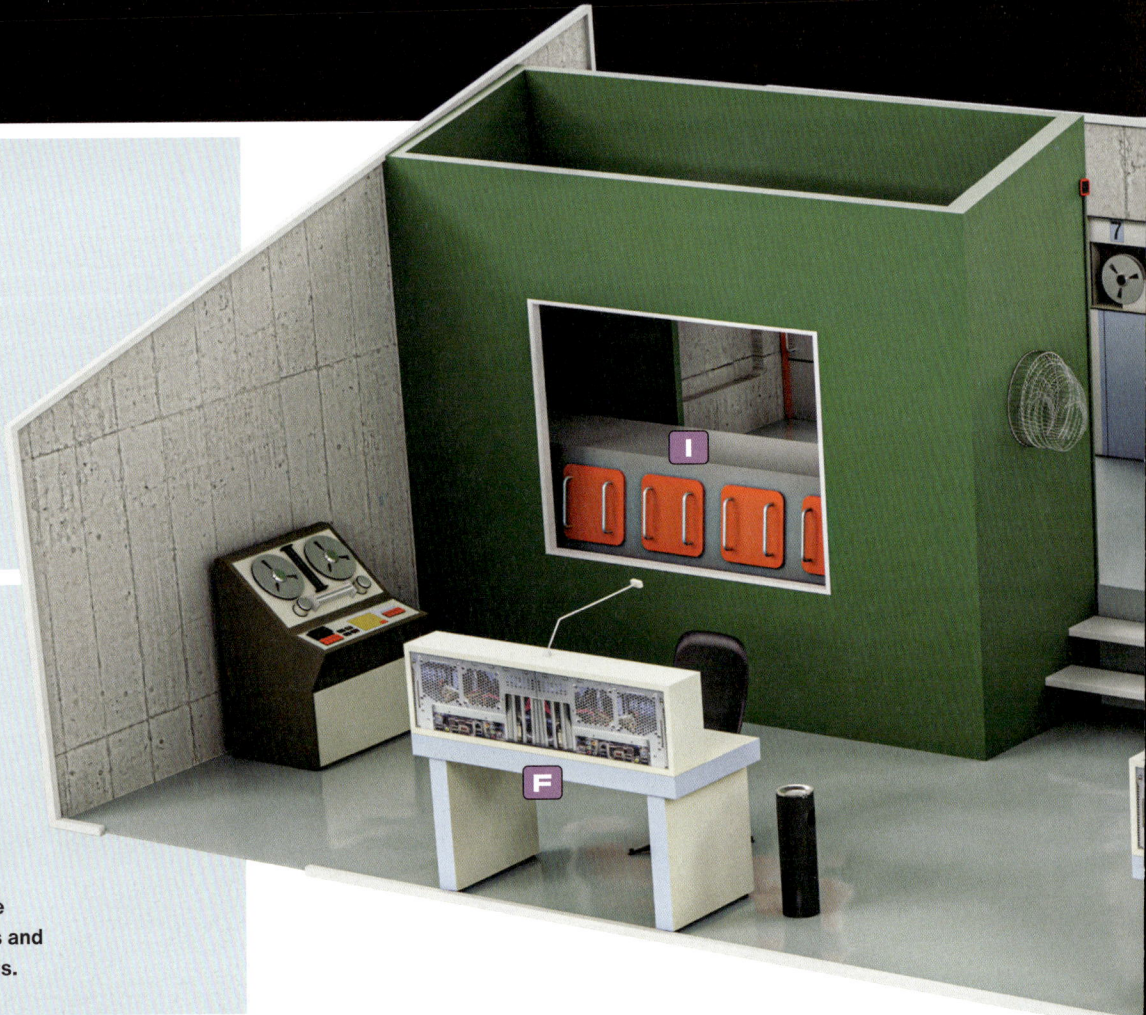

B **PRINTOUT STATION**
Used to decode telemetry into printed text or images; similarly, documents can be loaded into these machines and transmitted to other stations.

I

F

C **INTERNAL COMMUNICATIONS**
This station primarily deals with the running of SHADO HQ itself, keeping track of duty rosters, paging personnel and coordinating with security forces detailed to HS Studios.

D **LIBRARY STATION**
A comprehensive set of data cards electronically storing reports and archival data. An input keypad allows for the correct data card to be accessed within moments.

E **CONTROLLER'S STATION**
The primary controller's station with a direct line to Moonbase, the Skydiver fleet and other SHADO forces in the field. A monitor allows the controller to relay situation reports to the Commander and pass on information and commands.

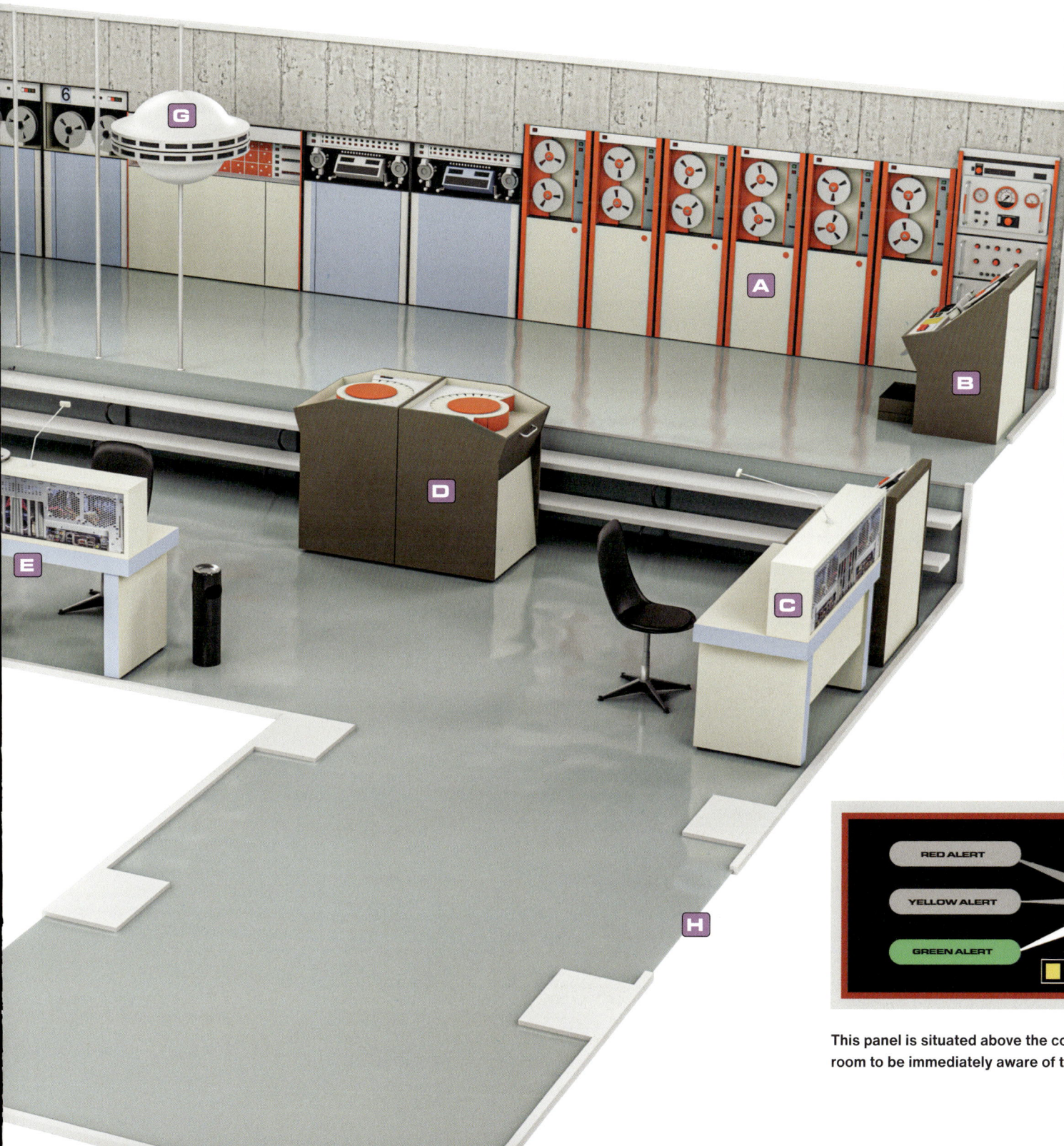

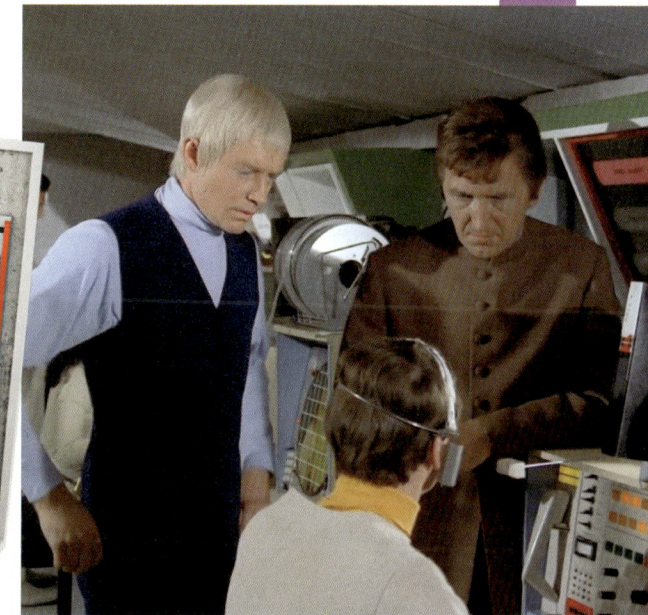

F SECONDARY CONTROLLER'S STATION
The secondary station has a similar function to the primary station, allowing the secondary controller to handle the administrative and generalised duties of the SHADO organisation when the primary station is dealing with an unfolding crisis or situation. Both stations are interchangeable.

G Space Intruder Detector (SID) primary speaker

H Exit to the Commander's office

I Electrical circuits

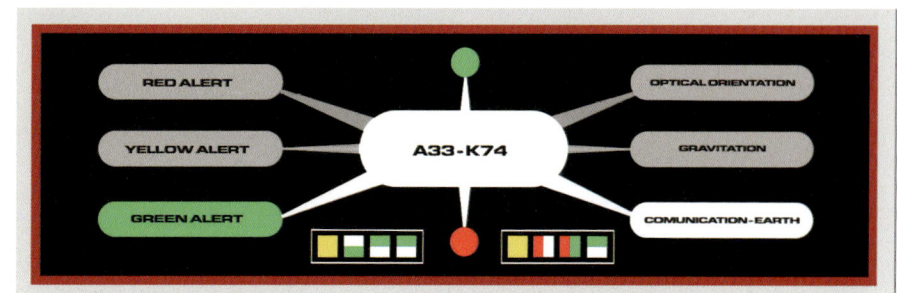

This panel is situated above the controller's desk, allowing for anyone entering the control room to be immediately aware of the communication and alert status of the organisation.

COMMANDER'S OFFICE

Located adjacent to SHADO Control is the Commander's office, a quiet area where Commander Straker and other command staff can conduct their business away from the hustle and bustle of SHADO Control. In many ways, this room is the real centre of SHADO, where all the key life-or-death decisions are made.

H COMMANDER'S DESK
The Commander's desk utilises the latest in videophone technology, allowing the Commander a direct link to any SHADO installation or civilian line.

A Desk

B Wall display

C Document vaporiser

D Drinks dispenser

E Conference table

F Videophone

G ESCAPE SHAFT
Given Commander Straker's inherently suspicious nature, he has had a secret escape shaft fitted within the wall display behind his desk, allowing escape to the surface within moments.

I WALL DISPLAY
This wall features various screens for displaying data, while also showing a small scale model displaying the Moon's current location relative to the Earth. The map screen can be cleared to be used as a whiteboard.

A Desk

B Window to garden area

C Headshots of various
   actors currently
   contracted to HS Studios

D Double-sliding doors

E Trophy wall

SURFACE EXITS

Given the secret nature of the SHADO facility, its various entrances need to be well camouflaged. For this reason, rather than simple hatches or accessways, more theatrical solutions have been employed.

Primary access for SHADO operatives is via the administration building, with lifts built into two of the production offices. Several additional lifts can be found in maintenance sheds that lead to vantage points around the studio.

EXECUTIVE ENTRANCE

In addition to his primary office, Commander Straker also has an office for his film studio work above ground, overseen by his secretary – SHADO operative Miss Ealand. This space not only acts as an office but also includes an elevator to Shado HQ, offering a more formal environment for the Commander to welcome high-ranking officers, diplomats and executives. A comms link and a hidden video screen allow the Commander to be up to date on the ongoing proceedings underground while carrying out his studio duties.

MISS EALAND

Acting as Commander Straker's personal secretary, Miss Ealand's role is to help the Commander balance his responsibilities above and below ground. As she presides over the executive entrance, she also provides ranking SHADO operatives with the relevant briefing material prior to their descent to SHADO HQ.

RECEPTION

Miss Ealand's office doubles as a reception to the Commander's office, with access only granted to a limited number of individuals. For many visitors from within the film industry, this will be as far as they go.

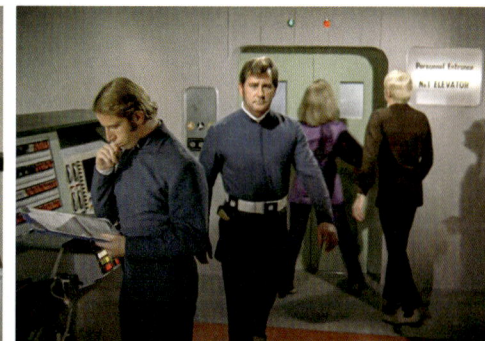

SECURITY CHECKPOINTS

Each surface entrance leads to a checkpoint manned by SHADO security. Here, voiceprint and fingerprint checks are conducted in conjunction with the ID check department on E level to ensure no unauthorised personnel can gain access to the base.

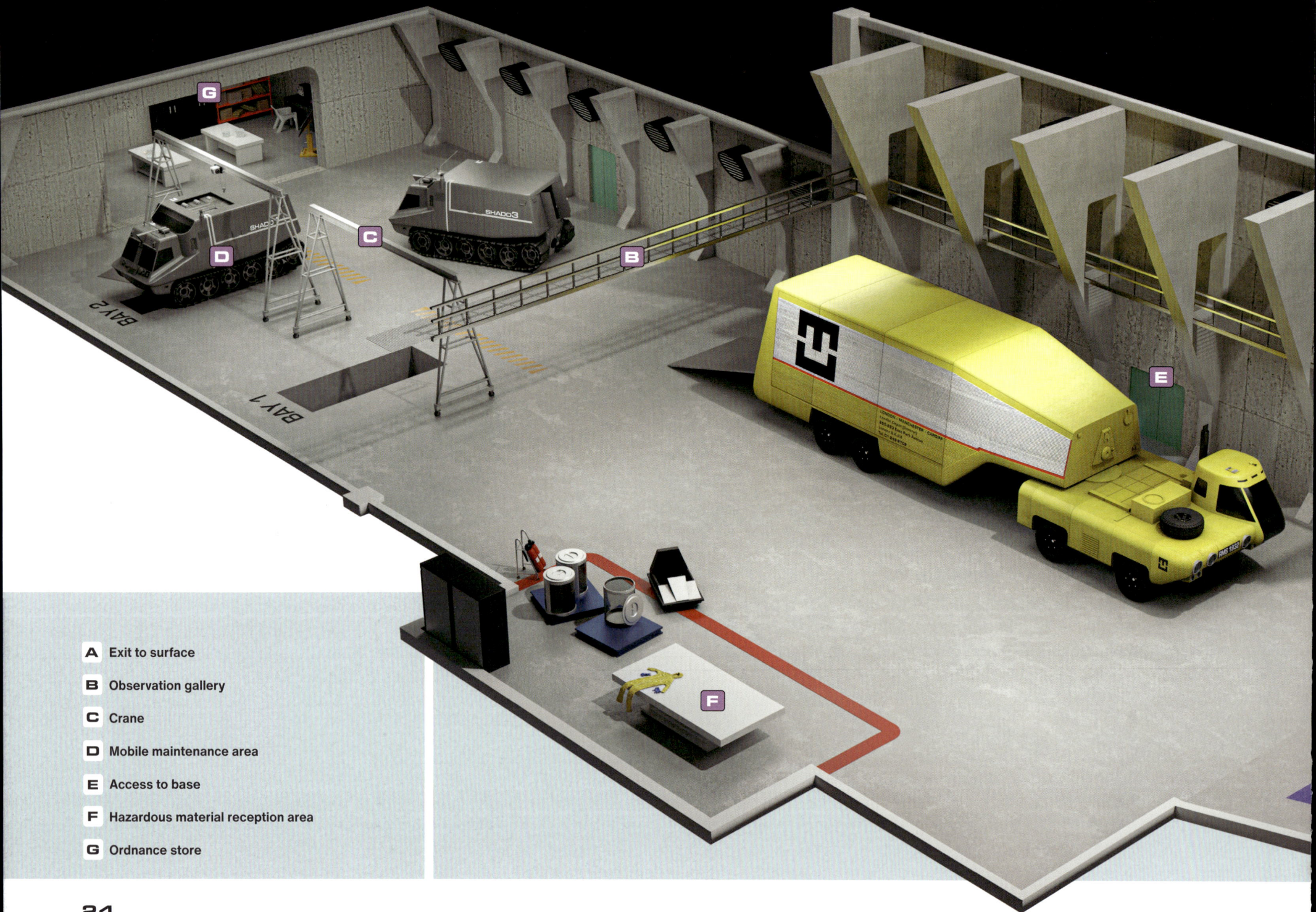

A — Exit to surface

B — Observation gallery

C — Crane

D — Mobile maintenance area

E — Access to base

F — Hazardous material reception area

G — Ordnance store

UNDERGROUND VEHICLE BAY

Concealed on levels D and E is SHADO HQ's extensive vehicle reception and maintenance bay. Here the fleet of SHADO Mobiles are maintained and prepared for transit aboard their carrier vehicles. It also functions as the reception area for alien materials, e.g. debris or bodies, arriving at the base.

When not in use, the carriers are stored in another bay nearer the surface, with their Mobile stowed on board ready for immediate deployment.

The open area of the vehicle bay can be used for research experiments, developing and testing larger weapons, or, in a few instances, can be soaked in a preservative mist to allow UFO debris or fragments to be handled with minimal degradation.

As SHADO's forces continue to improve and expand, it has become necessary to enlarge this area of the base. A new sub-level is in the process of being dug out to free up more space in the reception area.

Access to the garage can be found via two service exits at the rear of the studio. This prevents undue attention being drawn to unusual deliveries which cannot simply be passed off as props and scenery for the film studio. The exit for the SHADO Mobile carriers is built directly into the studio's loading dock and allows the vehicles to leave without suspicion.

The main access tunnel splits off into two separate areas, one leading to the Mobile carrier exit, the other for general traffic terminating in a hidden entrance built within the HS Studios multi-storey car park.

DEPARTMENT:

MOONBASE

MOONBASE

The most ambitious and therefore most expensive arm of the SHADO organisation is the squadron of space fighters that act as the first line of defence against UFO attacks. Central to their operations is Moonbase, a permanent base on the lunar surface that is able to deploy its fleet of Interceptors within minutes of a warning of approaching intruders.

The base itself sits on the Moon's exterior and is thus not exactly a secret. Moonbase is instead listed on many travel charts as a collaborative international military outpost which allows for a generous exclusion zone around the facility.

Five reinforced modules, each given a specific task, surround a central engineering unit which houses the main reactor and life support systems. A small garage level provides an entry and exit point for operatives performing an EVA.

BENEATH THE SURFACE

What makes Moonbase exceptional are the subterranean silos and equipment storage bays built on a scale unseen before (metaphorically and literally) when compared to other lunar programmes, with most other installations usually sufficing with prefabricated modular components. The extent of Moonbase's facilities allows the base's Interceptors and ground vehicles to undergo maintenance and refit in a safe, pressurised atmosphere, in order to maximise efficiency.

PERSONNEL

At any one time, Moonbase is staffed by up to 20 personnel. In the absence of any ranking Commander or Colonel, it is commanded by either Lieutenant Gay Ellis or Lieutenant Nina Barry.

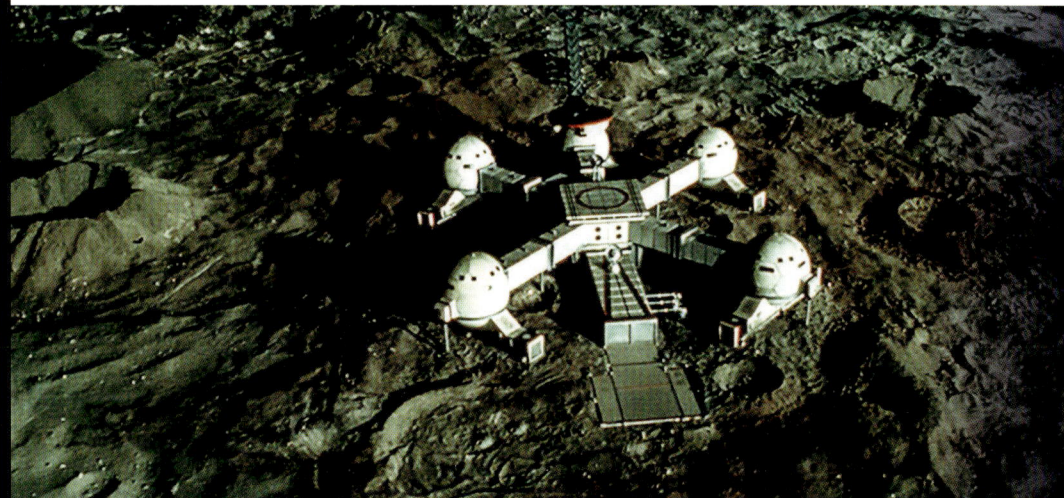

Moonbase was assembled in the foothills of the Montes Caucuses, which offers the base a degree of additional and incidental environmental protection. Any attacking UFOs are required to come in from above, rather than approach low level across the lunar surface.

MOONBASE STRUCTURE

At first glance, the visible surface structure of Moonbase presents itself as one of the largest structures on the Moon, with most other installations restricted to smaller single-use habitation modules. However, Moonbase's reactor can power a much larger installation – plus its subsurface components – almost indefinitely. But such a large surface structure makes for a very tempting target, as reflected in its significant defences.

VERSATILE DESIGN

Moonbase's design is such that, should the need arise, the base can be extended with additional modules and subterranean areas. Plans are under consideration to relocate SHADO's primary operational hub to the Moon in order to improve the security of the organisation, but this plan is largely dependent on being able to improve the interception rate of UFOs.

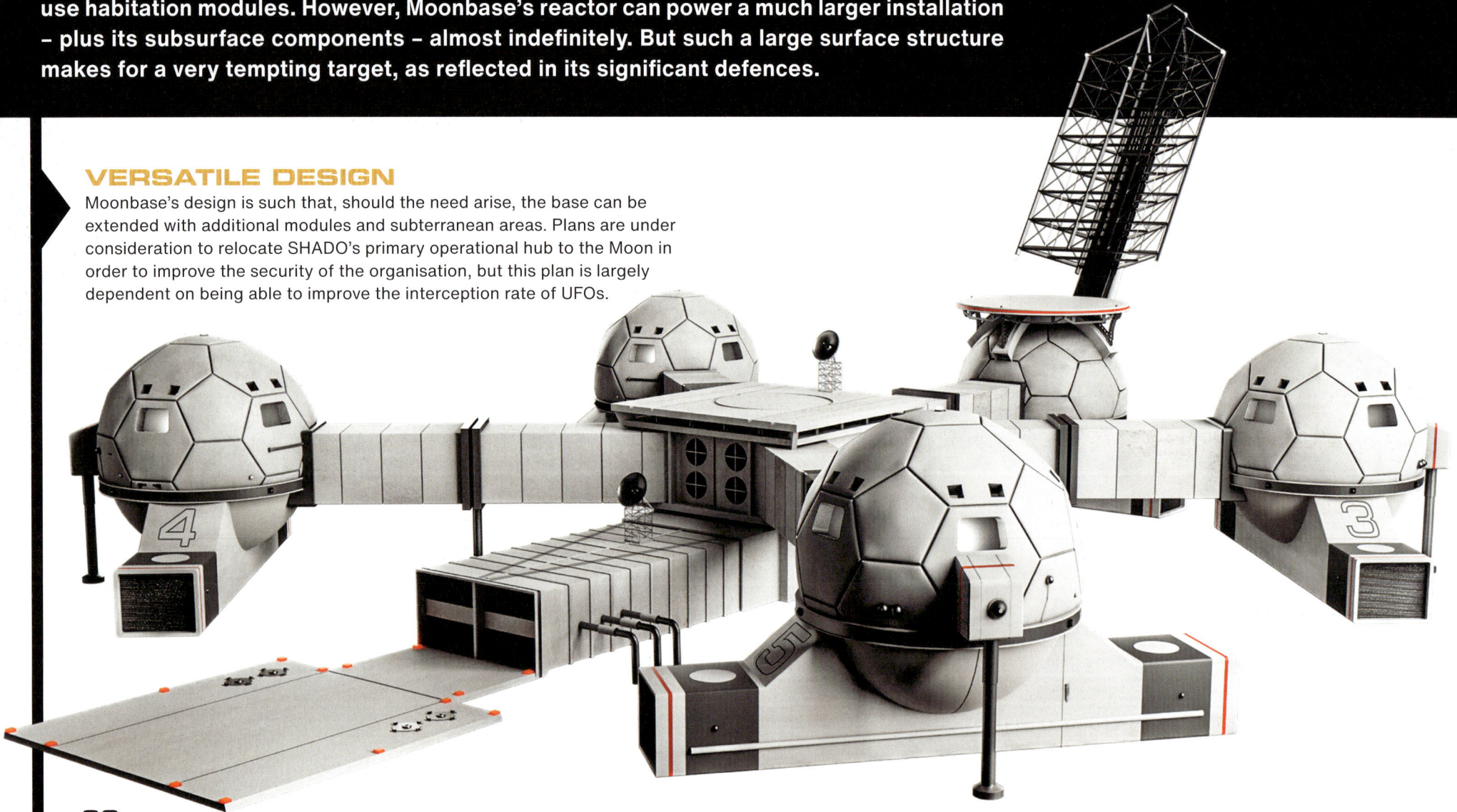

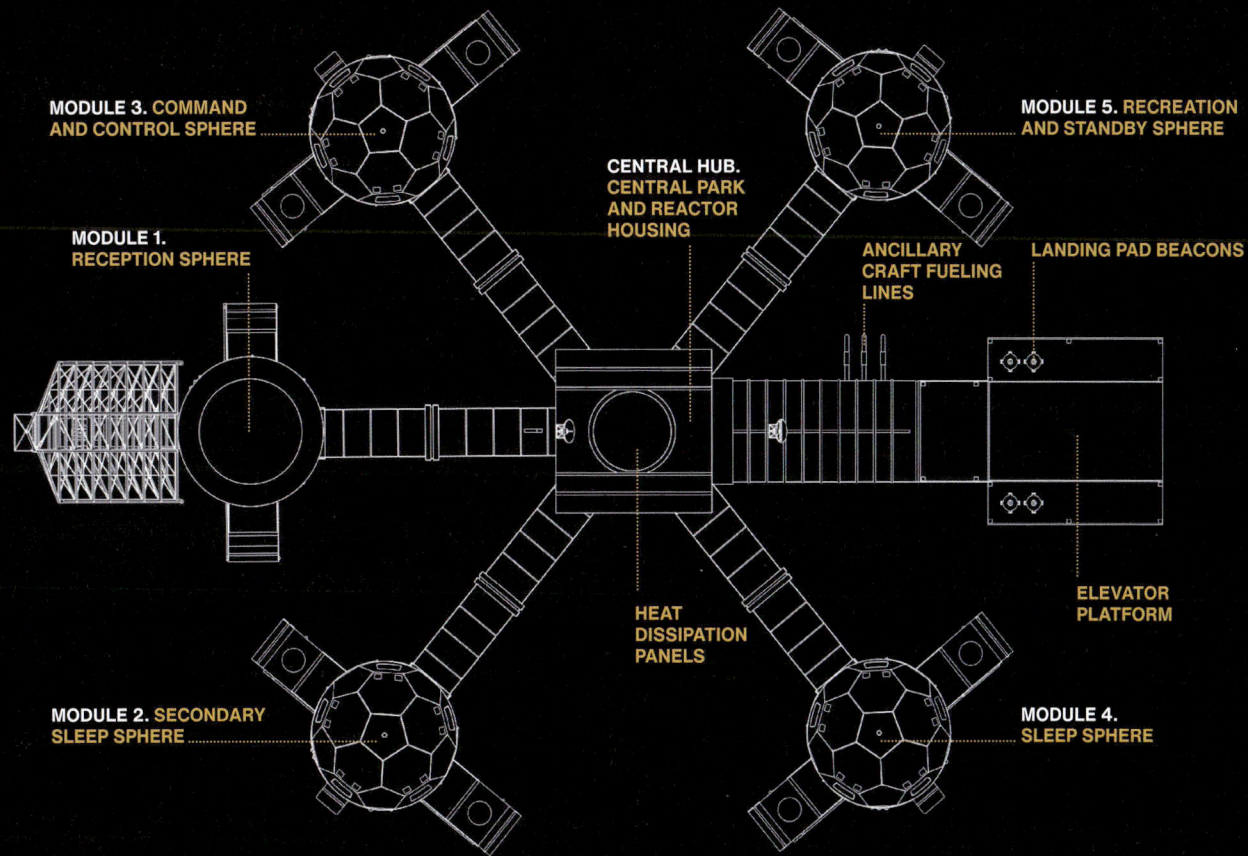

MODULE 3. COMMAND AND CONTROL SPHERE

MODULE 1. RECEPTION SPHERE

MODULE 2. SECONDARY SLEEP SPHERE

CENTRAL HUB. CENTRAL PARK AND REACTOR HOUSING

ANCILLARY CRAFT FUELING LINES

MODULE 5. RECREATION AND STANDBY SPHERE

LANDING PAD BEACONS

ELEVATOR PLATFORM

HEAT DISSIPATION PANELS

MODULE 4. SLEEP SPHERE

LANDING PAD

Module 1 acts as a landing pad and reception sphere, and is specifically designed to hold craft similar to or smaller than the Lunar Module. It has a retractable launch tower that folds back when not in use. However, this system is more a product of the rather rushed nature of Moonbase's design, and leaves the base vulnerable to crash landings and malfunctions. A larger off-site landing pad is currently being built a short distance away that will enable craft to land in a safer environment and also allow them to be stored underground.

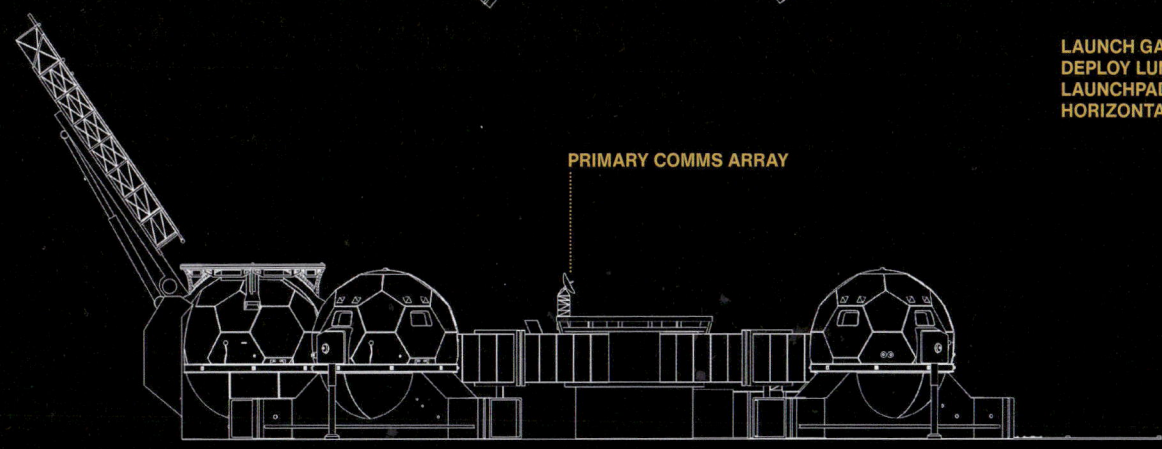

LAUNCH GANTRY. RAISED TO RECEIVE OR DEPLOY LUNAR MODULES ON THE LAUNCHPAD. LOWERS TO AN ALMOST HORIZONTAL POSITION WHEN NOT IN USE.

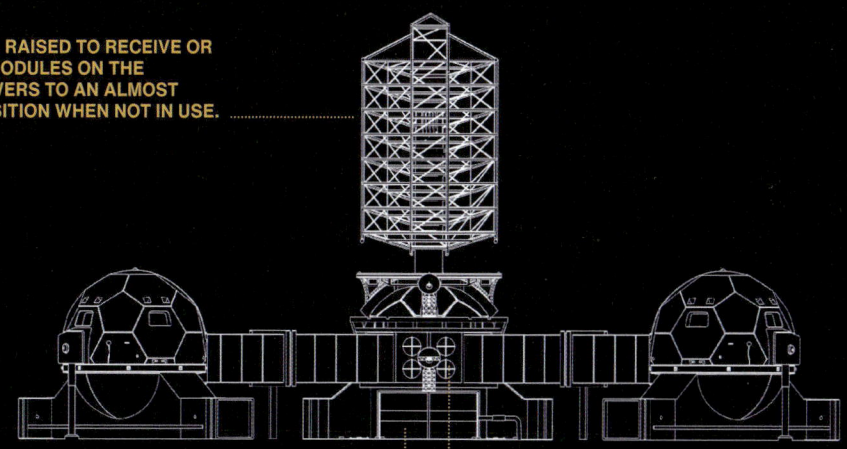

PRIMARY COMMS ARRAY

GARAGE DOORS. SMALLER VEHICLES ARE STORED IN THIS GARAGE, ALLOWING FOR QUICK ACCESS TO THE OUTSIDE.

REACTOR EXHAUST

TECHNOLOGICAL DEVELOPMENTS

As many technological developments by SHADO go on to be released into the public domain, much of the systems and technology developed for Moonbase have been used to improve the structural standards and quality of life on numerous lunar outposts. A newer, larger Moonbase is currently being constructed in Plato crater that utilises the same subterranean architecture that is used beneath Moonbase.

VITAL STORES

For additional safety, much of Moonbase's stores of air, fuel and water are located off-base in a well-protected depot. An obvious target for attack or sabotage, this secure facility makes it harder to destroy Moonbase's entire supply of vital stores and would only disrupt operations rather than stop them entirely.

MOONBASE & SURROUNDING AREA

A Moonbase

B Interceptor launch site

C Secondary landing pad

D Secondary garage access

E Supply base

Hashed area – Subsurface structures

CONTROL ROOM

The primary control sphere is the nerve centre of almost all of SHADO's space operations. There, operatives direct missions and flights with the assistance of the base's state-of-the-art computer system. Three operatives generally man this position, with the base Commander occupying the central terminal and a space tracker on either side. While defence and communication systems are controlled from this room, other day-to-day operations are overseen from the engineering section.

A   Main control station

B   Computer banks

C   Observation window

D   Secure locker for codes, classified files and small arms

E   Primary tracking station

F   Secondary tracking station

G   Alert status

H   Exit to central hub

MODIFICATIONS

The space around the control room is deliberately quite sparse to allow for modifications or to accommodate short-term consoles for specific missions. Four more stations are planned as SHADO and Moonbase operations expand in the coming years.

I   The far side of the control room is occupied by a large screen that displays a UFO's trajectory and interception point. This console is directly fed by live telemetry from SID, giving operatives a constant overview of the unfolding situation.

5

6

4

1

C

B

J

G

D

E

A

H

I

J A three-dimensional map of the Moon is housed on the wall, allowing for the Commander to coordinate SHADO resources on the surface and in orbit.

RECREATION ROOM

The recreation room is a multipurpose space that is designed to act as a dining hall, recreation facility and standby lounge for the Interceptor pilots.

With no functional kitchen on the Moon, operatives eat from a constantly restocked dispensary dominating one side of the room. Rehydrated meals can be selected and dispensed quickly and eaten at the adjoining dining tables.

The main central space is used by operatives to relax and unwind when off duty, making use of a library of books, games, music and films available from the Moonbase archives.

Lockers and chutes to the Interceptor bays make up the remaining space.

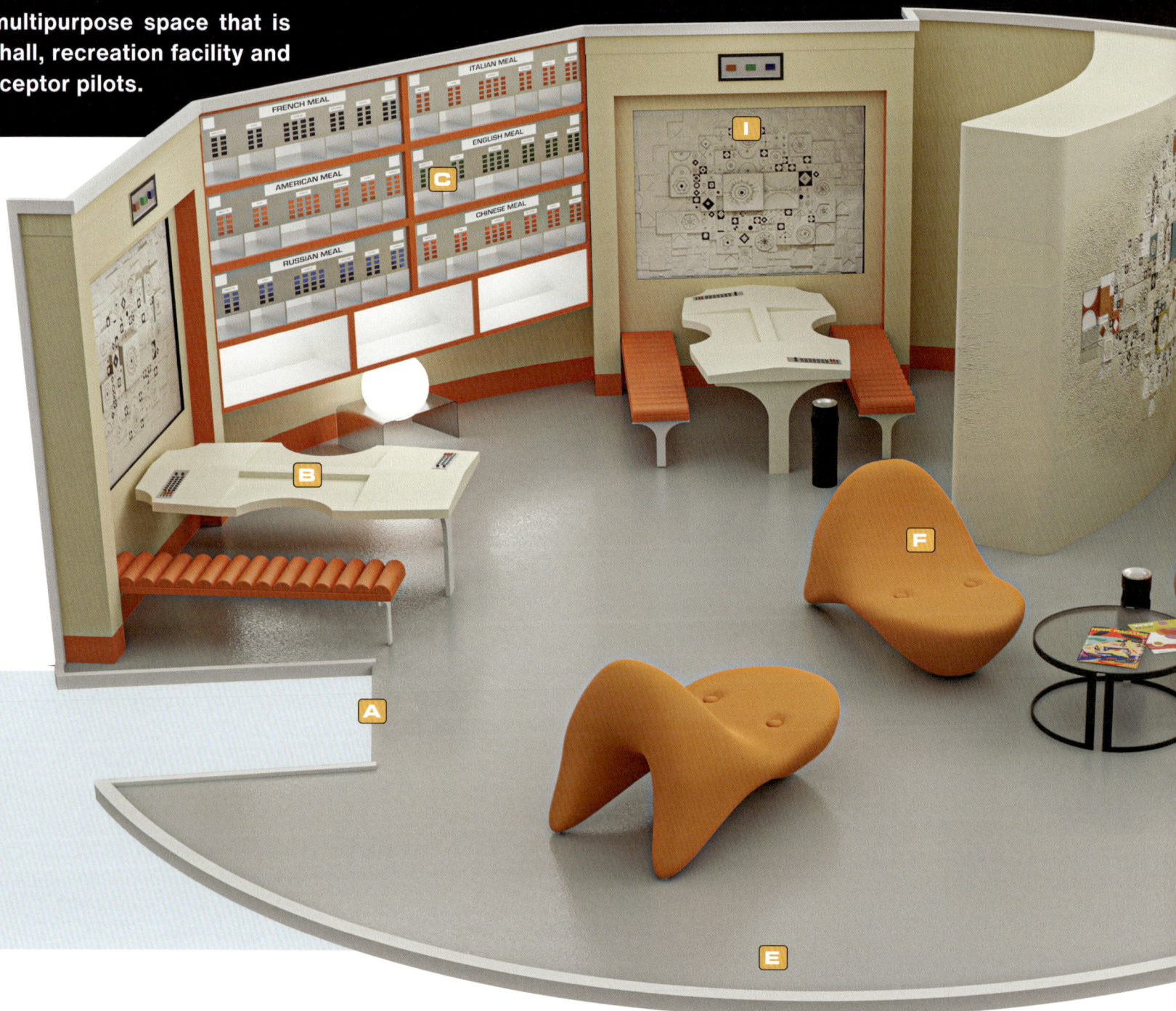

A   Entry

B   Dining area

C   Food and drink dispenser

D   Observation window

E   Archives wall

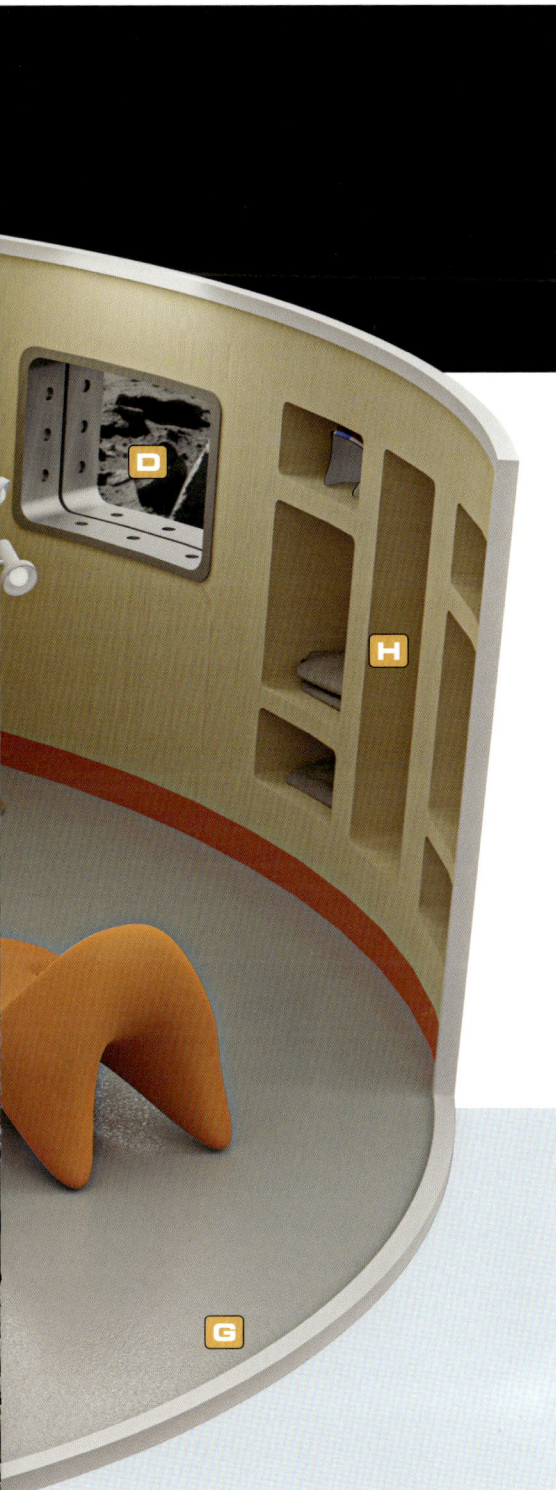

F Seating area: As with other areas on Moonbase, the space is designed to be easily and quickly adapted to other functions, in this instance, a briefing room for a large-scale space mission.

G The Interceptor chute wall offers the fastest method of getting the Interceptor pilots to their fighters. To conserve air, an airlock system is in place which only opens when the pilot is detected using the chute.

H A set of spacesuits are also housed here to allow Moonmobile or Lunar Module pilots to change in a comfortable environment while being briefed.

I Many of the communal spaces on Moonbase are decorated with fine art in order to break from the traditionally stark nature of Lunar outposts.

A Floral display

B Seating area

C Exit to control sphere

D Exit to recreation sphere

E Exit to sleep sphere 1

F Exit to sleep sphere 2

G Exit to reception sphere

H Exit to dormitories

I Lift

J Exit to washrooms

COMMON AREAS

The central module on Moonbase houses much of the primary engineering sections in the lower levels. The upper levels, however, accommodate some of the common areas which operatives will use in their downtime.

CENTRAL PARK

The convergence of the five access corridors at the centre of Moonbase has been affectionately nicknamed 'Central Park', partly for the small garden display in the centre of the room. Almost any trip across the base will require you to pass through this section and, as such, has been made into a seating area where operatives can meet, chat and relax.

ACCESS CORRIDORS

The primary access corridors that connect the five external modules on Moonbase are rather spartan, their design reflecting their initial inception as softbody constructions that were used in the early days of Moonbase's construction. They have since been covered with external armour plating.

GYMNASIUM

Beneath Central Park is the Moonbase gymnasium which operatives are required to utilise in order to maintain the very high level of physical fitness demanded by SHADO. The space normally houses a standard set of gym equipment but can be cleared for martial arts, or group activities.

SLEEPING AREAS

Multiple sleeping quarters are provided for the crew across the base. While far more spacious than those found on Skydiver, space is still at a premium and many personnel are expected to sleep in communal dormitories.

A Each sleep unit is colour-coded to make it immediately apparent which unit belongs to which operative. This also allows a small degree of personalisation in each unit.

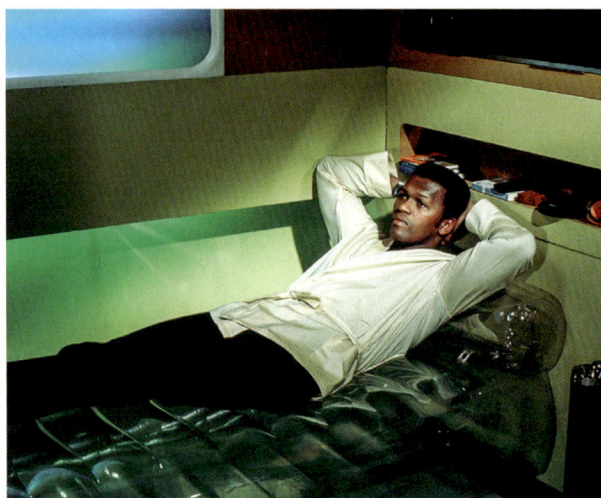

B In order to cut down on weight restrictions when importing materials from Earth, the beds on Moonbase are mainly air mattresses which can be easily moved or deflated as required.

C Private changing area: Hidden behind a one-way mirror is a small changing area that provides operatives with some privacy while changing in the washroom areas.

G

SICK BAY

Currently, there is no medical bay on Moonbase, which means the surgeon on duty will generally attend to operatives in their own sleeping areas.

PERSONNEL QUARTERS

A few individual quarters have been constructed in the two other external modules. These are generally reserved for visiting officers/ dignitaries and the base Commander.

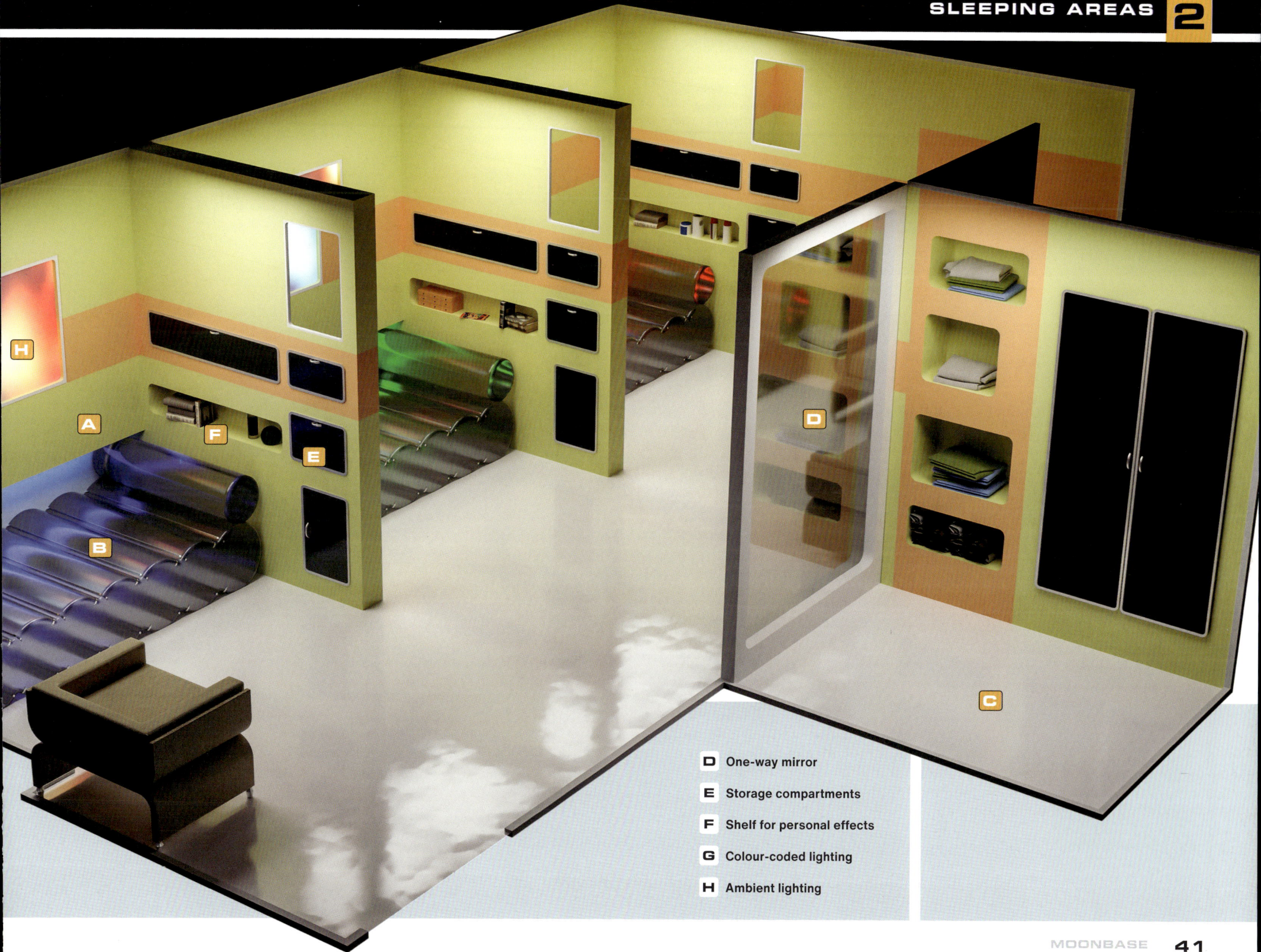

H

A

F

E

B

D

C

D One-way mirror

E Storage compartments

F Shelf for personal effects

G Colour-coded lighting

H Ambient lighting

VEHICLE GARAGE

Hidden beneath the main structure of Moonbase is the cavernous subterranean garage level which the base's central hub extends down into. Tunnelled out in secret after the hub was installed, the underground installation's tunnels and compartments extend out for over half a mile, 100 feet below the surface.

The main garage stores and maintains Moonbase's fleet of Moonmobiles and Moonbase Defence Vehicles (MDV) while also serving as a storage area for UFO debris awaiting study.

Three tunnels lead off this compartment, one to the surface ramp exit, one to the Moonbase supply base and the last to the Interceptor silos. Generally, craft will use the service elevator that depressurises then lifts the vehicle to the surface adjacent to the primary airlock while the crew are preparing their EVA suits to board the craft.

In theory, this section should be deep enough underground to be able to withstand the destruction of the base above in the event of an alien attack.

BUGGIES

In order to navigate the tunnel system quickly and also carry small loads, the same electric-powered buggies used in SHADO control are in use on the Moon.

MOONMOBILE

While extremely manoeuvrable in the lunar environment, the Moonmobile can be quite unwieldy when operating in Earth's gravity and is usually moved around on wheeled trailers. Fully serviced Moonmobiles are usually parked on the surface near an airlock.

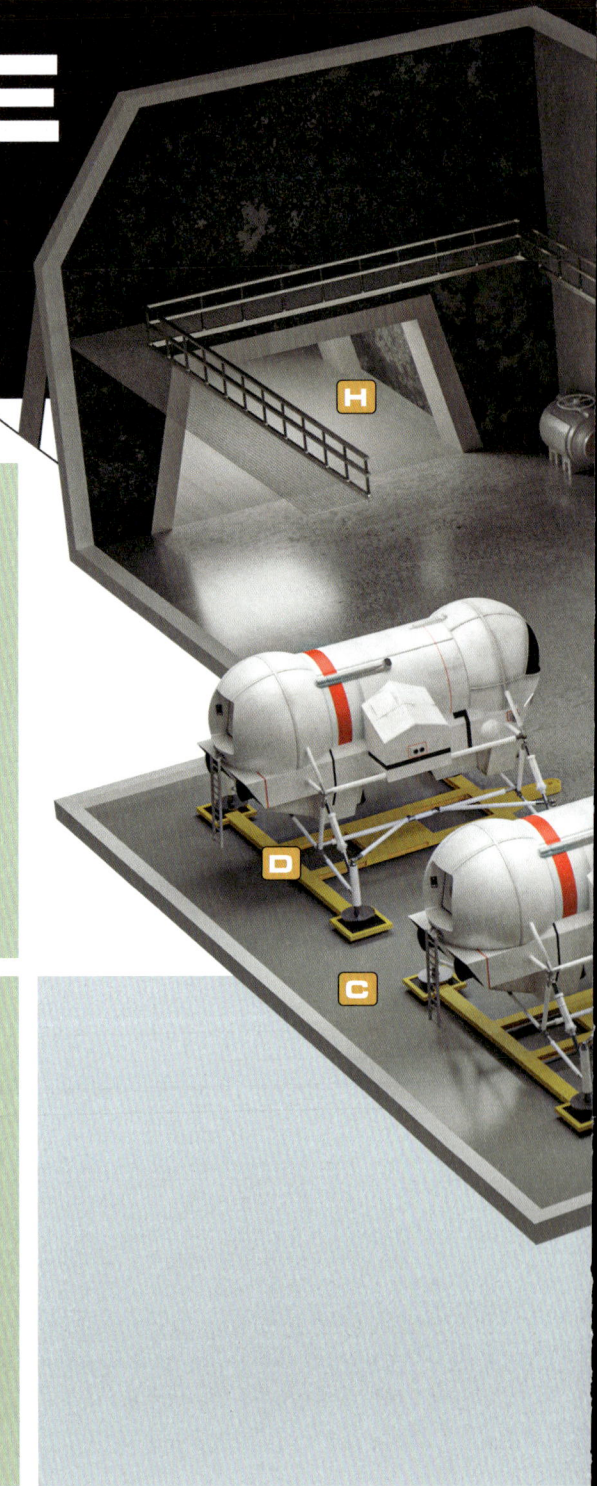

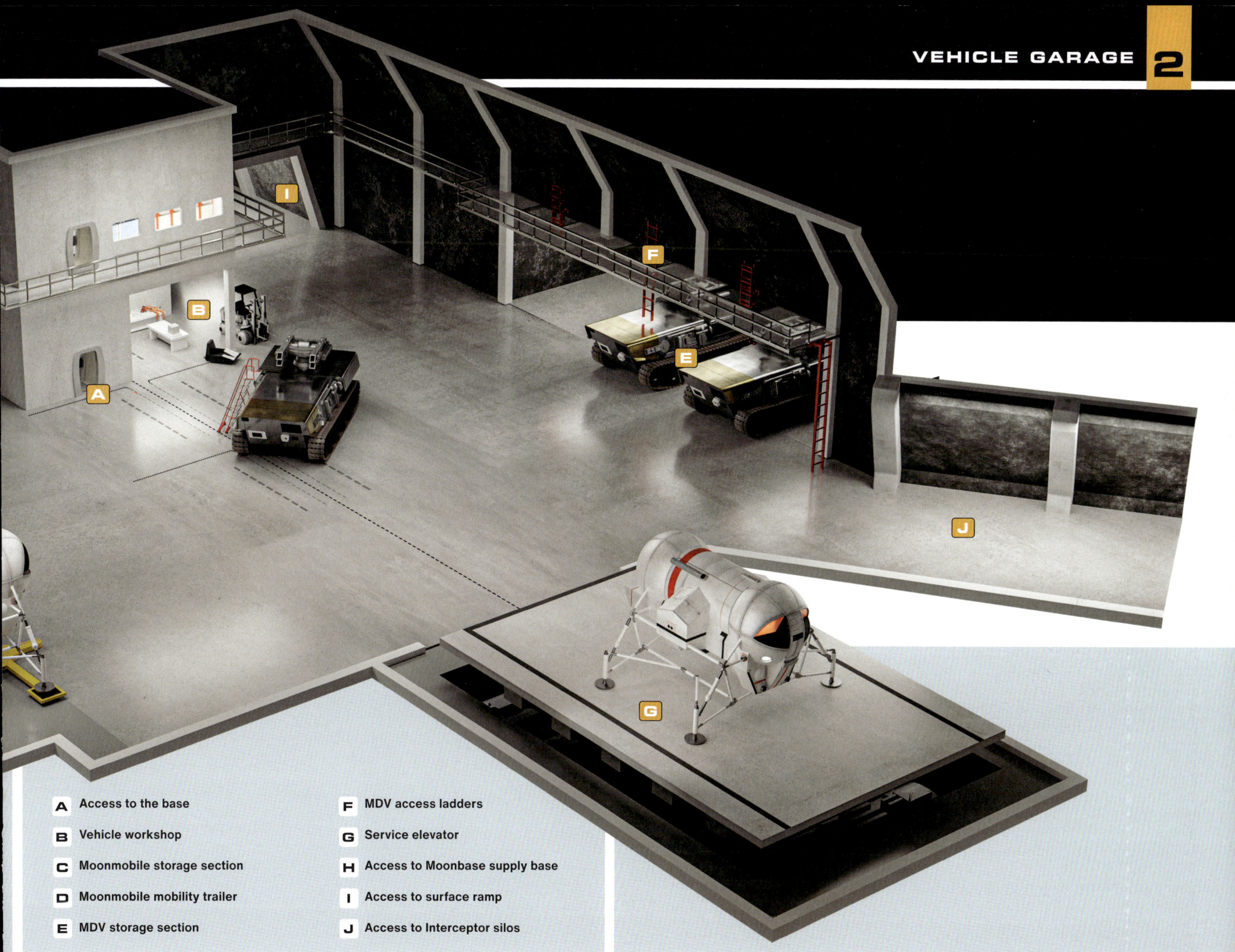

A Access to the base

B Vehicle workshop

C Moonmobile storage section

D Moonmobile mobility trailer

E MDV storage section

F MDV access ladders

G Service elevator

H Access to Moonbase supply base

I Access to surface ramp

J Access to Interceptor silos

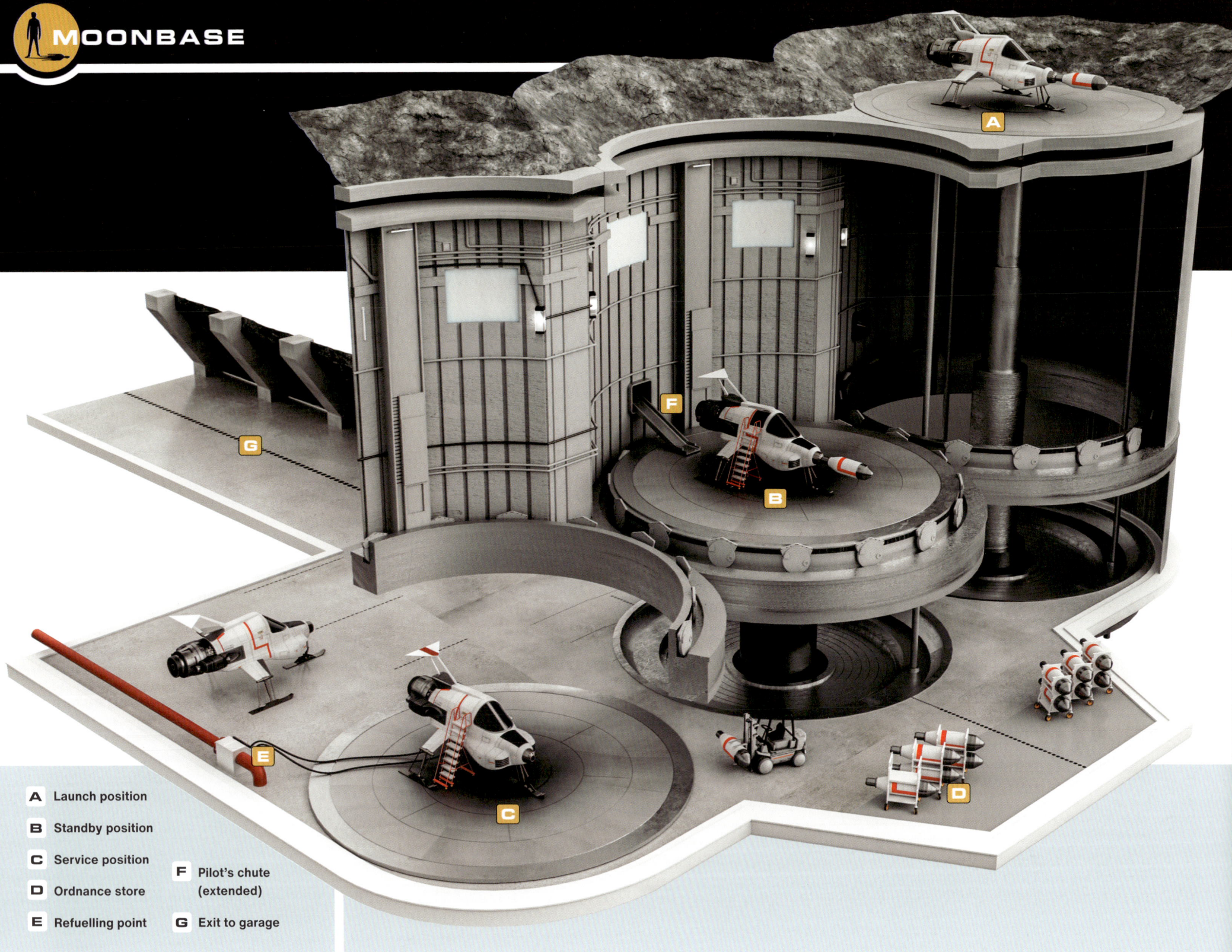

A Launch position

B Standby position

C Service position

D Ordnance store

E Refuelling point

F Pilot's chute (extended)

G Exit to garage

SUBTERRANEAN SILOS

Housed in a series of artificial craters a few hundred feet away from Moonbase are the Interceptor launch silos.
Three elevator platforms lift the Interceptor to the lunar surface or lower them into the main hanger.

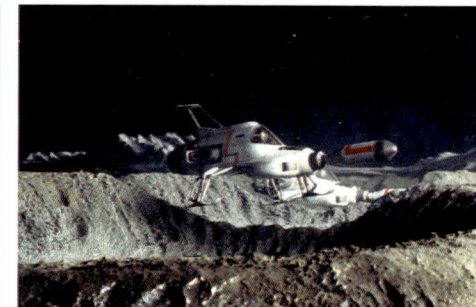

Disguising the silo doors as craters offers several advantages when launching the Interceptors – most obviously camouflage – and the high walls offer some cover if the Interceptors are being launched while the base is under attack. The natural circular shape also masks the regolith displacement caused by an Interceptor launch.

While somewhat comical in nature, the chute system is the fastest and most reliable way to get the Interceptor pilots to their craft. A sharp turn in the chute at its end slows the pilots before their arrival in the hangar.

The main hangar is a large open space connected to the base's garage level by tunnel. The hangar deck is where Interceptors are assembled, maintained, fueled, armed and repaired. Only when an Interceptor is flight-ready will it be elevated to the upper level, designated the standby level. Here the craft will stay until the Moonbase Commander calls "launch stations".

Once scrambled, the launch procedure begins. The craft is powered up and all its umbilicals are disengaged by the ground crew. The Interceptor pilot arrives via chute and enters the craft via the stepladder, which is then moved away. Once the ground crew have cleared the bay, the compartment is depressurised, the roof doors opened and the craft is raised to the lunar surface. When on heightened alert, the Moonbase crew should be able to accomplish this within two minutes.

MOONBASE DEFENCES

Despite its advantageous location on the lunar surface, Moonbase is still a rather exposed and tempting target for alien attack. Its destruction would have serious repercussions for the defence of Earth. It has been calculated that if it was destroyed, Moonbase (or its replacement) would take almost three years to become operational again, although these calculations do not account for attempts by the aliens to interfere with any building and/or reconstruction programmes.

MISSILE DEFENCES

At present, Moonbase missile defences are spearheaded by its small fleet of MDVs. However, after several of these were knocked out in late 1981, a proposal to replace them with permanent fixed launchers that can retract below the surface has been implemented. Three launchers are in the process of being installed at points around the base with the MDVs acting in support (while providing a degree of tactical flexibility).

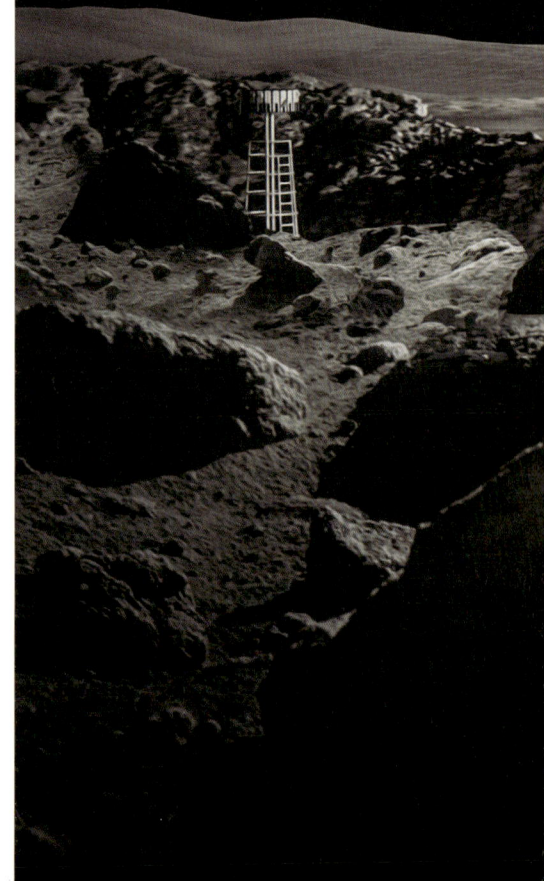

MISSILE SILO

Another defence strategy being implemented is the addition of a strategic missile silo to the base. While efforts are generally taken to disable and capture UFOs that land on the lunar surface, the silo's missile payload can be used in instances where a UFO poses a significant ground threat, ensuring the destruction of any attacking force.

POINT DEFENCE CANNONS

Located on four of the Moonbase modules are the base's point defence cannons. Their primary role is to protect the base from attack by ground forces (using the missile defences at closer ranges could result in damage to the base). However, the PDCs can be employed against UFO attacks.

The PDCs fire small-calibre explosive shells designed to damage EVA suits and equipment.

INTERCEPTORS

The Interceptors will be covered in much more detail elsewhere in this manual; however, it is obvious that the greatest way to protect Moonbase is to not let the aliens reach the Moon at all. History has shown that it is harder for the aliens to approach the Moon given the more advantageous vectoring the Interceptors have on incoming UFOs. However, sunspot activity or masking their presence with space debris has enabled the aliens to slip past the Interceptors altogether.

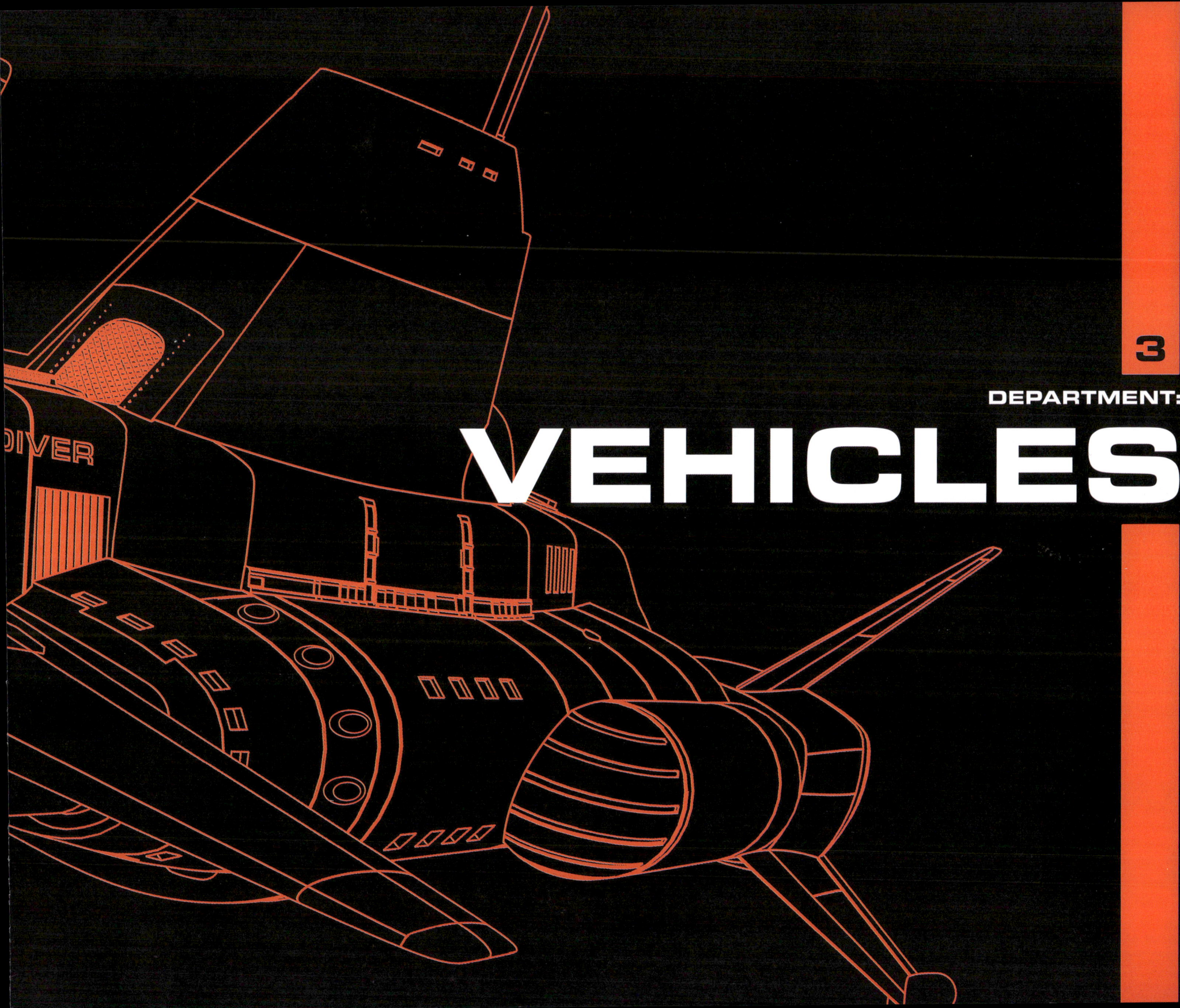

DIVER

VEHICLES

Commissioned for posterity and currently hanging in SHADO HQ's restaurant is this painting, showing all four of SHADO's field branches in action.

THE SHADO FLEET

Faced with a foe possessing technology far exceeding our own capabilities, the world's greatest minds were brought together to develop an effective response. It was clear that SHADO would be unable to design a vehicle that would match the UFOs in the arenas of space, air, land and sea. They could, however, design a selection of craft that could excel in their respective environments and use their home advantage to outmanoeuvre, outrun or outgun the UFO.

SHADO OPERATES FOUR FIELD BRANCHES:

THE SPACE FORCE
Operating between Earth and the Moon.

THE GROUND FORCE
A quickly deployable force of combat and utility vehicles.

THE NAVY
Patrolling Earth's oceans and ready to deploy atmospheric fighters at a moment's notice.

SHADair
SHADO's civilian airfleet, vital for maintaining the organisation's global infrastructure.

Over your career in SHADO, you will likely be rotated around these branches. This section will familiarise you with their primary equipment and functions.

A	Challenger jeep – 12 ft		**J**	Kingfisher VTOL – 43 ft
B	Javelin car – 18ft		**K**	Interceptor MkI – 55 ft
C	Executive car – 18 ft		**L**	Albatross – 90 ft
D	Mobile – 40 ft		**M**	SID – 98 ft
E	Moonmobile – 42 ft		**N**	Lunar Transport – 132 ft
F	MDV – 48 ft		**O**	Seagull X Ray – 149 ft
G	Mobile transporter – 92 ft		**P**	Skydiver – 155 ft
H	UFO transporter – 135 ft		**Q**	Neptune – 238 ft
I	Interceptor MkII – 41 ft		**R**	Valkyrie – 338 ft

SHADO SPACE FORCES

Space Force is the largest consumer of SHADO's resources, both financially and in terms of manpower and equipment. Much of the technology employed is experimental and, coupled with the harsh nature of the operational environment, a posting in space can be considered the single most hazardous role for any operative.

The two primary bases utilised by Space Force are Moonbase and Halton Space Port, a repurposed RAF base a few miles from SHADO HQ. In situations where heavier payloads need to be transported to orbit, SHADO is able to requisition launch sites from the International Space Commision, NASA and Eurosec.

Space Force also has a logistical role, supplying Moonbase and maintaining the SID satellite network, but its primary mission is as a first line of defence against the alien threat and ensuring no UFO makes it as far as Earth's orbit. In the event that all spatial lines of defence fail to prevent a UFO attack, it becomes the duty of Space Force to ensure that no UFO returns to its home planet.

SPACE INTRUDER DETECTOR

SID is a multipurpose sensor platform fitted with the latest utronic equipment recently developed by SHADO. While also serving as part of SHADO's communication network, SID's primary function is to scan for and monitor UFOs entering our solar system, tracking their exact velocity and bearing to provide a firing solution for Moonbase's Interceptors. This makes SID a vital part of the whole operation and, as one of the largest non-modular objects in Earth's orbit, its protection is vital. That said, direct attacks on SID have proven to be rare, as UFOs that attempt to decelerate into orbit are easy targets for the Moonbase Interceptors.

As well as scanning near space, SID is also tied into the terrestrial detection systems of many military organisations across the globe. This allows SID to be able to assist ground and air forces in intercepting UFOs that have been missed by the Interceptors.

As SID has to process and relay a massive amount of data, it was decided to give the main computer a voice command function enabling simple commands and information to be transferred over standard communication channels – more complex calculations can be transferred directly to screens and targeting computers. While seeming very lifelike, SID's onboard computer is only capable of a small number of vocal commands and will only recognise the voice print of certain SHADO operatives. This hasn't stopped some from affectionately referring to the satellite with he/him pronouns.

'MINI SID'

SHADO has many satellites in orbit in order to allow for guaranteed secure communication. Some of these satellites are also equipped with a smaller version of the detection equipment used by SID. These give coverage in the blind spots created by SID's orbit, while also providing redundancy in the event of system failure or damage aboard SID.

DEVELOPMENT TEAM

Astronaut Craig Collins headed up the SID design team under the supervision of Commander Straker. Many of the vital onboard systems had to be designed from scratch over the course of the 10 years it took to put SID into operation, and were farmed out to multiple satellite companies that were developed specifically for SHADO purposes.

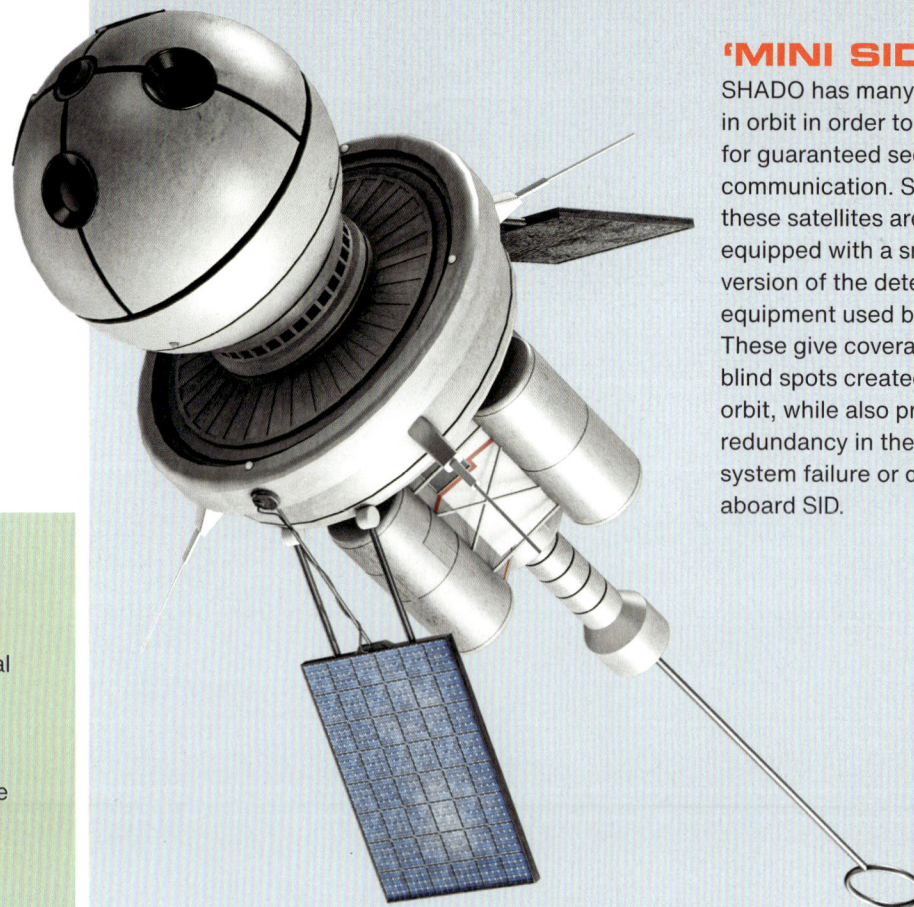

Access to SID's interior is provided through an airlock located beneath the forward section. Capture clamps in this area are designed to allow a variety of smaller vehicles to dock, such as Interceptors or one-man personnel shuttles. Conventional access is performed via spacewalk.

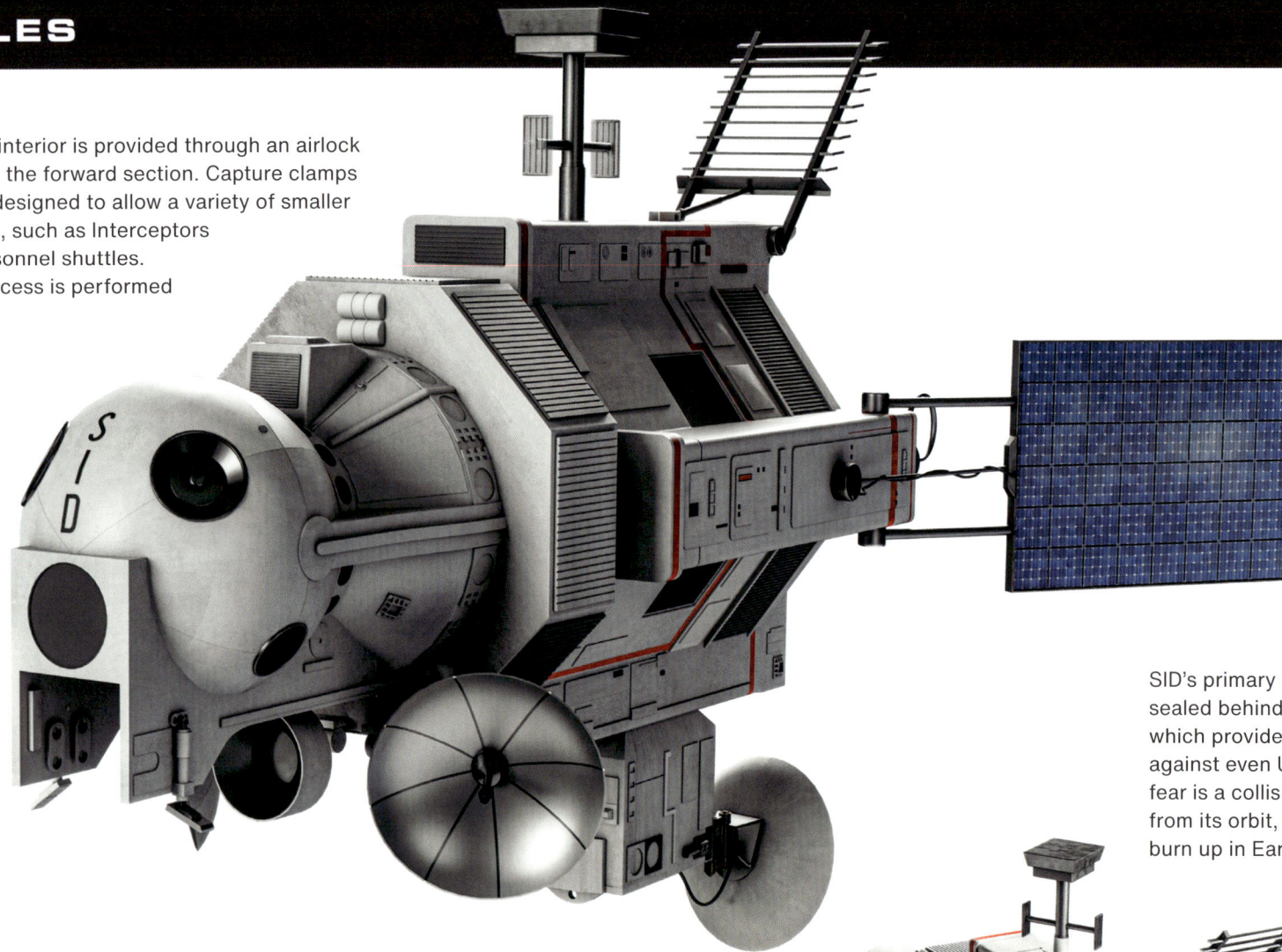

SID's primary computer section is sealed behind thick protective armour, which provides an effective defence against even UFO attack. The greater fear is a collision that could push SID from its orbit, causing the satellite to burn up in Earth's atmosphere.

DAMAGE

While there have only been a few near misses, SID has been rendered fully inoperable just once when a UFO broke formation and attacked the satellite. While the main computer was rendered non-operational, ground control was able to stabilise its spin using manoeuvring thrusters, and a repair operation was quickly organised.

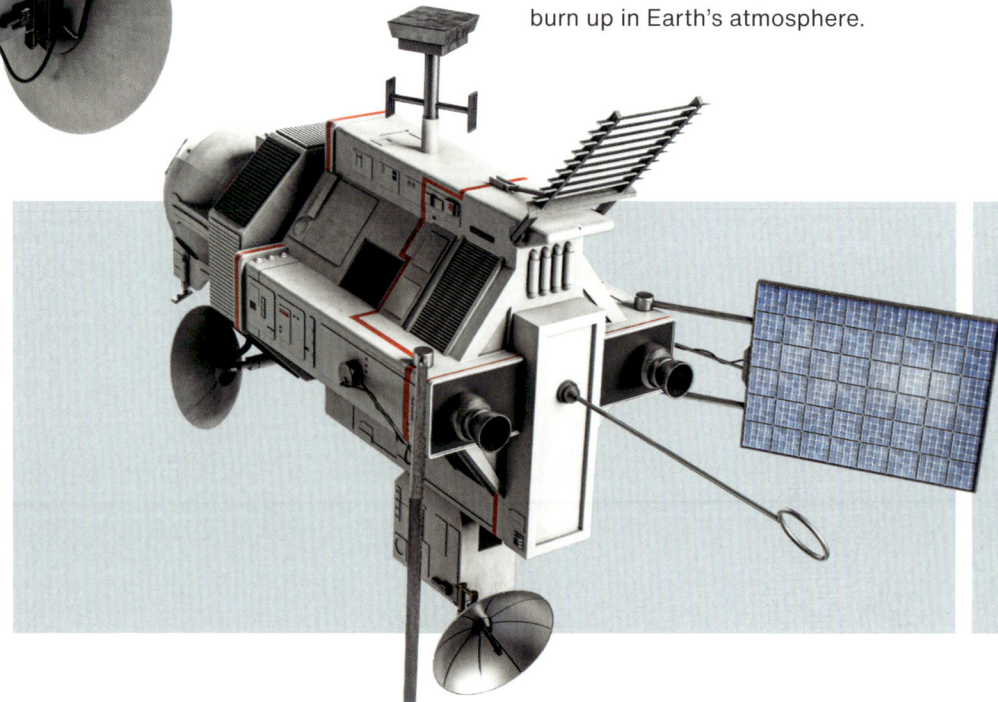

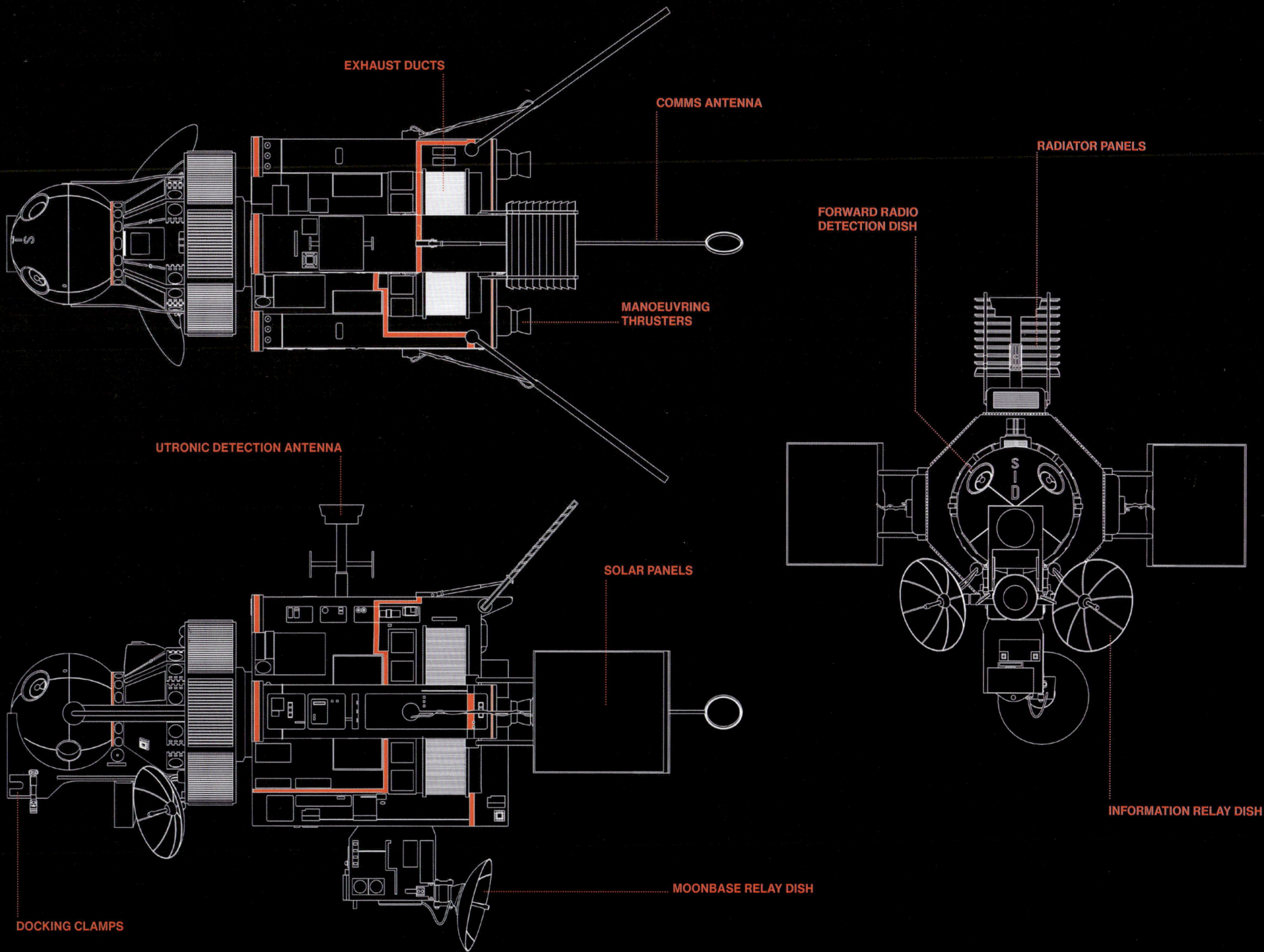

EXHAUST DUCTS

COMMS ANTENNA

RADIATOR PANELS

FORWARD RADIO
DETECTION DISH

MANOEUVRING
THRUSTERS

UTRONIC DETECTION ANTENNA

SOLAR PANELS

INFORMATION RELAY DISH

MOONBASE RELAY DISH

DOCKING CLAMPS

INTERIOR

The primary interior is split into three main compartments:

■ **THE DOCKING STATION:**
A compartment located below the primary sensor sphere that allows smaller craft to connect with the satellite without the need for a spacewalk.

■ **THE COMMAND MODULE:**
A confined space not dissimilar to the piloting areas on the old Apollo command modules, used for manual control and diagnostics.

■ **THE MAIN COMPUTER ROOM:**
The largest section of the interior – it houses the new X1 series computers.

SID has no artificial gravity systems or amenities, so is unsuitable for long-term habitation.

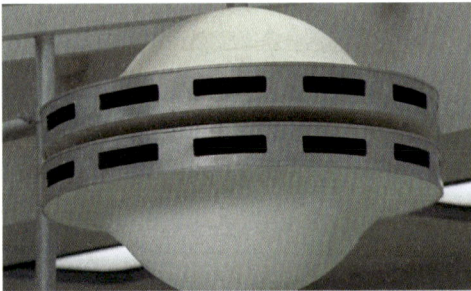

SHADO CONTROL

SID has its own dedicated vocal speaker system in SHADO control, which is used to provide real-time warnings plus updates to control personnel on the progress of intruding UFOs.

DOCKED PORT

The docking station below the sensor sphere is designed to connect to lunar transfer modules via an extendable boarding tube. During initial planning stages, SID was originally conceived as a manned space station and a second line of defence in the event that UFOs penetrated Moonbase's defences. As such, SID was adapted to have a single Interceptor stationed on board. A potential extension and refit of SID is currently in early development.

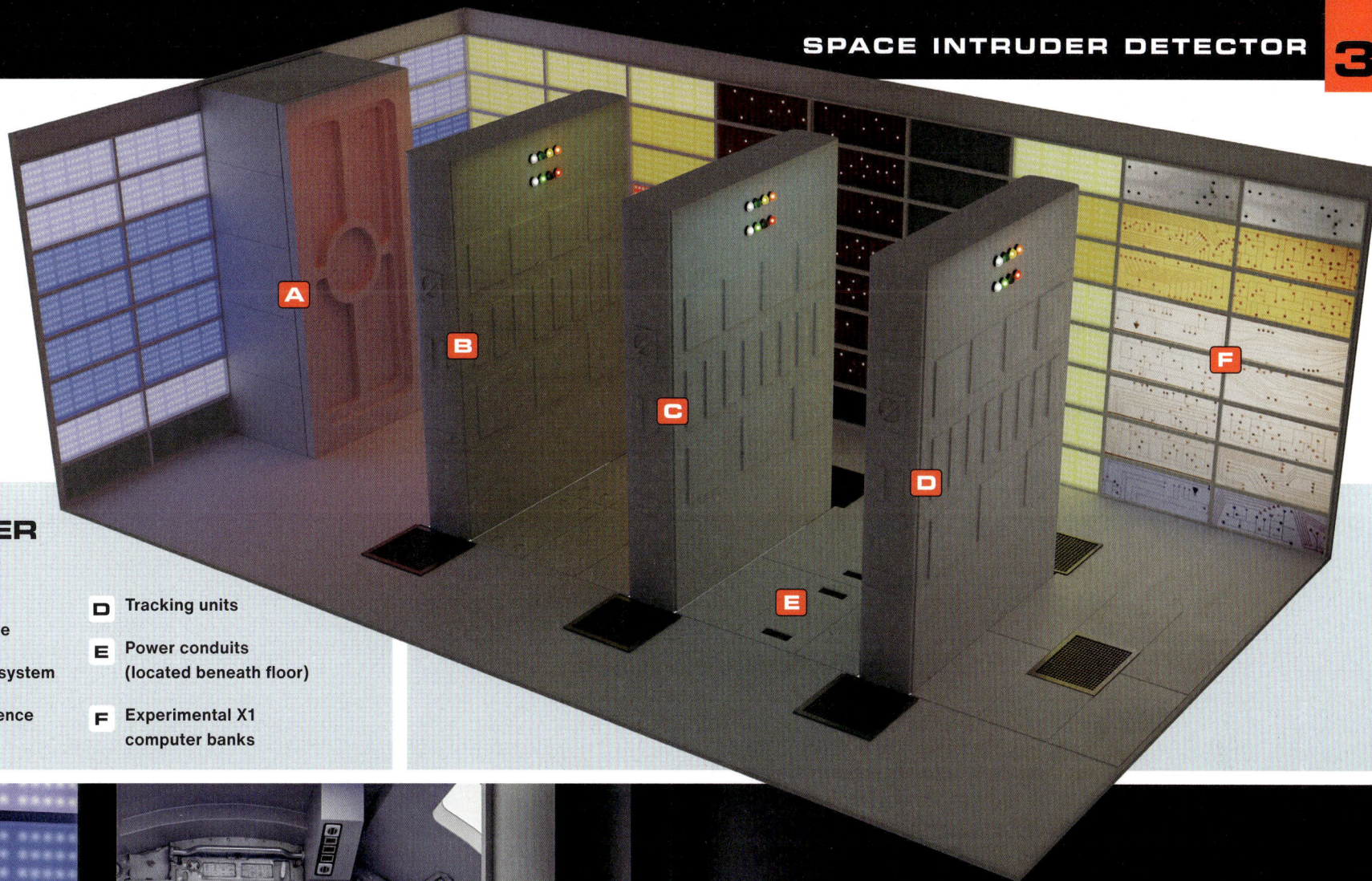

COMPUTER ROOM

A Access door to command module

B Attitude control system

C Artificial intelligence hub

D Tracking units

E Power conduits (located beneath floor)

F Experimental X1 computer banks

COMMAND MODULE

The command module provides direct access to SID's altitude control systems in the event that the automatic systems on board should fail. SID is capable of limited flight but only for orbital adjustment.

INTERCEPTOR

Humanity had only been exploring space for a decade, but the subsequent alien incursion challenged it into developing craft that could operate in and defend this new territory. A combat spacecraft was needed that could be deployed quickly and engage the technologically-more superior UFOs.

As the most expensive component of the entire SHADO venture, the Interceptor programme was derived from a series of three initial proposals put forward for combating the UFO threat. These were:

- An armed satellite network that could track and detonate missiles in the path of approaching UFOs. While promising, this was vetoed due to the sheer expense and manpower required.

- A 'mobile battleship' – a heavily armed and armoured spacecraft that could fulfil a similar role to its naval equivalent while maintaining a high orbit. Deemed to be beyond current technical capabilities, there were also concerns about placing such a high-value asset in a combat environment.

- Small-scale combat vehicles that could be deployed from a defensible base on the Moon. While this concept has many drawbacks, it was felt that it was the only option achievable in SHADO's 10-year plan.

The Interceptor is an extremely basic vehicle consisting of a cockpit with a life support system, propulsion system and launcher. Each of these components has been stripped back to the absolute bare minimum required to keep the vehicle mission capable. The result is an incredibly light and efficient craft that can quickly achieve a firing solution on its UFO target, then return to base.

DEPLOYMENT

While six Interceptors are maintained and on station at Moonbase, only three can be deployed at any one time. While the first flight of Interceptors can be deployed very quickly, it takes a further 10 minutes to be able to launch a second wave.

The protective hull around the Interceptor gives it an incredibly sleek and aerodynamic appearance. However, the craft is only rated for space and lunar flight. For delivery to the Moon, the Interceptor can be broken down to its component parts and shipped within the cargo bay of the lunar module over several trips.

The access hatch for the pilot is located above the cockpit and can be ingressed via a retractable stepladder that is removed by ground crew before launch. While not the most practical way to enter the craft, this method was chosen in order to allow the cockpit ejection system to function unimpaired.

HOLDING FORMATION

Once the missile has been deployed, Interceptors are required to remain in a holding formation until Moonbase has made the necessary fuel calculations to safely return them to base.

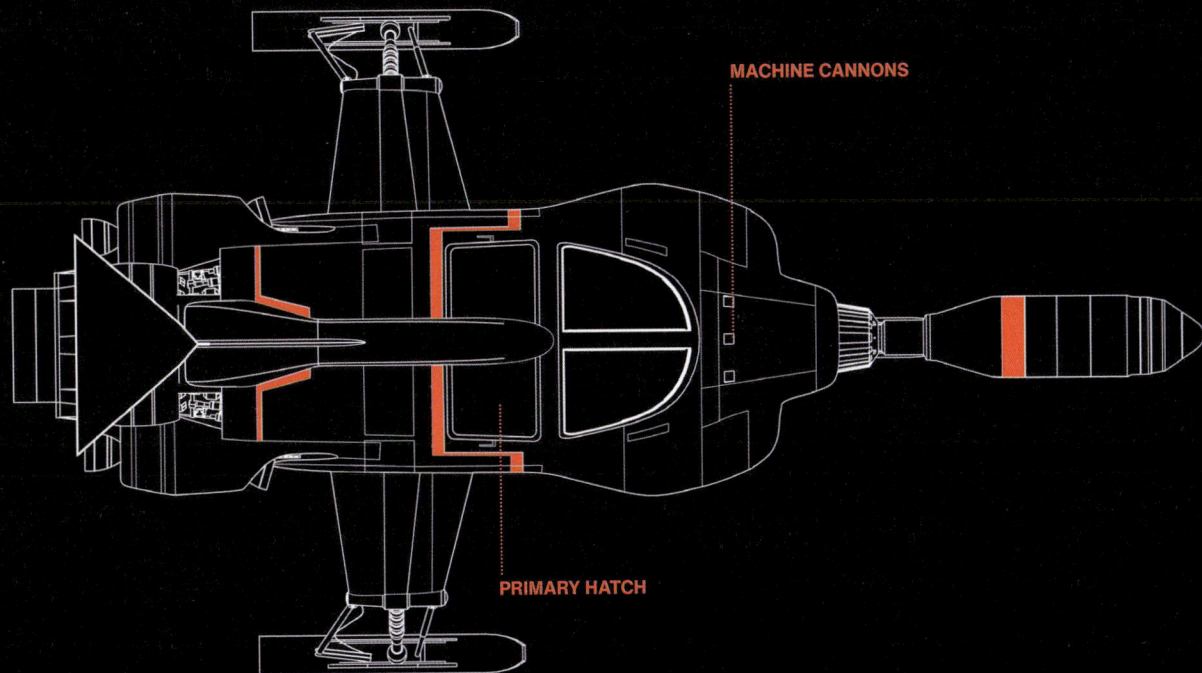

MACHINE CANNONS

PRIMARY HATCH

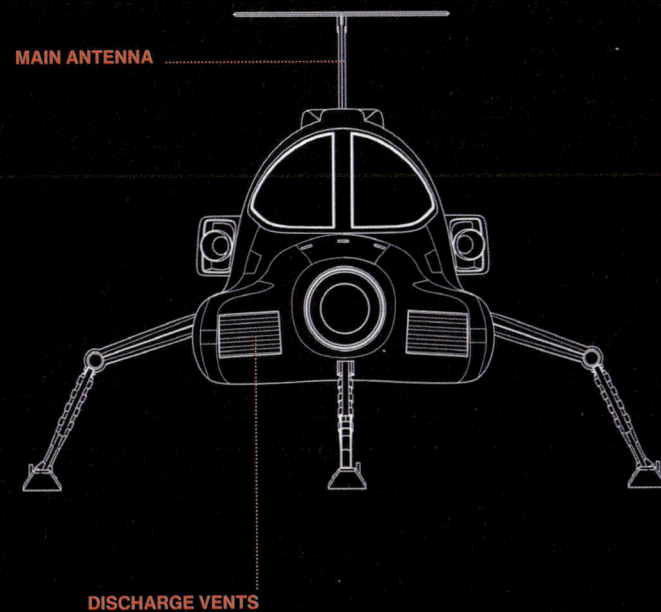

MAIN ANTENNA

DISCHARGE VENTS

COCKPIT

CLUSTER MISSILE

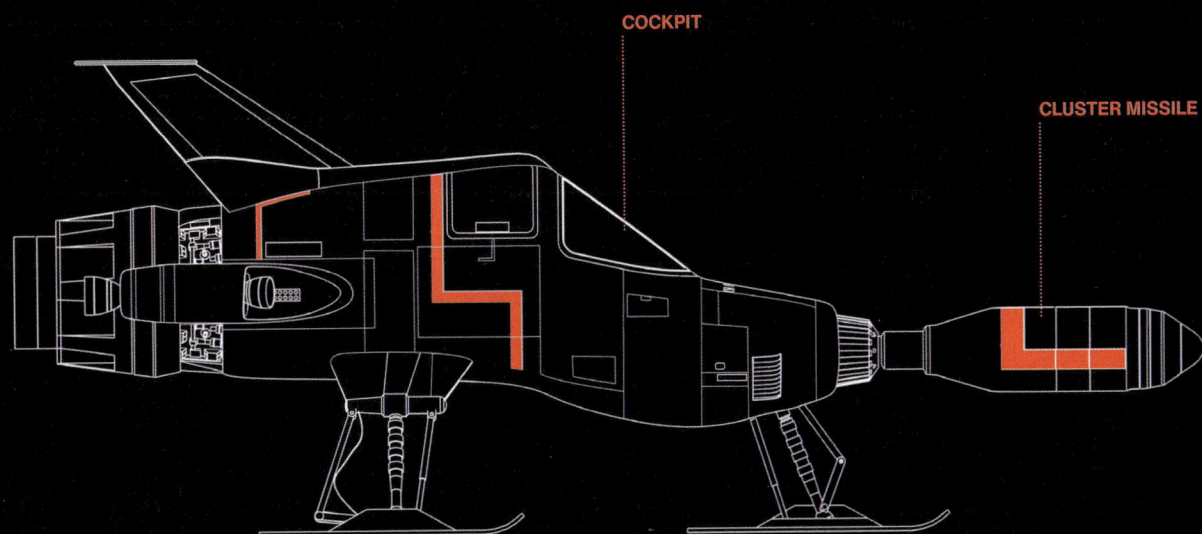

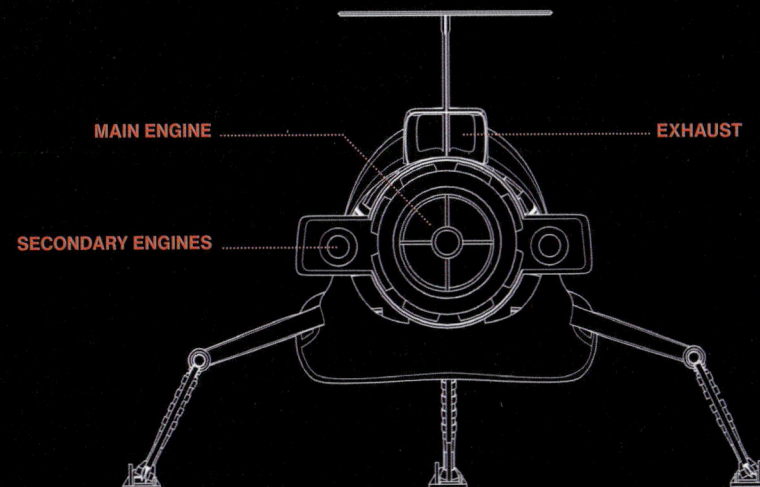

MAIN ENGINE

EXHAUST

SECONDARY ENGINES

PROTOTYPE

The first flyable prototype of the Interceptor was a larger, more robust craft, very much a holdover of established NASA and EUROSEC technology. Twin gimballed engines allowed for fast take-off and manoeuvring, and a cramped cockpit had enough space for a pilot and navigator. While this craft fulfilled the basic requirements of the brief, it was felt that a more efficient design could be created using the prototype as a basis.

The two-man cockpit was replaced by a single-seat version, the pilot augmented by data supplied by Moonbase's main computer. The primary propulsion engine was switched out for three smaller engines, while only a single gimballed liftoff engine was retained to further reduce weight.

Finally, a more compact cluster missile was developed as a replacement for the more expensive and heavier nuclear warhead.

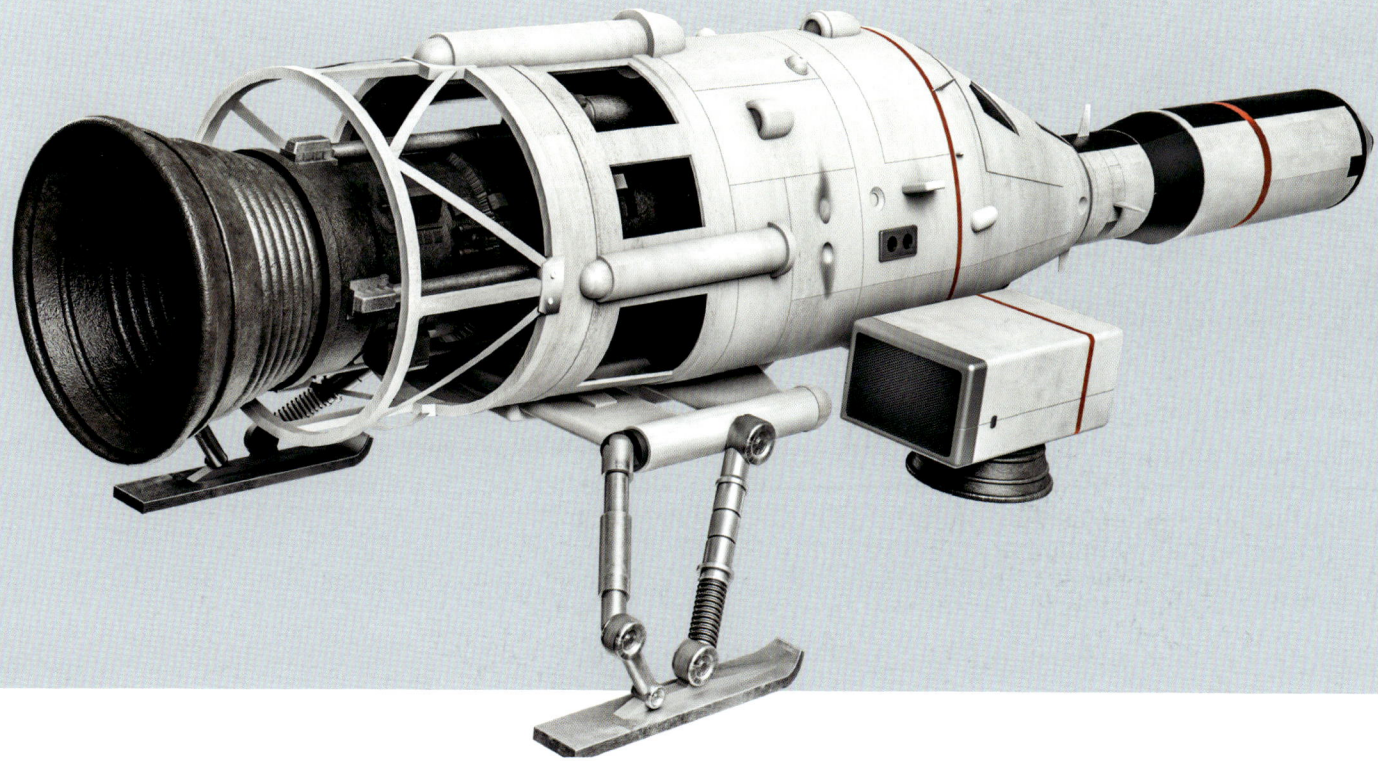

At present, the Mk1 is deployed on Moonbase, and it is also in the process of being modified for a secondary strike role that allows it to engage UFOs on the lunar surface. However, due to the critical disadvantages that SHADO craft have when engaging UFOs at close range, most of these plans have not left the development stage.

INTERIOR

The cockpit of the Interceptor is surprisingly spacious compared to many other fighter craft. This is partly to allow space for the numerous onboard computer and life support systems. The compartment is pressurised in order to allow the pilot to quickly transfer from the silo to the craft as fast as possible without the need to don a spacesuit.

COCKPIT

A Pilot's seat

B Emergency oxygen supply

C Life support system

D Radiator

E Flight controls

F Temperature controls

G Flight computer

The Interceptor's clear, single-piece canopy provides the pilot with a panoramic view rarely afforded aboard other craft. This greatly assists the pilot in those rare instances where a UFO is engaged visually.

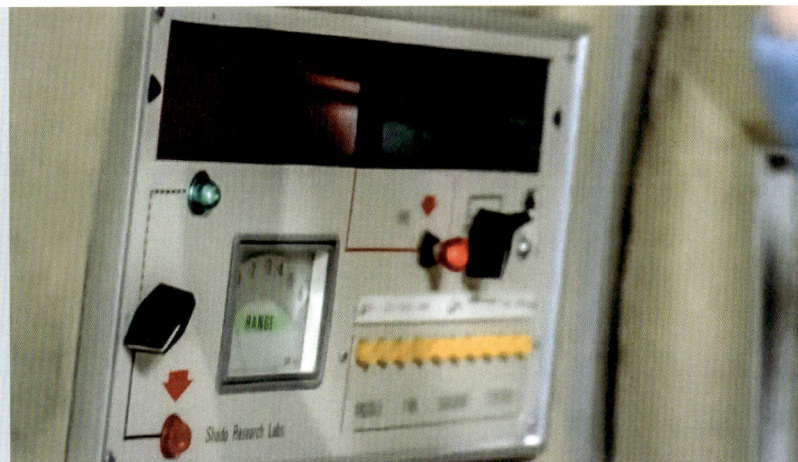

The primary antenna on the craft allows constant contact with Moonbase's main computer, allowing for important trajectory and fuel calculations to be made in real time. In exceptional circumstances, this link can be severed if an Interceptor needs to evade detection.

ESCAPE UNIT

Without a spacesuit, a traditional ejection by the pilot is physically impossible. Instead, the entire cockpit and VTOL engine unit can separate from the rest of the craft and blast clear from the main body. However, this is considered a last-ditch manoeuvre as the Interceptor's theatre of operations means any ejection can leave the escape unit out of range of any SHADO forces that could affect a rescue.

SPACE COMBAT

Trying to engage an enemy in the vast arena of space is very different to traditional aerial combat in Earth's atmosphere, particularly as the attacking UFOs are significantly more adept at navigating the environment than the slower, more fuel-reliant Interceptors. However, as SHADO forces are operating on the defensive, it means they can take advantage of a key weakness in alien technology.

UFOs have to travel relativistic distances at the speed of light in order to make the journey from their home planet. However, SHADO forces utilising the latest utronic technology can spot and track the alien craft with a reasonable degree of accuracy. UFOs are forced to decelerate to avoid hitting Earth's atmosphere at fatal relativistic speeds, and it was observed that during this process, their ability to manoeuvre is severely compromised. This means their course, speed and an intercept point can be calculated.

"YOU ONLY GET ONE SHOT"

Given the speeds, physics and geometry involved, and the mass of the missile required to be effective, Interceptors are only outfitted with one missile. A second would increase the craft's mass, reducing manoeuvrability and accelaration, and therefore requiring more thrust to move the Interceptor into position. While further design modifications have been suggested to remedy this, for the time being, the single-shot Interceptor is the only effective solution.

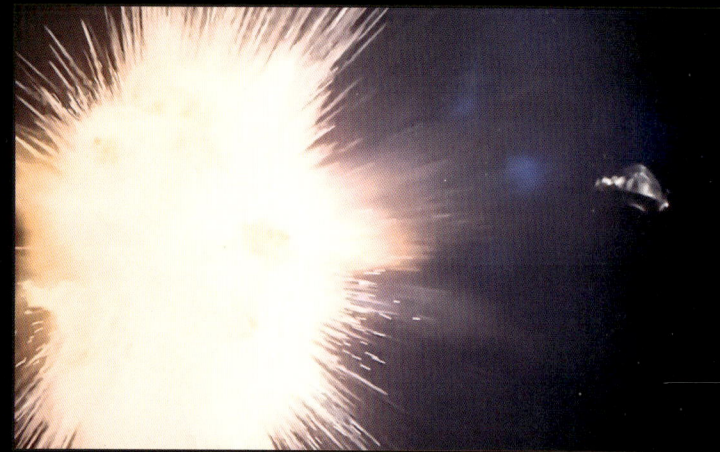

WARHEAD

Unfortunately, even the most powerful computer would not be accurate enough to provide a firing solution for conventional weapons to create a blast close enough to destroy or damage a UFO. In the first year of SHADO's operation, nuclear warheads were used, but this led to numerous political, environmental and ethical issues. And while effective when detonated close to the target, at longer distances it appeared that a UFO's shielding was quite capable of repelling much of the energy produced by the atomic explosion. In addition, the use of nuclear weapons was prohibited when UFOs were close to assets such as Moonbase or SID. Nuclear weapons are also expensive, and SHADO was quickly encountering supply issues.

A solution was found when it became clear that UFOs had a weakness to SHADO's less advanced kinetic weaponry. It was decided that instead of using a single warhead, the missile would use a payload fitted with six smaller missiles that would disperse and detonate, creating cones of shrapnel over a wide area which the UFO would then impact into at sublight speeds, damaging or destroying it. The cluster payload can be rendered inert at close ranges in order to protect nearby SHADO units.

MOONMOBILE

Navigating the lunar surface is a significantly bigger challenge than it might initially appear. The terrain is frequently rocky and heavily cratered, while the fine regolith makes it difficult for heavier tracked vehicles to maintain a grip on the steeper slopes. It became apparent that a fuel-efficient vehicle that could cover difficult ground at speed was required in order to make lunar operations viable.

The earliest Moonmobiles were not dissimilar to NASA's 'flying bedstead' from the Apollo programme. Essentially an engine in a simple framework, this contraption could transport a small crew over the lunar surface using low-powered VTOL rockets that would hold the craft 15–30 feet off the ground while horizontal rockets would propel it forward.

The variation of the Moonmobile employed by SHADO is a slightly larger and more robust craft than the commercial models used on the Moon, and made up of three primary compartments – the cockpit, a configurable engineering mid-section and the rear airlock. While not best suited for combat, these craft provide Moonbase's primary response force in the event of a UFO incursion managing to secure a foothold on the Moon.

Too large to fit in Moonbase's surface garage, Moonmobiles are kept in an underground hanger and lifted to the surface via an elevator. A fleet of five are kept on station and are on constant standby.

Larger models of the Moonmobile have been trialled as a cargo-carrying variant. Instead of utilising its VTOL rockets to hover above the surface, this model would use them in short bursts to 'hop' across the surface several hundred feet at a time. While showing initial promise, the lack of manoeuvrability and crew comfort meant that this variant was quickly withdrawn from service.

OPERATIONAL USE

SHADO's research and development division has been working to develop Moonmobile operating procedures and tactics in order to improve the survival rate of SHADO operatives. Modifications under consideration include redesigning the engine array to maximise thrust/weight ratios and manoeuvrability, and increasing the size of the craft to allow the introduction of ablative armour. However, current practice is to leave the Moonmobile at a safe distance and engage the UFO on foot using portable rocket launchers.

VARIANTS

Each Moonmobile can look subtly different from each other depending on the mission-specific modifications made during the particular vehicle's operational service. Some may have additional sensors and antennas which improve the craft's detection capabilities, while others may have augmented armament including additional missile launchers or cannons. However, due to the nature of the craft's construction, any modifications are carefully considered so as not to unbalance the Moonmobile's stability or excessively increase weight/mass.

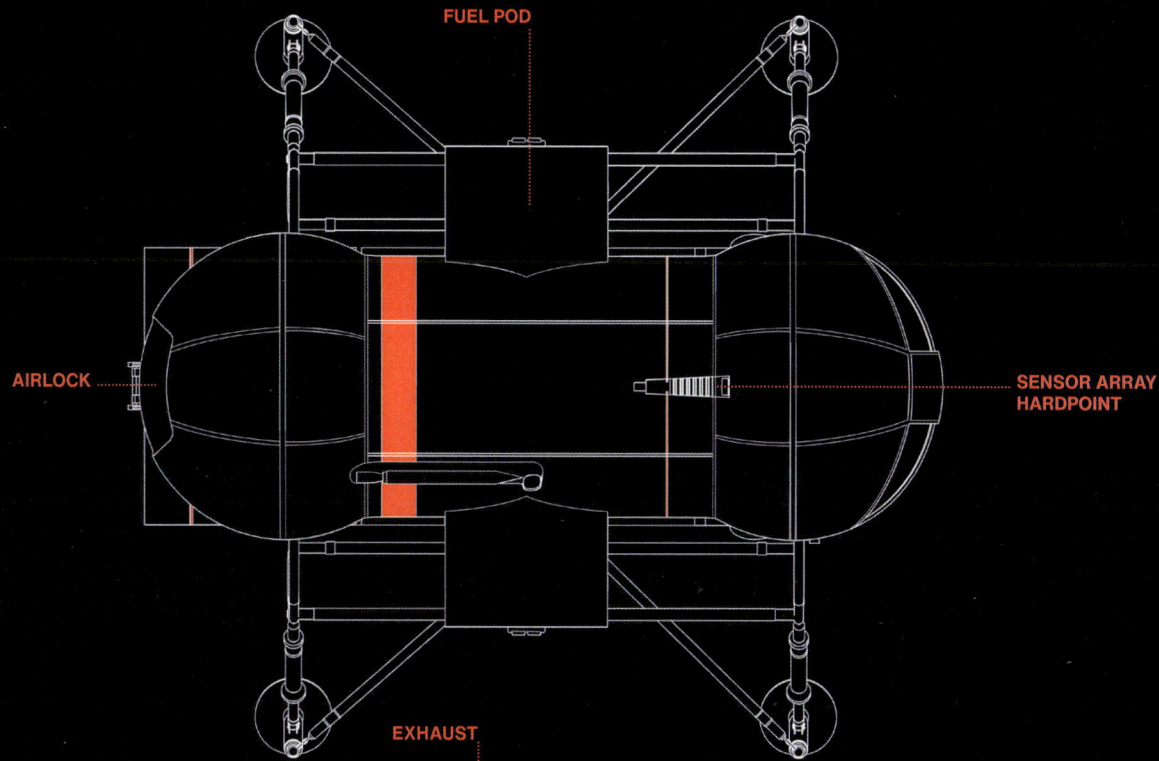

FUEL POD

AIRLOCK

SENSOR ARRAY
HARDPOINT

ARMAMENT

Initially not designed with a combat role in mind, Moonmobiles are lightly armed. Tactically, they work better when deployed on an elevated vantage point and using their rocket launchers from a distance.

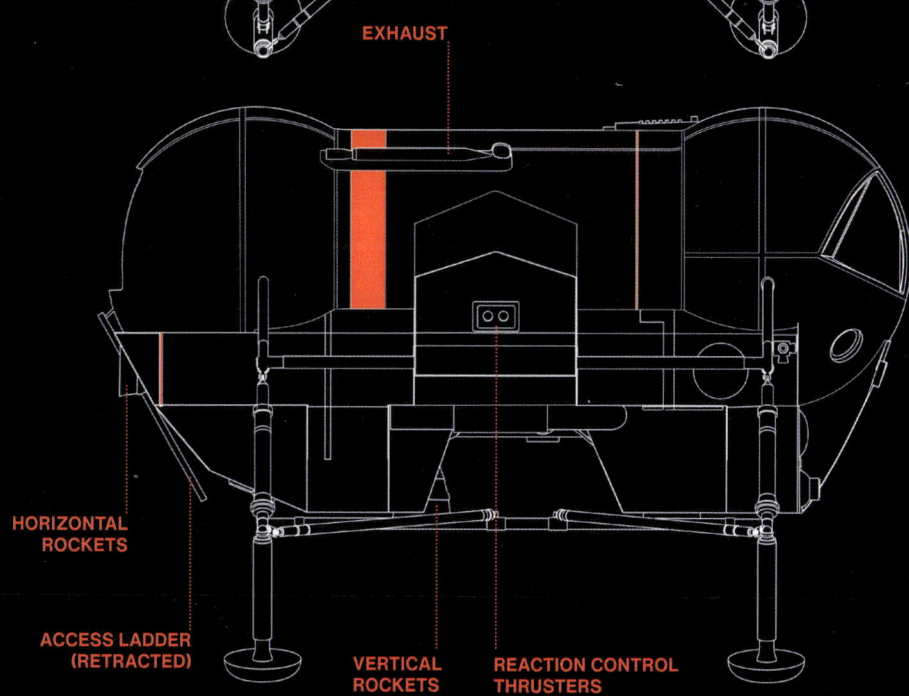

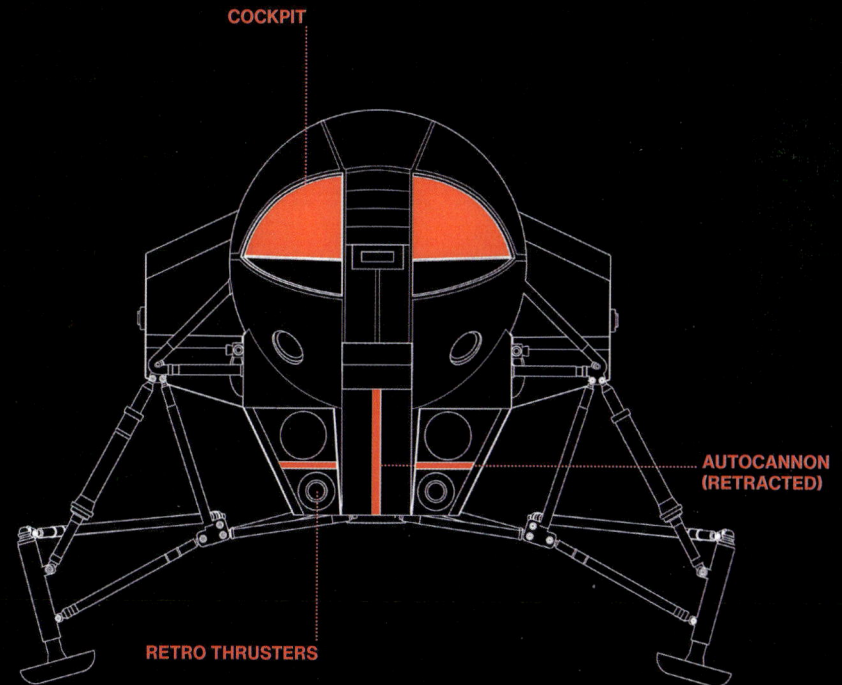

EXHAUST

COCKPIT

HORIZONTAL
ROCKETS

AUTOCANNON
(RETRACTED)

ACCESS LADDER
(RETRACTED)

VERTICAL
ROCKETS

REACTION CONTROL
THRUSTERS

RETRO THRUSTERS

INTERIOR

The interior of a Moonmobile is a small space rated for two pilots and a maximum of four passengers in the mid-section. While the interior is pressurised, for safety reasons crew are expected to wear EVA suits in the event of a pressure leak or explosive decompression; this further restricts the crew's movements. Many components of the vehicle's construction are carried over to its Earth-bound counterpart, the SHADO Mobile.

COCKPIT

A Pilot's station

B Co-pilot's station

C Life support controls

D Gun rack

E Umbilical air supply

F Sensor readouts

G Damage control readouts

H Air filtration system

I Access hatch leading to the craft's mid-section

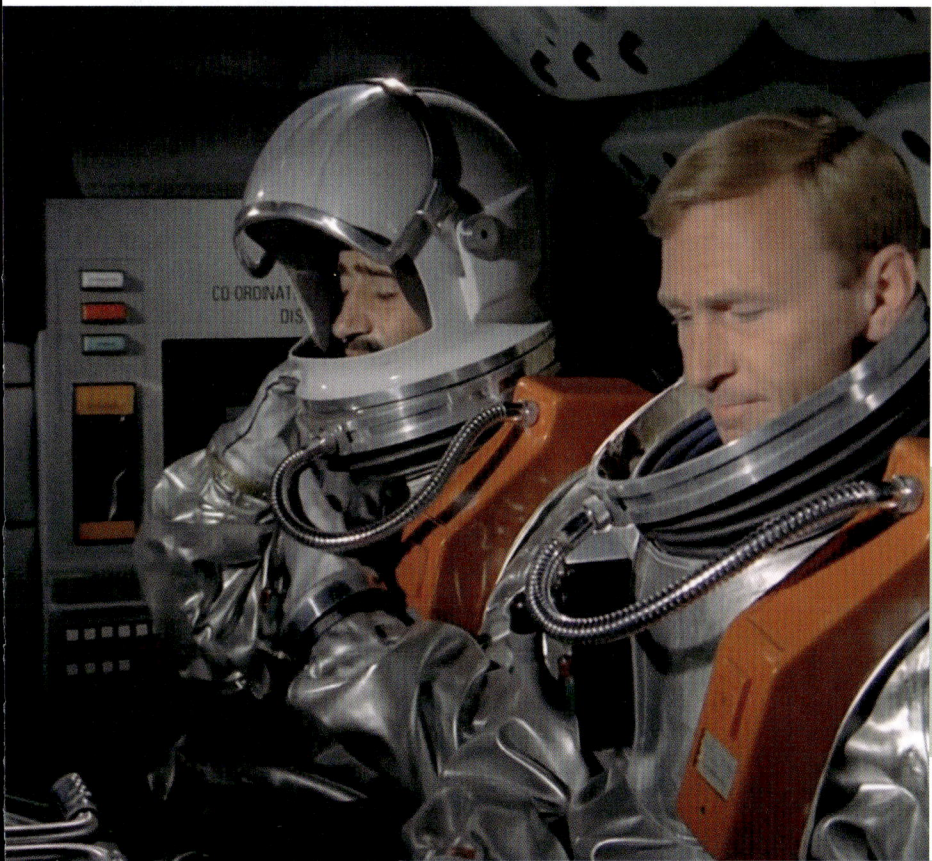

VARIANTS

As with the exterior, the interior of some Moonmobiles may vary depending on the age and use of the craft. For the most part, the controls and systems are the same, but additional panels may be added or moved in order to accommodate any internal modifications to the craft.

FLIGHT CONTROLS

The Moonmobiles are piloted using a similar system to the Interceptors. The yoke controls pitch and yaw, while a series of levers control vertical and horizontal thrust. These can also be pre-programmed for automatic control through simple terrain, though oversight is advised.

MOONBASE DEFENCE VEHICLE

When SHADO became operational in early 1980, the pace of alien attacks increased in frequency and intensity as their supply of humans was cut short. Soon it became apparent that Moonbase's existing defences would be unable to protect it effectively against the massed UFO attacks. Alternatives were needed – and quickly.

MDVs were the rather hastily-assembled response to this dilemma. Utilising existing terrestrial technology, MDVs are, essentially, hardened armoured personnel carriers, disassembled and shipped to the Moon using requisitioned cargo modules from the Moonbase Alpha project. The vehicles were adapted to operate on the lunar surface. Power was provided by electrical generators, and the interior cabin was replaced with a smaller armoured module that allowed the exterior of the vehicle to act like a second skin, greatly increasing the survival rate of the crew when engaging UFOs.

A guided missile launcher was fixed to the top of the vehicle, manned by a second operative. Capable of rotating a full 360 degrees, the launcher is fed by a magazine housing 12 missiles. Effective engagement range is over 1.8 miles, the missile defences now forcing UFO attacks to come in low over the lunar surface.

Currently, two of the five MDVs shipped to the Moon are still in operation and are in the process of being replaced by armoured turret systems.

LIMITATIONS

While the launchers are effective at long range, the speed and manoeuvrability of UFOs offers major advantages over the missile system at closer ranges where the alien reaction times degrade the missile's effectiveness. Even so, the threat the launchers provide has led to a change in UFO tactics.

ROUND THE CLOCK VIGILANCE

Until more permanent missile defences can be installed, the MDVs patrol the exterior of Moonbase with crews operating in 12-hour shifts. As the aliens have proven capable of evading detection, crews maintain a state of high alert as an attack could happen at any moment.

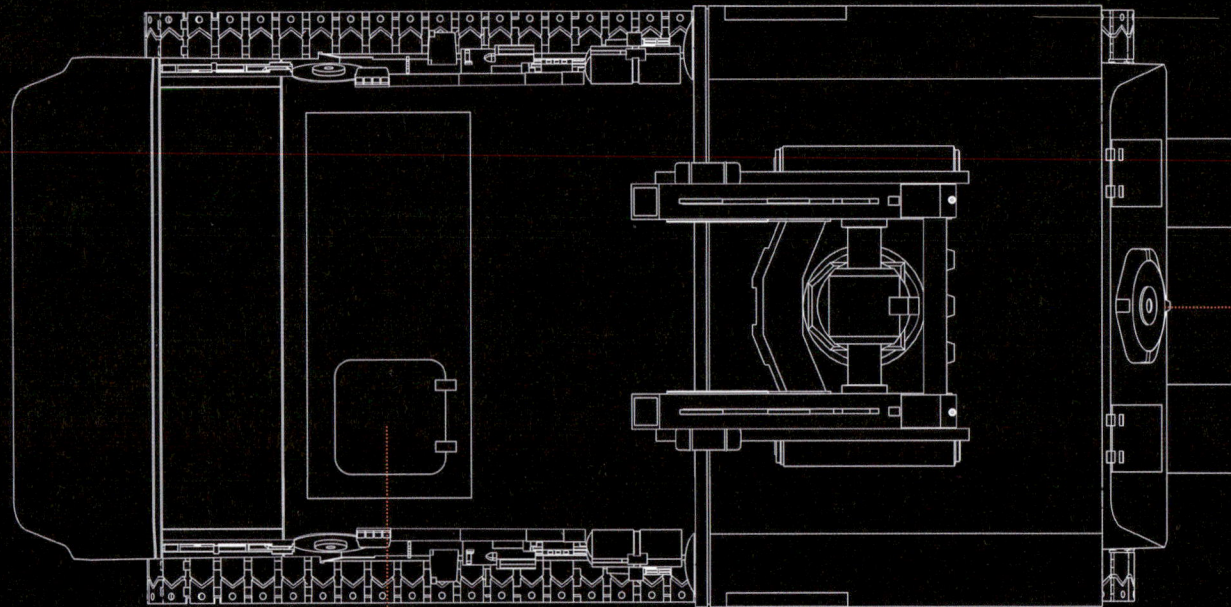

REAR ACCESS HATCH

ROCKET LAUNCHER

DRIVER'S VIEWPORT

DORSAL ACCESS HATCH

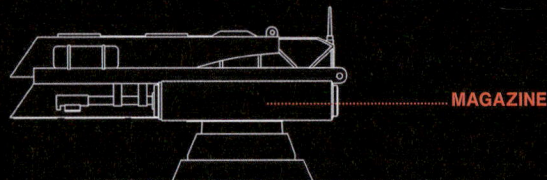

COMMS ARRAY

MAGAZINE

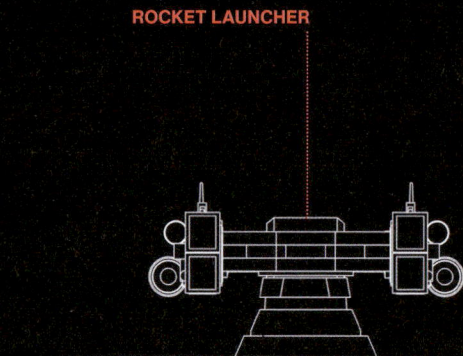

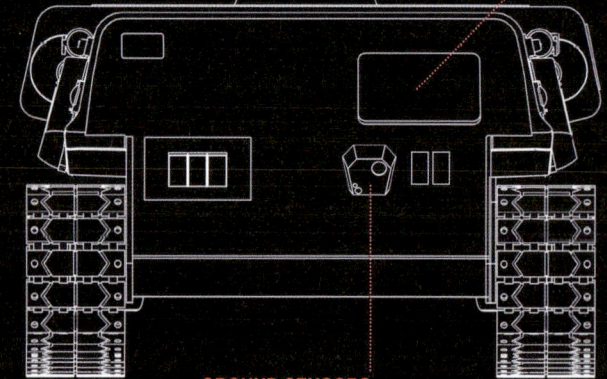

GROUND SENSORS

BATTERY COMPARTMENTS

The main vehicle the MDVs were adapted from was an experimental programme of armoured personnel carriers designed for use in jungle and swamp or wetland environments. The amphibious nature of the vehicle made it ideal for adaptation to the lunar environment, while the thick armoured shell offered more protection from the alien weaponry than the flimsier materials used on SHADO's other space vehicles.

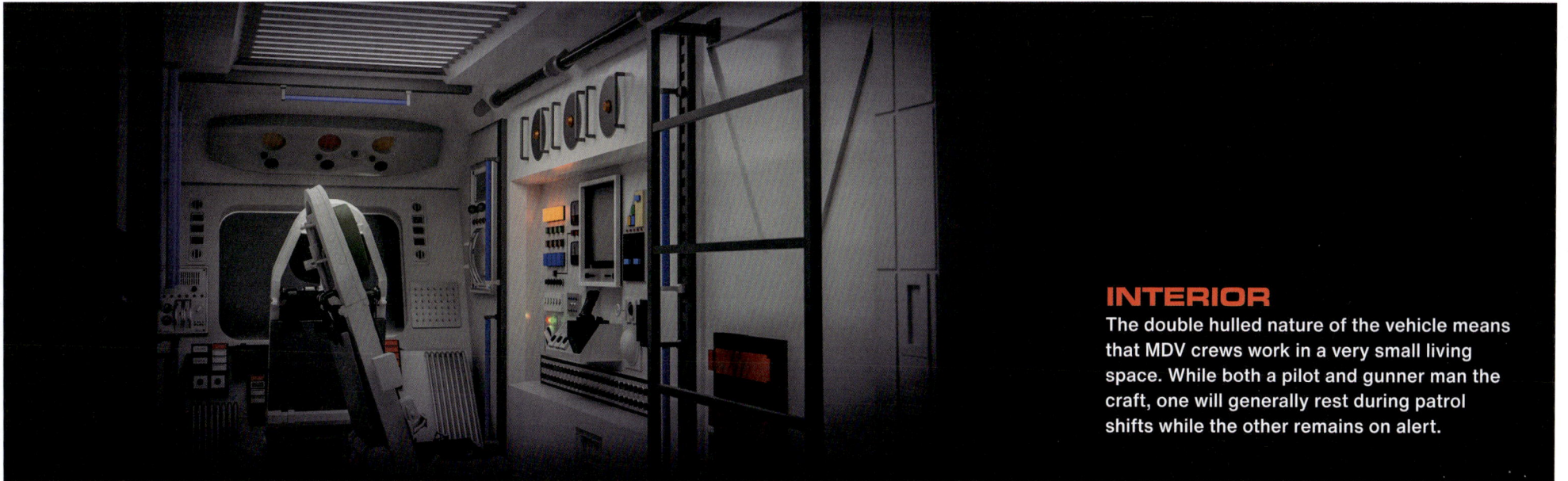

INTERIOR

The double hulled nature of the vehicle means that MDV crews work in a very small living space. While both a pilot and gunner man the craft, one will generally rest during patrol shifts while the other remains on alert.

LUNAR CARRIER

From the early 1960s, the primary method of lunar transit would be in small capsules, launched into orbit with massively inefficient rockets. The whole process needed years of preplanning, required huge budgets and had little margin for error. While this method continued through the early 1970s, it became clear that if SHADO was going to build and supply the first permanent installation on the Moon, they would need to design a craft that could reliably make the journey and be cost effective, versatile and, most importantly, reusable. The answer to this was the Lunar Module.

CONCEPT

Conceived from its inception as a two-stage vehicle, the concept for the Lunar Module called for the spacecraft part of the vehicle to be airlifted to the edge of the atmosphere by a larger carrier aircraft. The spacecraft would then separate and leave the atmosphere under its own power. While this method would limit the payloads that the Module could carry, the fuel (and money) saved means that flights to the Moon could become as easy as a commercial flight on Earth.

Upon return to Earth, the Module, protected by its heat shield, would decelerate to a speed where it could re-enter the atmosphere and rendezvous with the Carrier. Once safely captured, the craft could be reused after a brief safety evaluation.

HALTON SPACEPORT

Lunar Modules and Carriers are kept and maintained at a reconfigured RAF base in Halton, England. Flights from Halton operate under the guise of commercial traffic to near-Earth orbit or the Moon and on occasion will transport genuine scientific teams to maintain the deception. This allows SHADO to maintain control over their operations and ensure they are not disrupted by outside commercial and scientific endeavours.

The unusual shape of the Carrier makes it a rather tricky aircraft to fly. However, the design provides enough lift to carry the Module to the edge of the atmosphere. The craft makes a very tempting target for attacking UFOs, so Carriers are grounded and operations ceased immediately upon any sightings.

TWO CRAFT

The Lunar Carrier and Lunar Module are two separate entities even after they have been conjoined. There is no way to transit between the two craft, and in an emergency situation, the Module is detached and its emergency parachutes deployed while the crew on the Carrier perform a standard ejection.

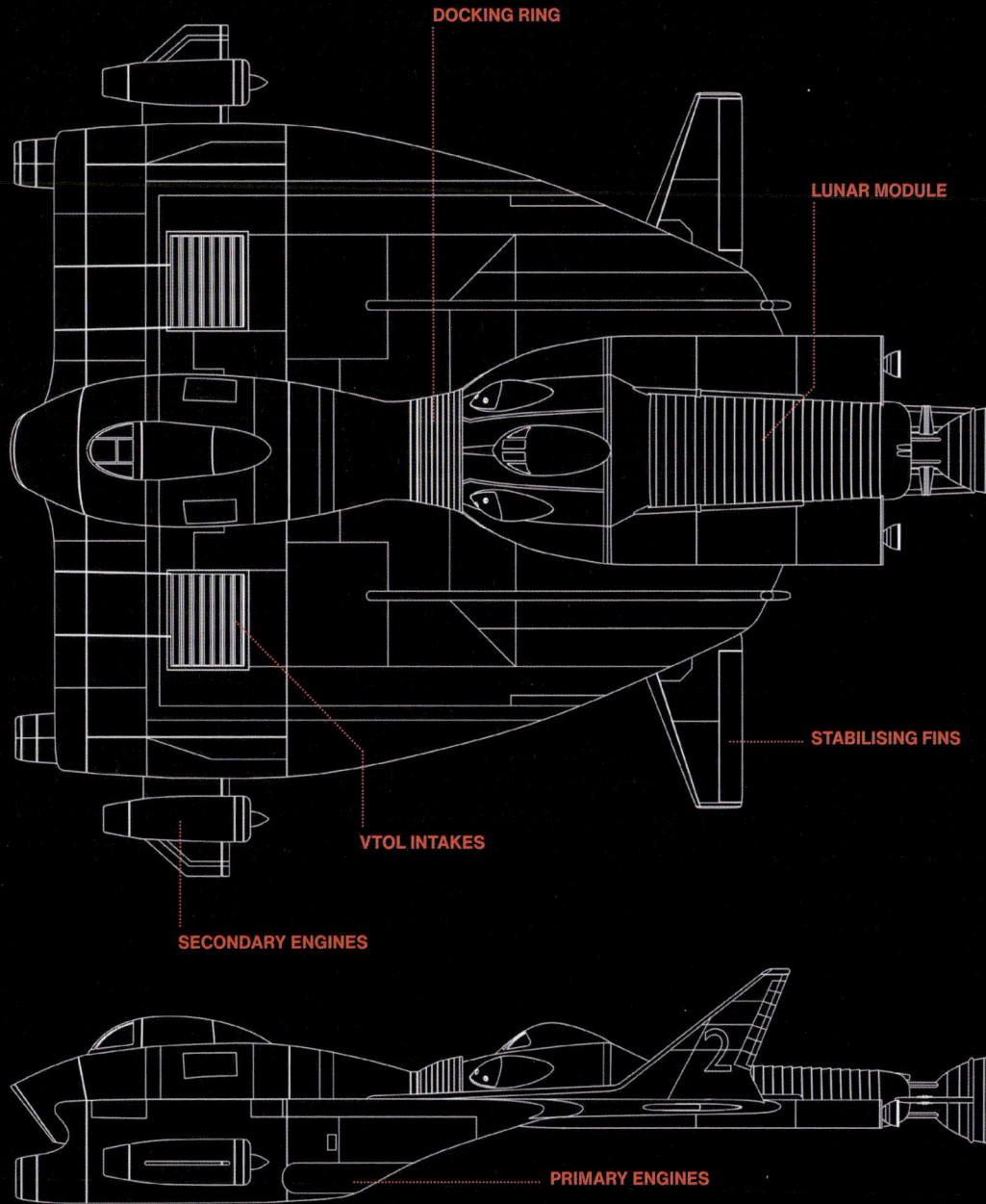

DOCKING RING

LUNAR MODULE

STABILISING FINS

VTOL INTAKES

SECONDARY ENGINES

DOCKING
The Carrier and Module are connected by a series of magnetic clamps.

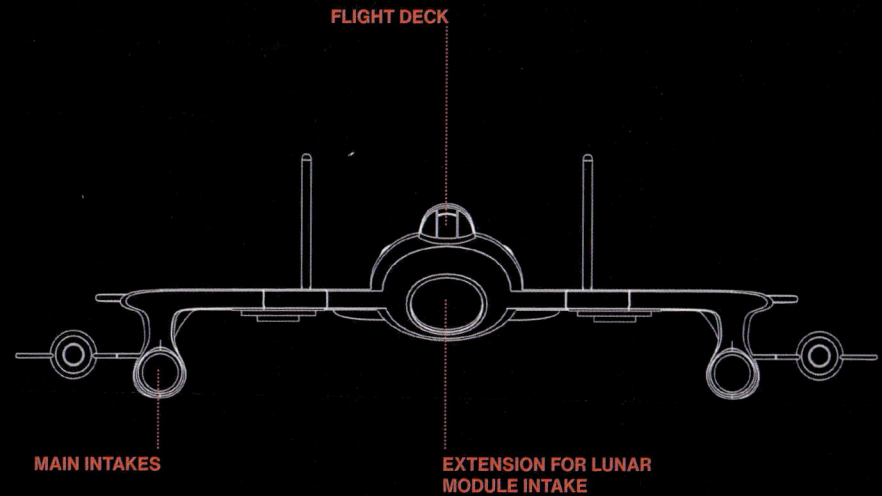

PRIMARY ENGINES

FLIGHT DECK

MAIN INTAKES

EXTENSION FOR LUNAR MODULE INTAKE

LUNAR MODULE

Compared to similar craft, the Module has a much tougher design – unsurprising given its role as the first truly reusable spacecraft. In theory, a Module should be able to return to Earth even in the event of superficial damage to its heat shield. Once recovered and returned to base, the craft is put through a rigorous testing programme to look for wear and tear to the exterior, a process that can take two days and cannot be accelerated. For this reason, extra Modules were built and are constantly rotated through operational cycles.

OPERATIONAL RANGE

The operational range of a Module is limited between Earth and the Moon, but it can remain in orbit for protracted periods without resupply. This allows crews to undertake lengthy satellite maintenance or orbital surveys in a single trip.

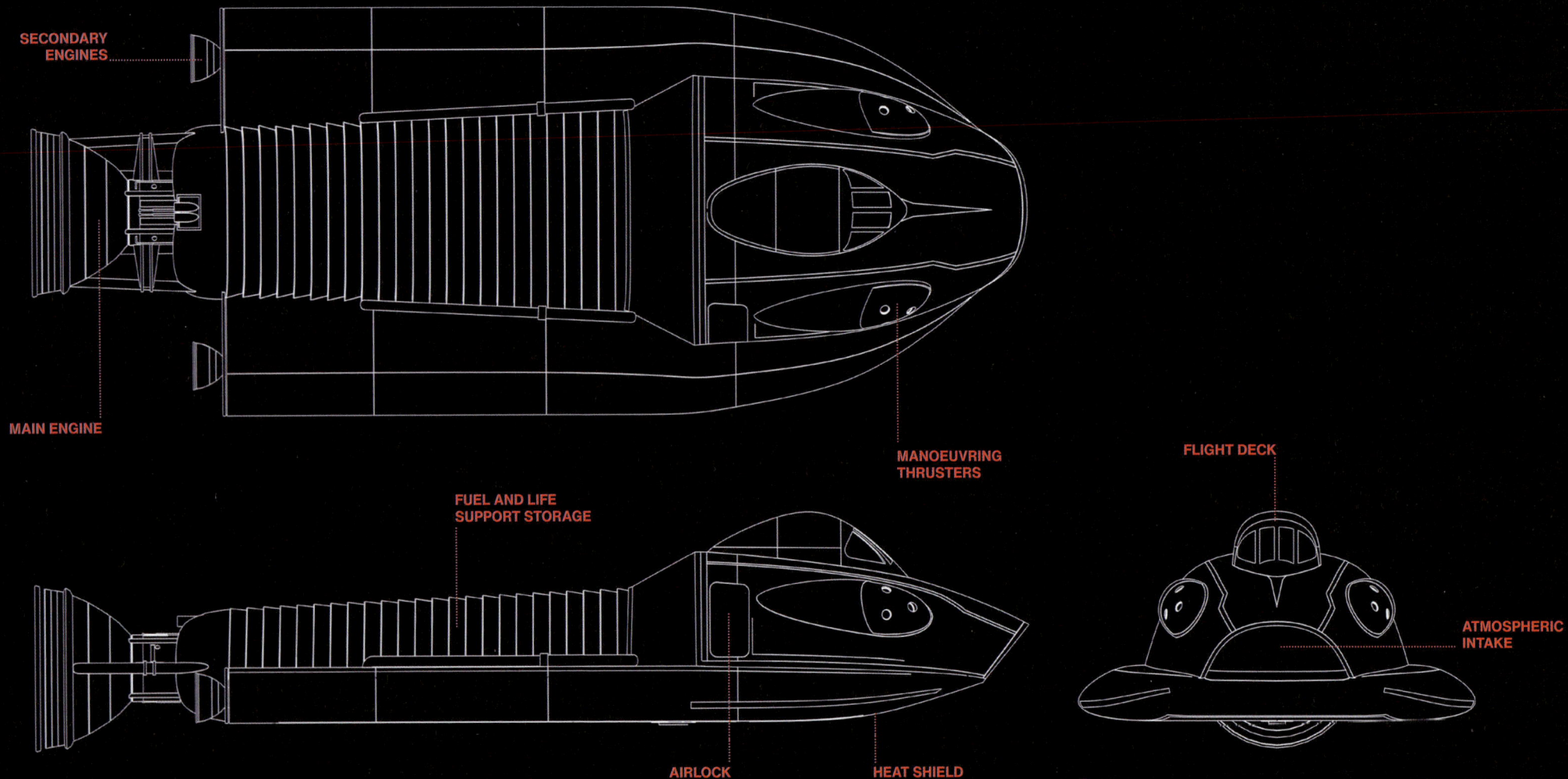

SECONDARY ENGINES

MAIN ENGINE

MANOEUVRING THRUSTERS

FLIGHT DECK

FUEL AND LIFE SUPPORT STORAGE

ATMOSPHERIC INTAKE

AIRLOCK

HEAT SHIELD

SENSORS

The Module is outfitted with multiple sensors that are retracted into the hull to protect them during reentry.

RE-ENTRY

The Module's re-entry into Earth's atmosphere is a precision manoeuvre controlled by precise calculations and timing to ensure its rendezvous with the Carrier. If the two craft fail to dock, the Module can use its single VTOL engine and parachutes to land safely, but damage to the craft is almost inevitable.

MODULE INTERIOR

The interior of the Module is separated into three compartments:

■ **A two-person flight deck where the craft's primary control functions are performed.**

■ **A passenger section with room for four people.**

■ **A small cargo compartment for supplies bound for Moonbase.**

In specific circumstances, the passenger section can be stripped to make a second cargo bay and vice versa.

The flight deck is fitted out with controls suitable for piloting the craft effectively in both the zero-*g* of space and in Earth's atmosphere.

COCKPIT

A Pilot's chair

B Co-pilot's chair

C Manual controls

D Computer entry controls

E Computer display panel (retracted)

F Observation window

G Onboard computer

H Air vents

I Life support panel

COMPUTER DISPLAY

The primary computer display can be lowered in front of the observation window during re-entry and landing. This provides a more accessible heads-up view of the computer readouts for the pilots while also protecting them from the intense glare of re-entry.

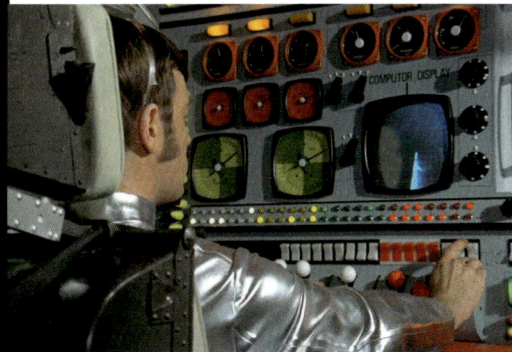

VARIANTS

As with many of SHADO's other spacecraft, there are subtle differences between each individual craft – the result of field modifications as new technology enters service and is retrofitted to particular craft, depending on their primary mission. A fleet-wide modernisation programme is underway to standardise each Module.

NEPTUNE SPACE MONITOR

The rapid expansion of the space programme through the 1970s had greatly increased the amount of activity in near-Earth orbit, and many existing spacecraft were now starting to show their limitations. It was quickly becoming apparent that to sustain humanity's foothold in space, new craft would need to be designed that could remain in service for longer, while also having an increased operational range.

The Neptune series was designed using developments taken from existing space station technology. Essentially, it was a large-scale mobile platform that would be launched into space in sections and assembled in near-Earth orbit. For efficiency, parts would be mass-produced, and during any construction phase, three Neptunes would be assembled at the same time.

The sheer versatility of the Neptune space frame, coupled with the mass-produced nature of the craft, means it is one of the most common sights in Earth orbit.

The largest section, containing the primary engines and fuel tanks, would be launched into space as one unit and the rest of the craft would be assembled around them. The command module would then be attached to the front with additional life support elements added along a central spine. A superstructure would then be assembled around the craft to hold all the parts securely in place. From there, the design would generally shift in the direction of whatever mission parameters that particular Neptune had been given.

Many Neptunes are retrofitted with radio telescopes and sensor equipment, allowing them to observe deep space. Additional passenger modules could be added in order to allow the craft to become a transfer module from Earth to the Moon. Two are operated by the International Space Commission and are specifically outfitted for surveying space junk in Earth orbit, which can be destroyed with mines where necessary.

SHADO currently operates a number of Neptune craft as part of their deep space probe programme. These have been militarised to track and identify UFOs outside SID's operational range. This is one of the most dangerous jobs within the organisation, as Neptunes are completely defenceless and make for tempting targets. Once SHADO realised that the aliens were beginning to stop short of Earth and abduct crews from these vessels, the deep space probe missions were shelved and SHADO's Neptune fleet were relegated to Moon transit and maintaining the SID satellite network.

LIFESPAN

Generally, Neptunes are designed to have an operational lifespan of about 10 years. However, given their modular nature and the constant redevelopment and introduction of new equipment and systems, it is possible that some of the Neptunes in service today will remain in service for the foreseeable future.

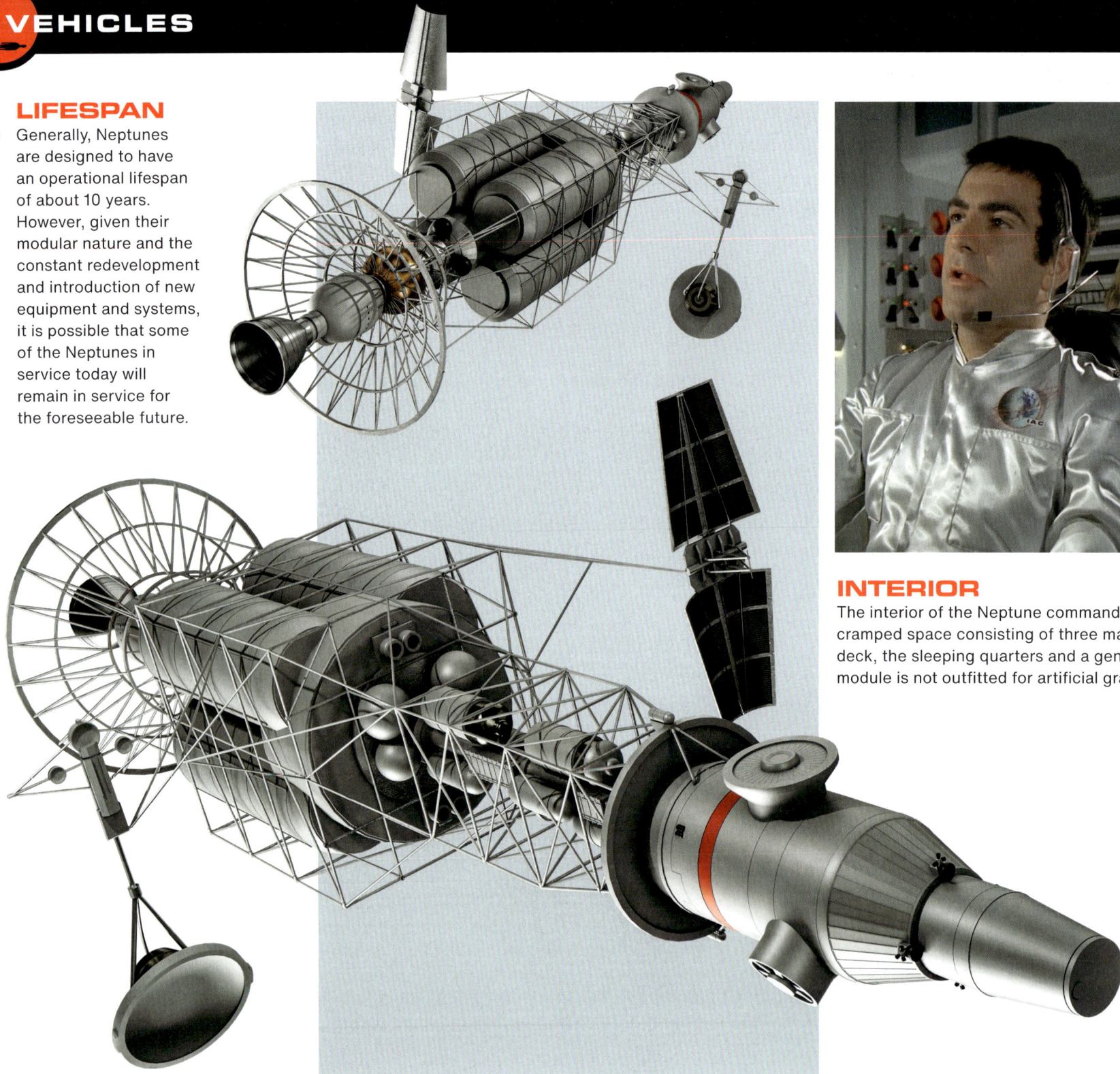

INTERIOR

The interior of the Neptune command module is a small, cramped space consisting of three main sections: the flight deck, the sleeping quarters and a general living space. The module is not outfitted for artificial gravity.

COMMAND MODULE

RETRO THRUSTER

RADIO TELESCOPE

DOCKING RING

EVA AIRLOCK

LIFE SUPPORT
STORAGE TANKS

COMMUNICATIONS ARRAY

FUEL AND POWER
PLANT MODULE

MAIN ENGINE

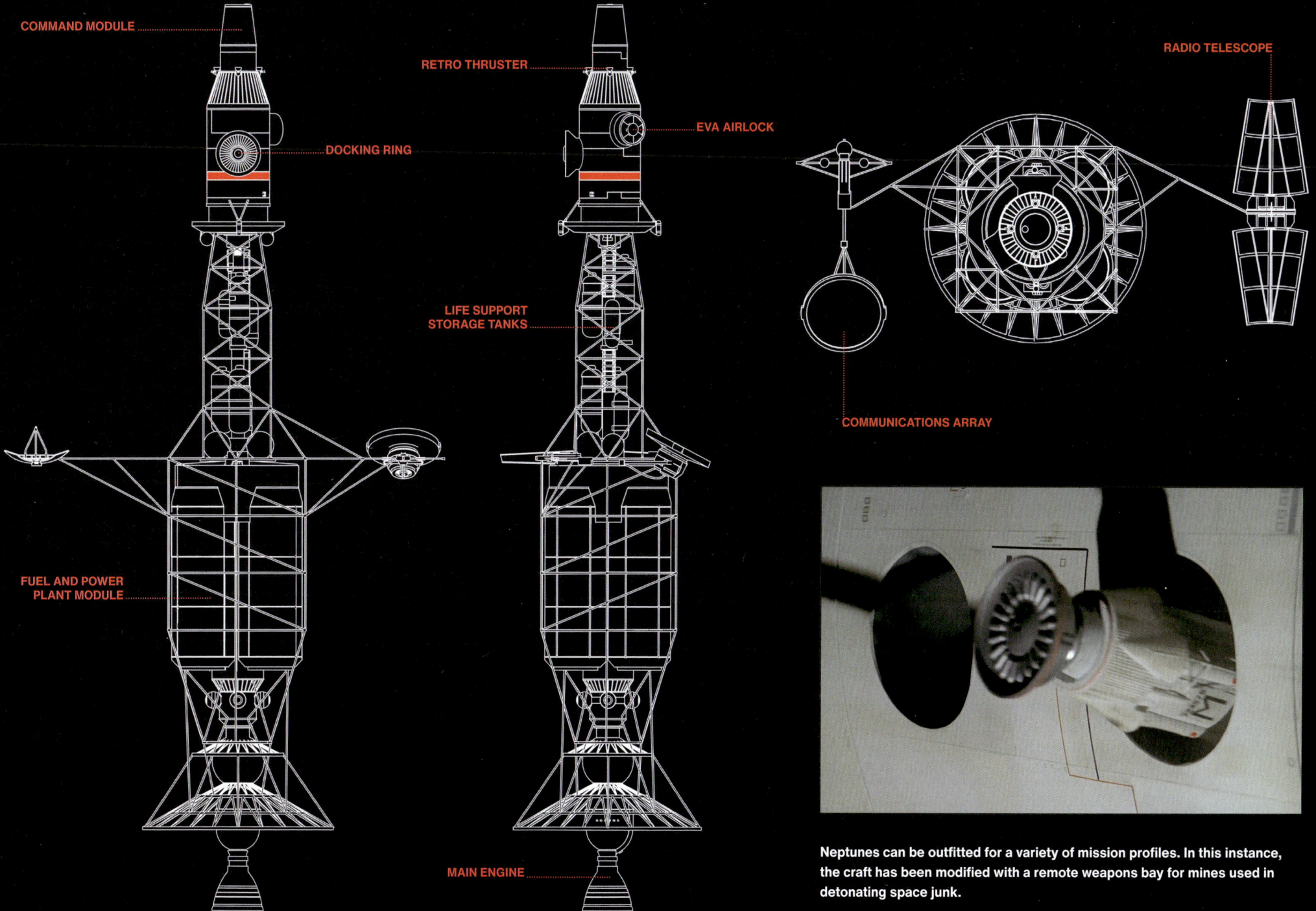

Neptunes can be outfitted for a variety of mission profiles. In this instance, the craft has been modified with a remote weapons bay for mines used in detonating space junk.

THE SHADO NAVY

Operating as Earth's second line of defence the SHADO naval force, particularly the Skydiver fleet, an ever-expanding number of submarines that patrol the seas and are ready to launch fighter aircraft at a moment's notice. The rest of the navy occupies more of a support role, making sure the various Skydivers are supplied and supported while on station. This includes a series of commercially-bought recovery vessels and seaplanes.

Several naval bases are in operation around the globe, with the primary construction yards hidden within an old classified submarine facility located at Scapa Flow in Scotland.

Out of all the postings, a position in the SHADO Navy is probably the safest but conversely the most gruelling, with much of the time on station spent in tight compartments maintaining the craft. For this reason, naval and space personnel are constantly rotated.

SKYDIVER

In the event of the Moonbase Interceptors failing to destroy an incoming UFO, a second line of defence was required to intercept UFOs within Earth's atmosphere before they could affect a landing. This would require advanced experimental fighter aircraft to be hidden all over the globe in positions where they could be launched instantly to defend key targets or population centres. Operating such a force on land, even in remote areas, would draw unwelcome attention to SHADO's operation, so engineers were directed to develop a craft that could be launched from a concealed underwater platform. The result of this research was the Skydiver fleet.

While small for a submarine, the technology in Skydiver is leagues ahead of any submersible in operation today. Completely invisible to sonar when running silent, and able to remain underwater for weeks at a time, the Skydivers patrol the seas waiting for the call to leap into action.

The real breakthrough is the submarine's ability to deploy an advanced Skyfighter from the front of the vessel. At launch depth, the vessel pitches up to a sixty-degree angle while the pilot transfers via chute to the Skyfighter. Once the angle is achieved, the Skyfighter's boosters ignite, blasting it clear of the vessel and to the surface, not unlike an ICBM. This means that SHADO can have a Skydiver at key points around the globe, allowing for almost certain interception.

At present, SHADO's manufacturing plant at Scapa Flow can only produce three Skydivers at a time. Following the destruction of Skydiver three, only five remain on active stations in the Pacific, Arctic, Indian and east and west Atlantic Oceans. The final three vessels, due to launch in early 1984, will complete the network, allowing for total coverage across the world.

In comparison to the fledgling space force, a hundred years of exploring the sea and sky has enabled SHADO to create a formidable vessel capable of levelling the playing field against the alien threat. As of writing, only one Skydiver has been lost to enemy action.

SENSOR ARRAYS

As an additional role, Skydivers can use their onboard suite of sensor arrays and communication systems to monitor objects in orbit. This is vital in maintaining SHADO's network of SID satellites.

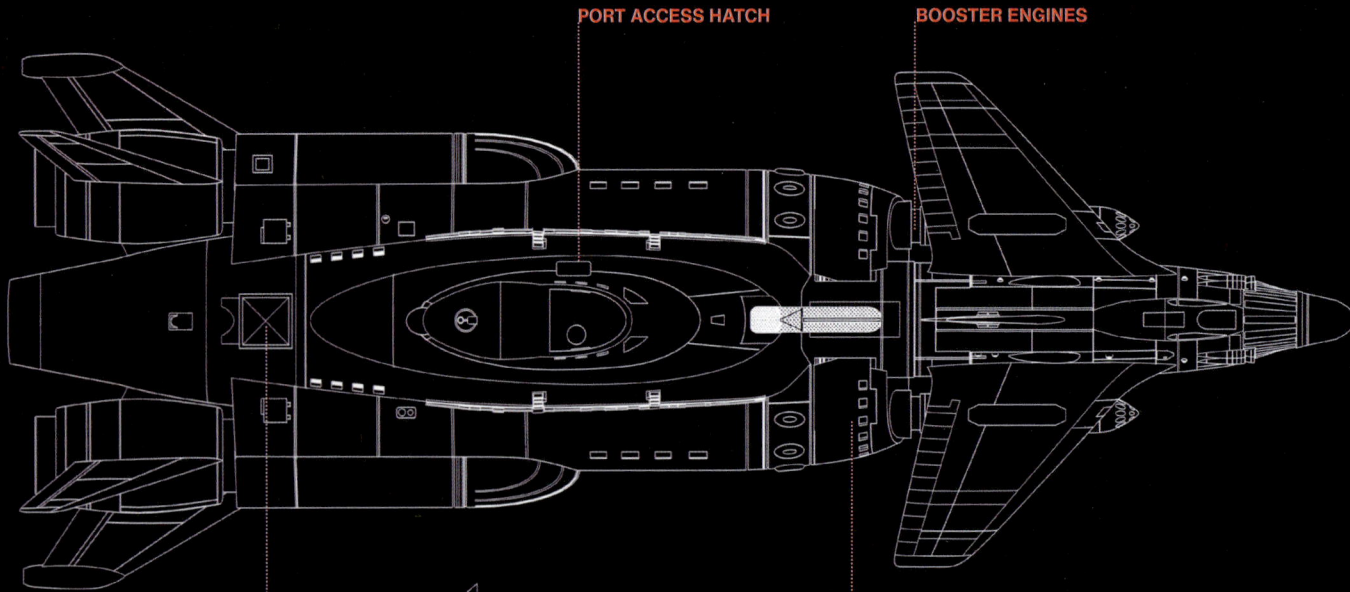

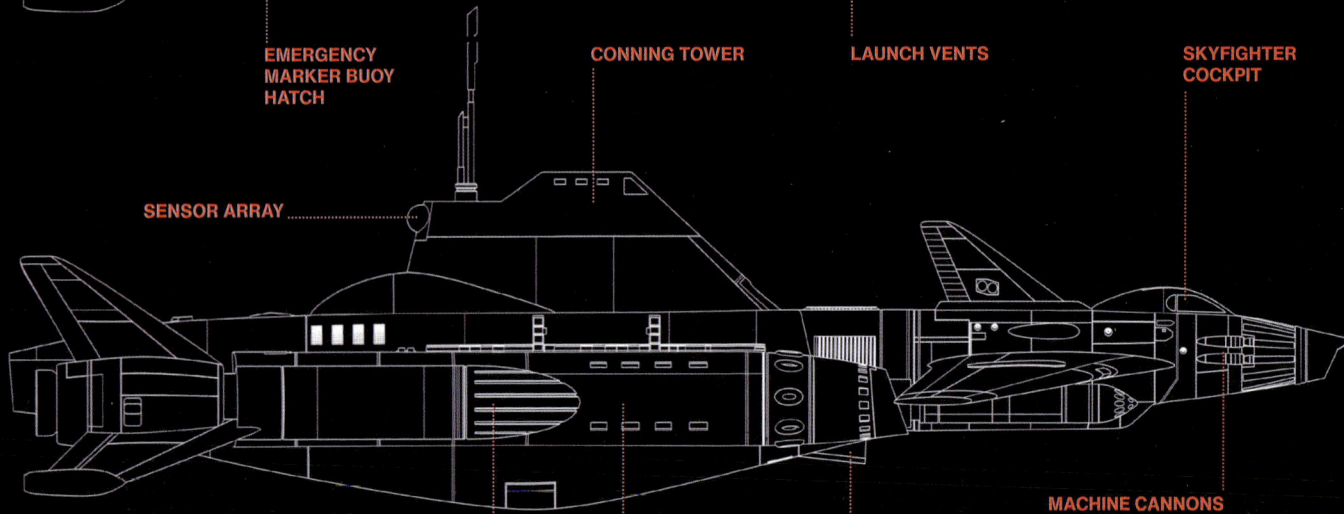

PORT ACCESS HATCH

BOOSTER ENGINES

PERISCOPE

EMERGENCY
MARKER BUOY
HATCH

CONNING TOWER

LAUNCH VENTS

SKYFIGHTER
COCKPIT

PRIMARY ENGINE

PRIMARY ENGINE

SENSOR ARRAY

CLEAR-VU SENSORS

SECONDARY INTAKE

MACHINE CANNONS

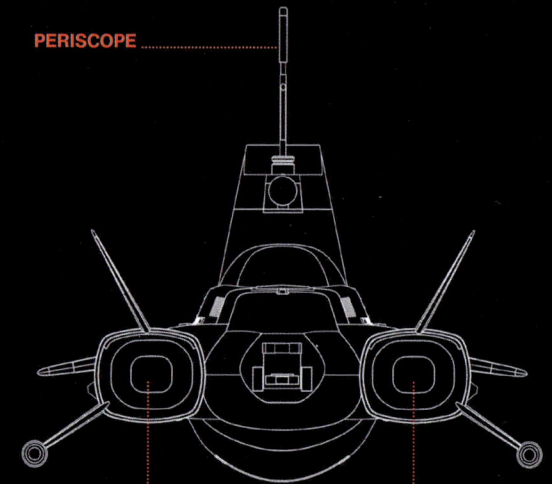

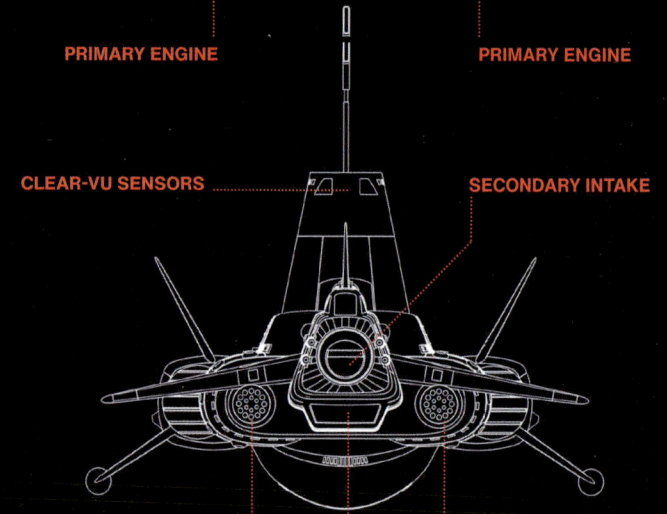

WEAPON POD

WEAPON POD

INTAKES

LIGHTING ARRAY AND
TORPEDO TUBES
(DEPLOYED)

PRIMARY INTAKE

A weapons pod is located on each side of
the Skyfighter. Each holds a selection of
air-to-air and air-to-ground rockets that can
be interchanged, depending on the location
of the target.

BALLAST TANKS

One of the advantages of being able to incorporate aerodynamics into the design of Skydiver means the craft can to a small degree function as a ground effect vehicle. In situations where a Skydiver needs to proceed to a target area at speed the craft can 'sea skim'. Essentially the combination of the large turbine engines at the rear and the craft's wings can lift the majority of the craft out of the water allowing it to skim across the surface with little to no water resistance. Sea skim can only be conducted out of sight of surface contacts and in calm seas.

In the event of a critical system failure, Skydivers have various safety features to ensure the survival of the crew. An emergency marker buoy is launched in order to mark the location of the craft on the surface while creating a direct telephone link. The survivors can then either escape using the hatches or wait for SHADO divers to arrive by seaplane.

SUPPLY SHIPS

SHADO have bought and modified several catamaran ocean mining vessels in order to keep the Skydiver fleet resupplied with fuel, supplies and munitions. A Skydiver can dock between the twin hulls of the vessel for servicing. Generally it is recommended that a Skydiver will do this after every successful launch to maintain its reserve supply.

INTERIOR

While being an impressive vessel by many standards, Skydiver's functionality requires the craft to be quite small compared to other submarines. A crew of six occupy the tight space inside and will generally be on a tour of duty for months on end.

COMMAND AND CONTROL SECTION

The main control area of Skydiver is housed within the conning tower of the craft. Two decks tall, it is the largest area of the submarine, and houses the helm, navigation, life support and computer processing stations.

A Skydiver's helm station is located in the upper level, in order to minimise disruption to the pilot during launch stations. Experimental 'clear-vu' cameras mounted in the conning tower give more visibility than would be possible on an ordinary submarine, while other sonar mapping instruments allow the pilot to navigate the craft safely.

B Surface hatch controls

C Skydiver has three escape hatches in the event of a Subsmash incident. One is housed beside the helm station, while the other two are in the port and starboard compartments.

D Ladder to conning tower

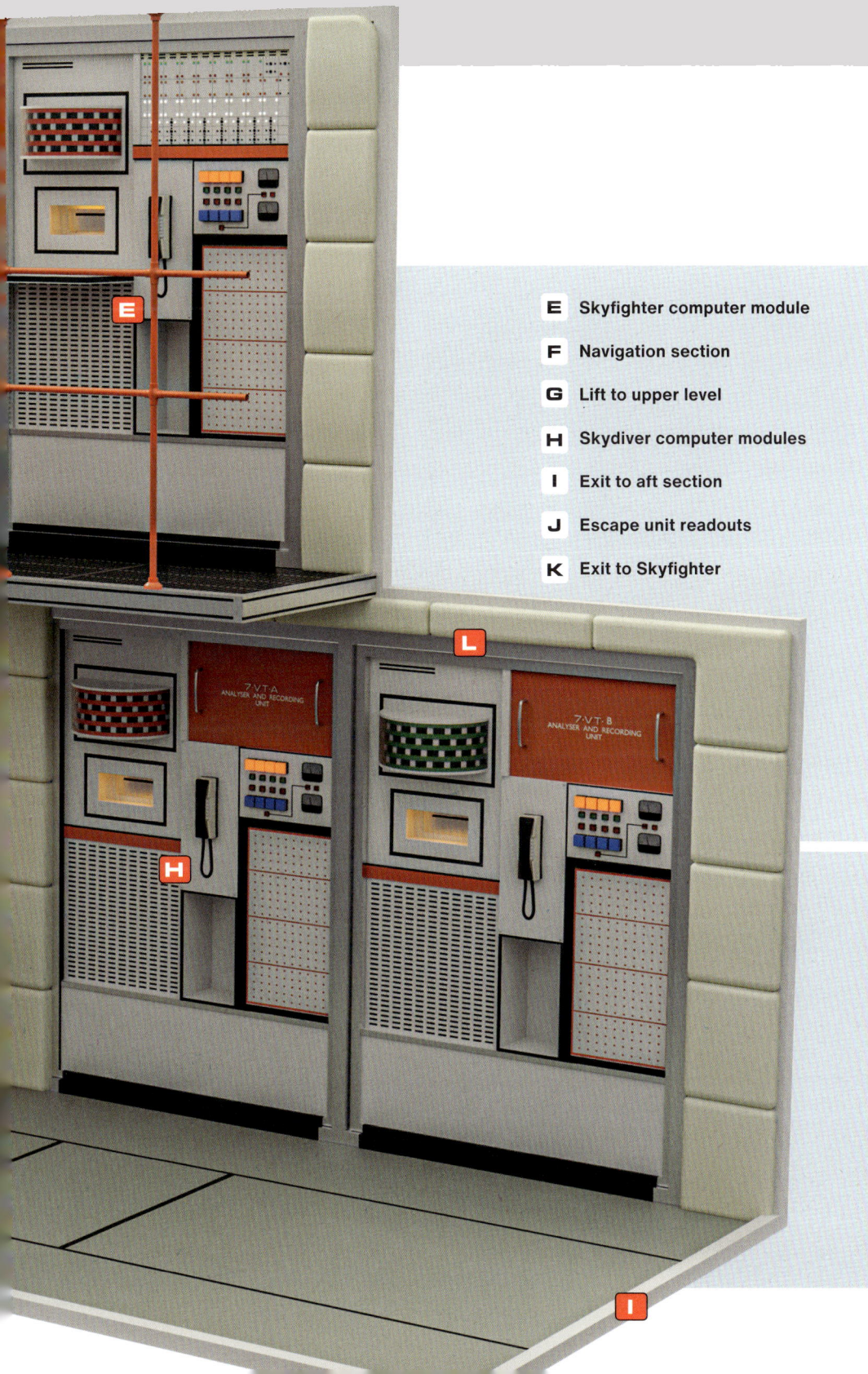

E Skyfighter computer module

F Navigation section

G Lift to upper level

H Skydiver computer modules

I Exit to aft section

J Escape unit readouts

K Exit to Skyfighter

L The periscope is mounted at the back of the compartment and is usually stowed in the ceiling ready for use. Generally, it is used by the Captain or executive officer (XO) to scan the horizon before the craft can surface.

M The far side of the compartment houses the sonar station, life support equipment and a locker containing small arms in case of emergencies.

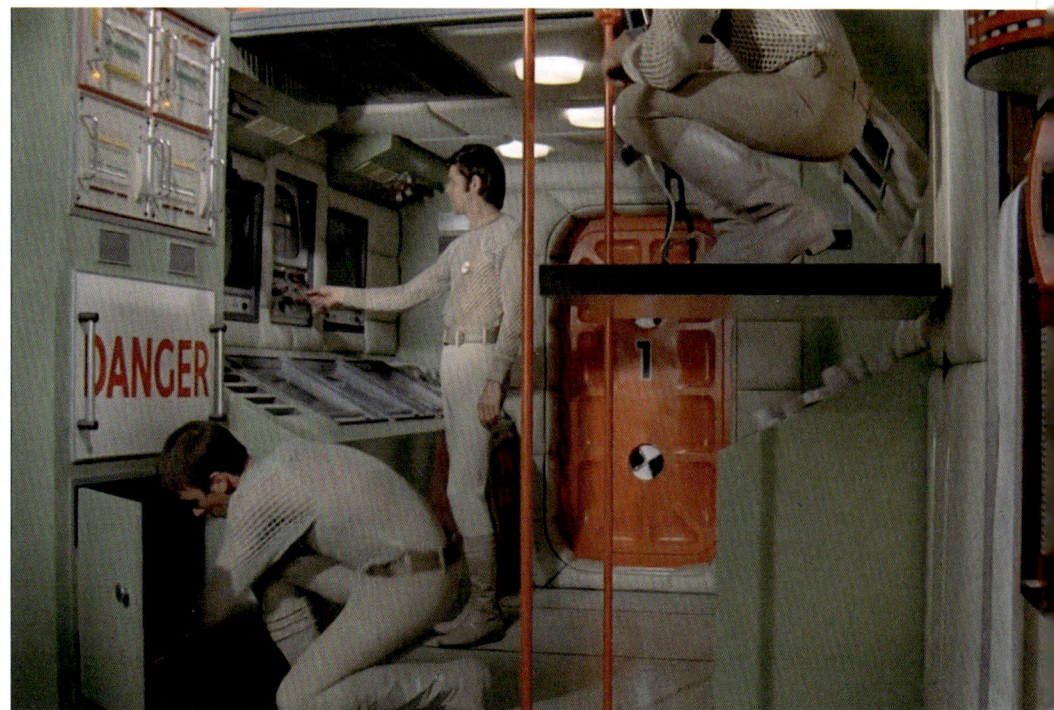

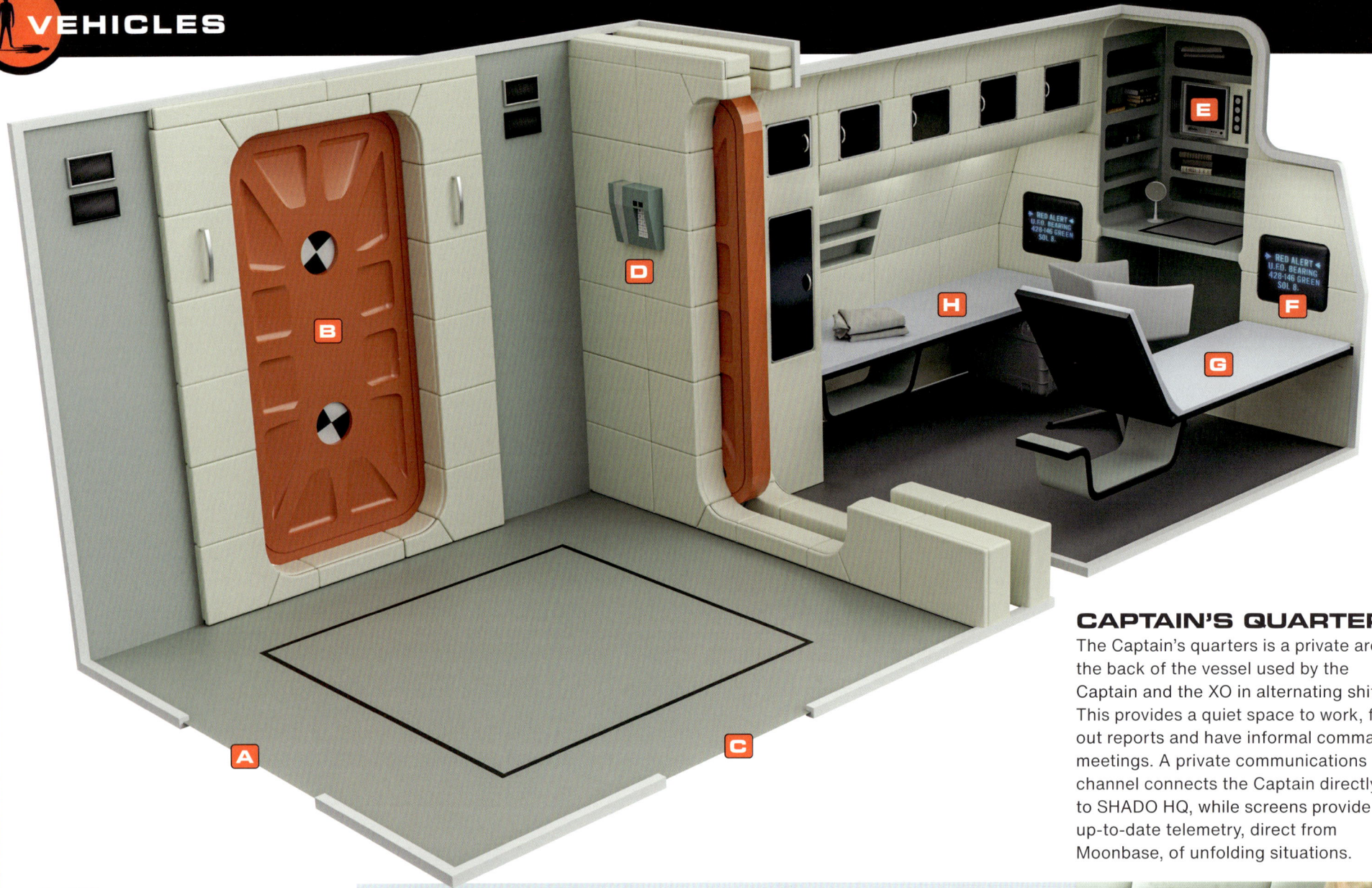

CAPTAIN'S QUARTERS

The Captain's quarters is a private area at the back of the vessel used by the Captain and the XO in alternating shifts. This provides a quiet space to work, fill out reports and have informal command meetings. A private communications channel connects the Captain directly to SHADO HQ, while screens provide up-to-date telemetry, direct from Moonbase, of unfolding situations.

AFT COMPARTMENT

The rest of the interior space of the vessel is primarily dedicated to living space and engineering. A compartment past the aft door of the command deck acts as a thoroughfare between the Captain's quarters and the port and starboard sections.

A Access to command deck

B Access to starboard quarters

C Access to port quarters

D Intercom

E Workstation

F Information screens

G Captain's bunk

H XO's bunk: As space on Skydiver is at a premium, the furniture needs to be as adaptable as possible. Each of the sleeping bunks can fold up into a seating position to make them comfortable when off duty. The Captain and XO are seated opposite each other to facilitate command meetings.

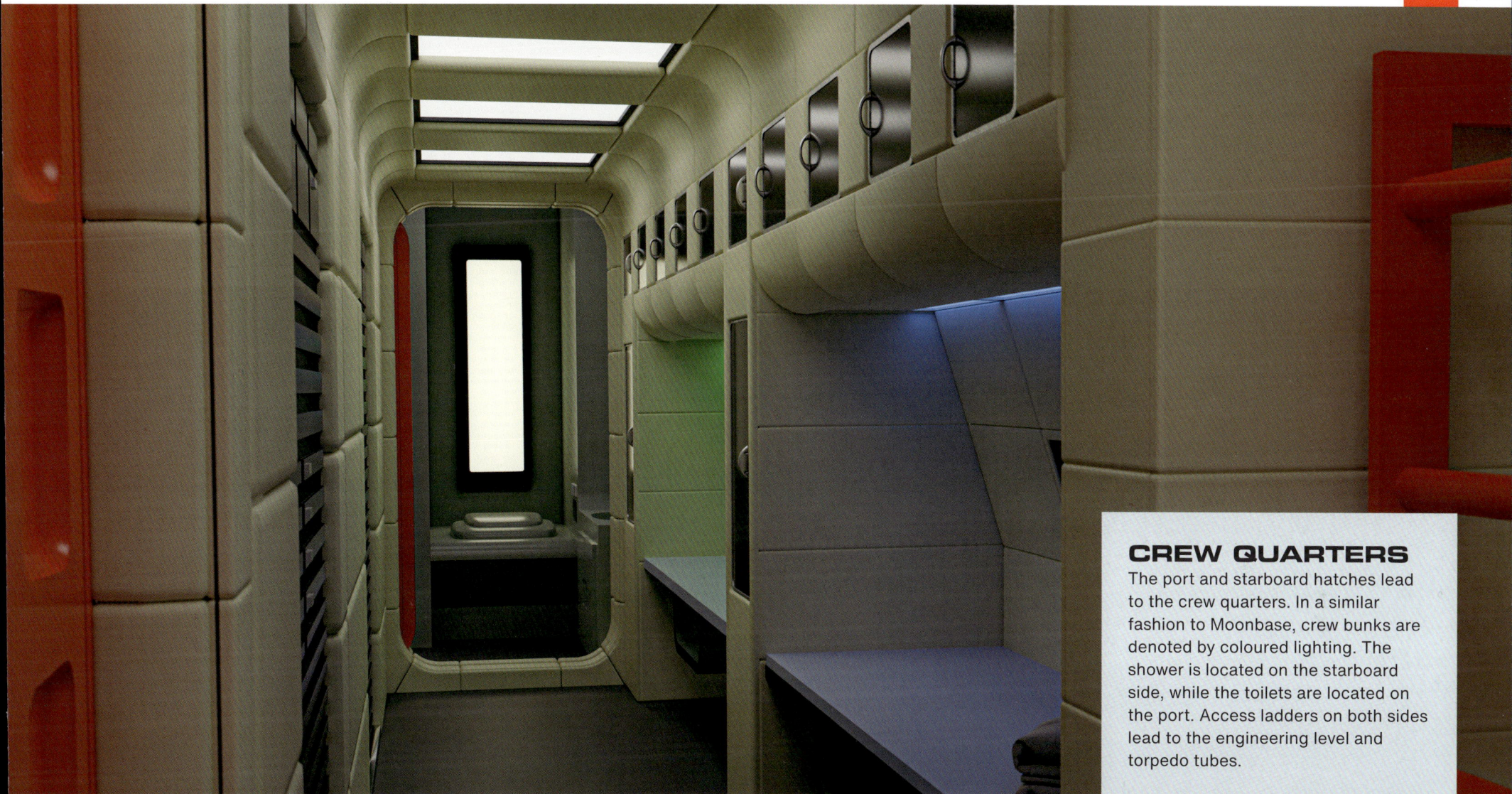

CREW QUARTERS

The port and starboard hatches lead to the crew quarters. In a similar fashion to Moonbase, crew bunks are denoted by coloured lighting. The shower is located on the starboard side, while the toilets are located on the port. Access ladders on both sides lead to the engineering level and torpedo tubes.

LOWER LEVEL

The lowest level is mostly a crawl space that allows access to the vessel's engineering systems and the forward torpedo tubes. In the event that the escape hatches are compromised, the torpedo tubes can be used as an alternative.

THE SKYFIGHTER

Designed to cross the vast abyss of space, UFOs greatly outclass any SHADO craft in that arena. Once in Earth's atmosphere, however, much of that advantage is stripped away. The challenge facing SHADO's engineering team was to develop a craft that could not only go toe-to-toe with the enemy, but also function as part of a larger vessel and deploy from underwater.

DEVELOPMENT

Development on the Skyfighter was conducted in parallel with the Skydiver team as both craft needed to work symbiotically, plus it was important that the amphibious nature of the craft would in no way impede its combat effectiveness in the air. This required extensive modelling and testing over the 10 years of SHADO's development.

The resulting craft is a powerful supersonic fighter, able to fly fast enough to outmanoeuvre the directed energy weapon used by UFOs and deliver a devastating barrage of rockets to destroy the alien's defences.

At any one time, there will be two Skyfighters to one Skydiver, with one being on station and the other back at a SHADair base for rearming and maintenance.

RETURNING TO BASE
When returning to base, the Skyfighter lands like a traditional aircraft on regular runways. Once down, the craft are quickly hidden in special hangers to keep them from public view. The unusual nature of the craft makes them difficult to handle at slow speeds, their only real design weakness, so only the most experienced pilots are rated to fly the Skyfighter.

BOOSTER FUEL
A secondary tank of booster fuel is held on the Skydiver, allowing for the Skyfighter to be launched twice before the submarine needs to rendezvous with a supply vessel. As this can take days, SHADO HQ needs to be sure a UFO is present and interceptable before authorising a launch and risking Skydiver being out of action for some time.

SKYFIGHTER COCKPIT

Smaller than the cockpit used on the Interceptor, the Skyfighter's interior is much more akin to a conventional aircraft. The pilot's chair is adjusted into flight position from the entry chute once the pilot is aboard. The main canopy is also hardened to protect it from launch and re-entry into the ocean. While this adds protection to the pilot, it does somewhat restrict their field of view.

A Pilot's seat	**E** Ejection system
B Life support equipment	**F** Yoke
C Elevator platform	**G** Pilot's seat (undeployed)
D Entry chute	**H** Entry hatch

EJECTOR SEAT

In the event the craft is irreparably damaged, a traditional ejection system can blast the pilot to safety. Explosive bolts activate in several sections across the armoured canopy, separating it from the fuselage a split second before rocket jets blast the pilot to safety.

G Canopy
The Skyfighter is optimised for fast and manoeuvrable hit-and-run strikes in order to combat the slower UFO's 360-degree field of fire. The focused design of the cockpit canopy highlights this.

SKYDIVER LAUNCH PROCEDURE

Launching the Skyfighter is a complex manoeuvre that requires the crew to implement the launch procedure to the letter in order to maximise the success of the launch and the safety of all operatives involved.

PHASE 1: UFO SIGHTED

- Upon SID detecting a UFO, all SHADO forces are put on immediate alert. All operational Skydivers ascend to launch depth and survey the surface for contacts. In the event of nearby shipping, the Skydiver will head for open water at maximum speed.

PHASE 2: UFO HAS BREACHED MOONBASE DEFENCES

- SHADO control begins calculating UFO trajectory. The nearest Skydiver is notified.

- Navigation readies the relevant charts for the Captain to look over while SHADO narrows down the UFO's trajectory.

PHASE 3: LAUNCH STATIONS

- The Captain calls "launch stations" and transfers to the Skyfighter via chute. The XO assumes command of the submarine. The operative manning the helm brings the submarine to a full stop.

- Once the Captain has reached the cockpit, the helm will slowly vent the forward ballast tanks and begin to pitch up the nose to a sixty-degree angle. This can take up to 30 seconds.

- The flight control technician primes the Skyfighter's boosters and opens the exhaust vents while the Captain performs a final instrumentation check.

- Upon reaching the sixty-degree angle, the Captain will wait for his system panel to have a green light from each crew member.

- The Captain will ignite the boosters as the magnetic clamps holding the craft disengage, blasting the Skyfighter clear of the surface to a point where the conventional propulsion system can kick in.

- The Skyfighter is now clear to engage.

PHASE 4: RECOVERY

- Guided by telemetry from Skydiver, the Skyfighter can roughly determine the location and direction of the craft. The Captain will circle until cleared for landing.

- Upon receiving clearance, the pilot will pitch the aircraft into a sixty-degree crash-dive towards the ocean, using the aerodynamic frame and shape of the craft to dive back into the ocean.

- Coming to a halt, the Captain will flood the onboard ballast tanks to hold the craft roughly in position.

- The Skydiver will use its laser guidance system to match the attitude of the Skyfighter. Helm will close the distance on minimum power.

- Once in range, the magnetic clamps will reactivate, drawing the Skyfighter the last few feet to connect with Skydiver.

- Now connected, the Skyfighter powers down and the Captain transfers back to Skydiver.

HIDDEN PEN

In order to minimise the amount of time a Skydiver has to be taken off patrol, submarine pens have been hidden all over the world that allow the sub to be maintained and serviced in absolute secrecy.

For the most part, SHADO's sumbarine pens are concealed within cliff faces or inside natural subterranean caverns with artificially added navigation hazards to keep civilian traffic away. Some sort of surface installation, disguised as an observation station, radar post or lighthouse acts as an entrance for crew as well as a post for SHADO security to do checks.

A Exit to open sea: As much as possible, SHADO utilises the natural environment to hide the presence of the hidden pen. In some instances, the Skydiver is able to depart submerged, but in other sites, the craft has to leave under the cover of nightfall until it can reach deeper water.

B Boarding tube

C Equipment store

D Supply depot

E Secondary berth

F Fuel depot

G Once past whatever cover installation is in place, a security checkpoint confirms the operative's identity using ID, voice and biometric checks. The operative will then move to a containment cell between the checkpoint and the pen while they wait for their identity to be confirmed.

H Access gangway to surface: The surface entrance to the pen generally looks pretty low-key so as not to attract any attention from outsiders. A secondary entrance is usually also present for heavy vehicles to deliver supplies and equipment, but they are searched with a similar level of scrutiny.

SHADAIR

Unlike the other clandestine branches of SHADO, SHADair is actually a public face of the organisation, operating transparently in the open. On the surface, SHADair is a publicly-owned freight haulage and VIP transport organisation that trades on the stock market and is frequently employed to transport cargo and passengers all over the world. This cover allows the organisation to inconspicuously ferry SHADO personnel and supplies without raising suspicion. SHADair's role as a commercial operation also provides SHADO with a cover when operating in countries that are not signatories of the international agreement that give the organisation free access to airspace and territory.

SHADair currently operates out of three bases: London, Los Angeles and Rome. These storage depots secretly house SHADO ground forces that can be loaded aboard a transport and deployed to airfields around the world once a UFO's landing position has been calculated. Smaller craft can be used to quickly transfer command staff to an incident scene or crew to a Skydiver at sea.

SHADair operates a wide selection of commercial aircraft but this section of the manual will cover only those specifically modified for SHADO operations.

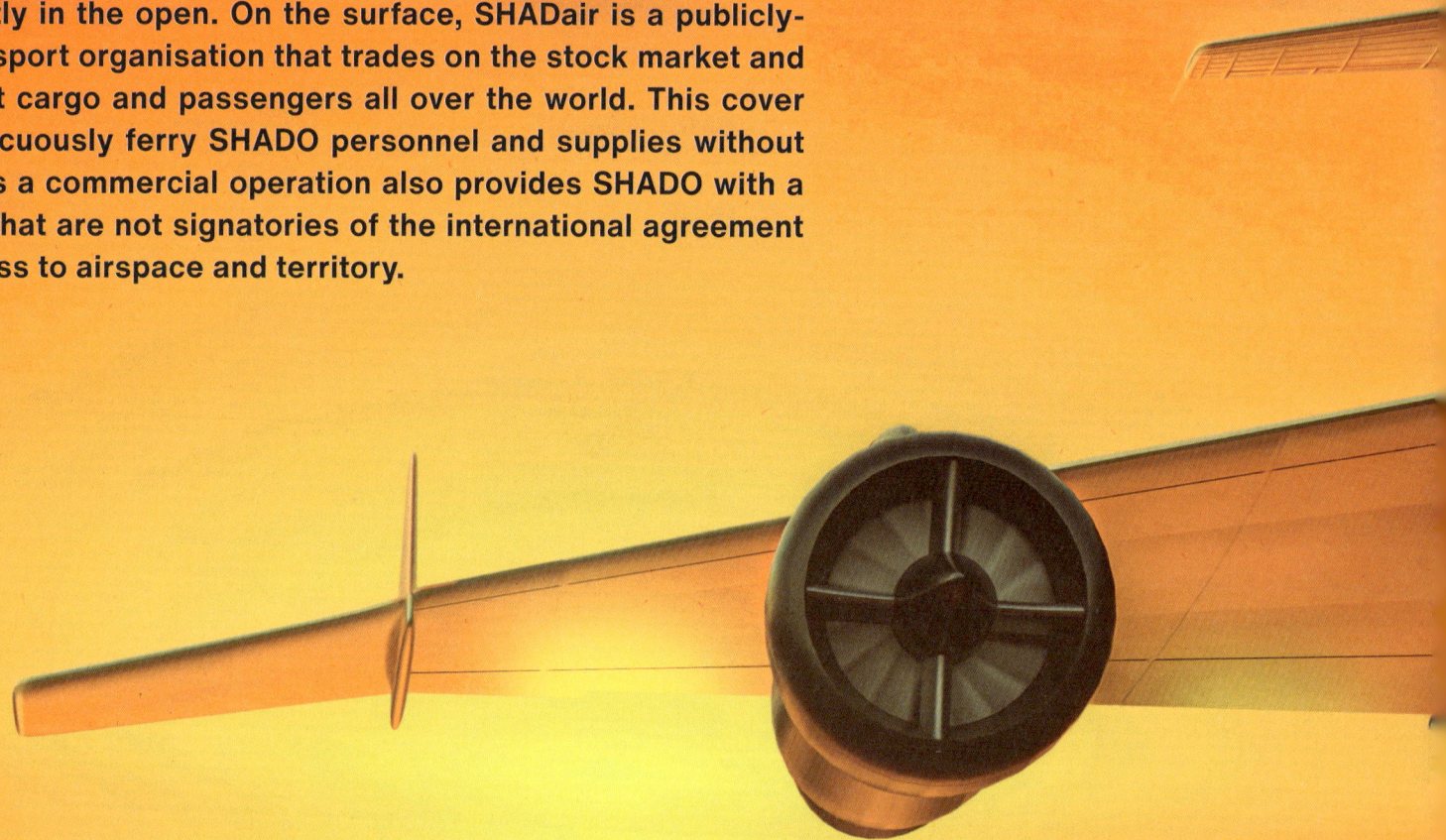

VALKYRIE

The two most essential parts of SHADair's operations are, firstly, to quickly transport SHADO forces to a UFO landing site, and secondly, to take advantage of infrastructure and facilities local to the incident.

The solution to the first requirement came in the form of the USAF's Valravn transport aircraft. At the time, it was the largest operational transport plane, used to globally transport heavy military equipment and aid. Under the guise of creating a civilian variant to the Valravn, SHADO bought two from an upcoming production order, with specific modifications included. This new variant was known as the Valkyrie.

While able to haul huge payloads over great distances and at speed, the Valravn had issues with take-off and landing, requiring a very long runway to accommodate the aircraft. SHADO's first task was to find a solution to reduce take-off and landing distances by half,

thereby greatly opening up the number of potential operating sites available to the Valkyrie. The answer was provided by the ability to gimbal the primary engines, and the addition of booster and braking rockets that could quickly accelerate or decelerate the aircraft much more quickly than its military cousin. Deployment of the rockets can be dangerous and spectacular, so this procedure is generally reserved for emergencies.

At present, SHADO's two Valkyries are stationed at SHADair airbases at Heathrow and LAX. Despite their cover as civilian-heavy transport, they are only occasionally used in this capacity, allowing them to be deployed on SHADO missions at a moment's notice.

SHADO TRANSPORT

The Valkyrie is large enough and fast enough to transport four SHADO Mobiles to most airports and bases around the world. Should no landing site be available near the UFO incident, Mobiles can be loaded onto platforms and airdropped with reasonable accuracy. This is only done occasionally as, in most instances, SHADO prefer to destroy a UFO found in a remote area, rather than expending additional resources while attempting to capture it.

DESIGN

Given the huge success of the Valkyrie design, more have been placed in production, with the intention of having one able to operate from every SHADair depot across the planet. An additional armed version of the aircraft has been proposed, the intention being to provide SHADO with the option to either use freefall bombs or conduct stand-off missile strikes against UFOs that may not be accessible by land, and also provide air support to Mobiles in the field.

LIVERY

The brightly-coloured livery of the Valkyrie is a deliberate attempt to obfuscate the actual purpose of the aircraft, with the burnt orange SHADair colours now a regular and iconic sight at various airports around the world. While the craft is unarmed, concealed countermeasures are fitted to protect the aircraft from missile attacks.

With a length of 338 ft and wingspan of 312 ft, the Valkyrie is the largest aircraft currently in service. In addition to its voluminous cargo bay, the aircraft also includes a two-tier passenger compartment located just aft of the flight deck. This can be quickly converted into a mobile operating station and planning area.

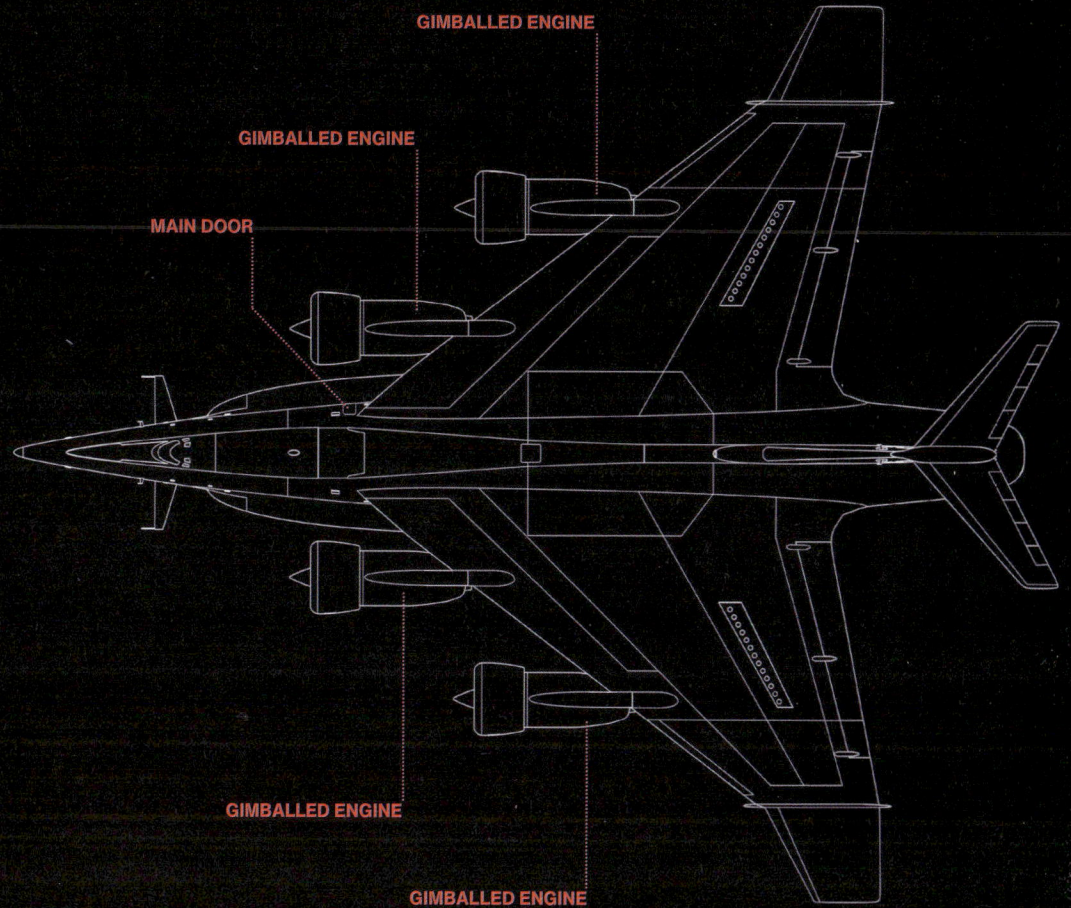

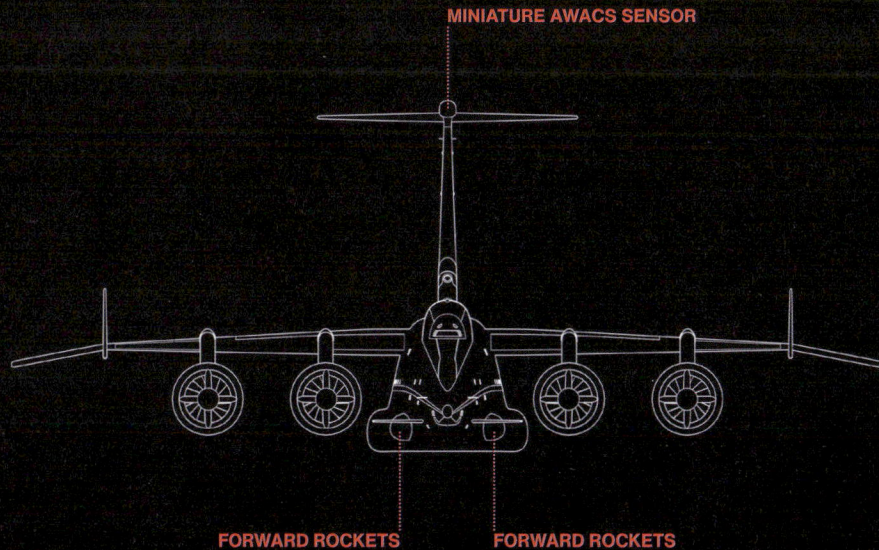

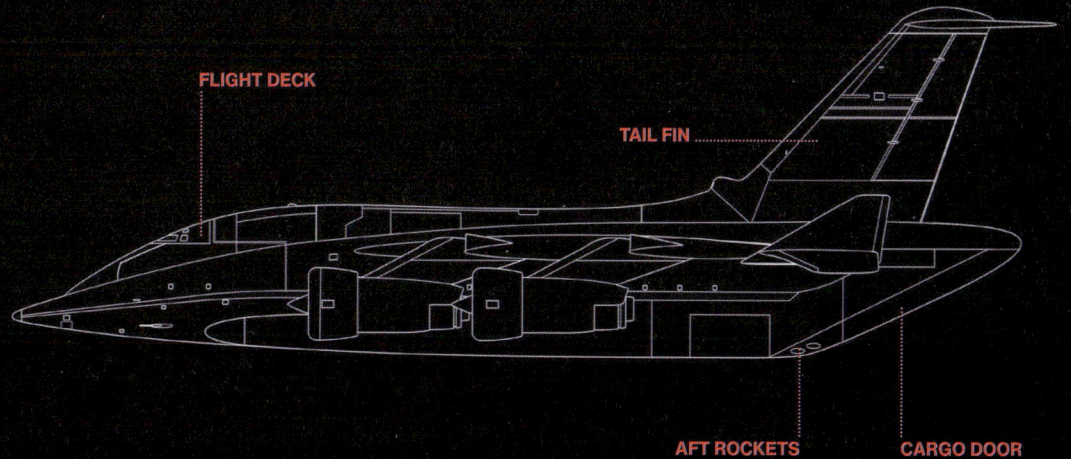

GIMBALLED ENGINE

GIMBALLED ENGINE

MAIN DOOR

GIMBALLED ENGINE

GIMBALLED ENGINE

MINIATURE AWACS SENSOR

FLIGHT DECK

TAIL FIN

FORWARD ROCKETS

FORWARD ROCKETS

AFT ROCKETS

CARGO DOOR

SEAGULL X-RAY

Designed by an external civilian contractor, the Seagull series of aircraft were created to serve as a supersonic executive jet with a particular focus on high-value clients. It was even put forward by the contractor during the evaluation competition for the next Air Force One type for the USAF. Unfortunately, while excelling in speed and security, the craft was deemed too small to handle the diplomatic and presidential requirements needed aboard the aircraft. It was at this point that the project came to SHADO's attention.

HEATHROW AIRPORT

When not in active use, Seagull X-ray is stationed at the SHADair depot at Heathrow airport, a 15-minute flight away from SHADO HQ. Most commonly, the craft will be used to ferry operatives between SHADO's American and UK operations, but sometimes it will be called upon to transport international delegations.

As a global operation at the highest level of the United Nations, SHADO needed to be able to transport its command staff, executives and various political dignitaries around the world quickly and safely. As such, and given the increasing risk of UFOs targeting SHADO personnel directly, an aircraft would need the performance and the requisite countermeasures to evade attack. The Seagull project was deemed perfect for this task.

Capable of a top speed of Mach three, the Seagull uses three turbojets mounted in the aft section of the aircraft, not unlike a military fighter. Twin vertical stabilisers assist in the manoeuvrability and stability of the craft, while a variable-geometry nose cone cleans up the aircraft during transonic flight. This enables the pilots to lower the nose to increase their field of view during take-off and landing.

Currently, SHADair operate two Seagull craft, Seagull X-ray and Seagull Lima, often stationed on opposite sides of the Atlantic, ready to ferry operatives when required.

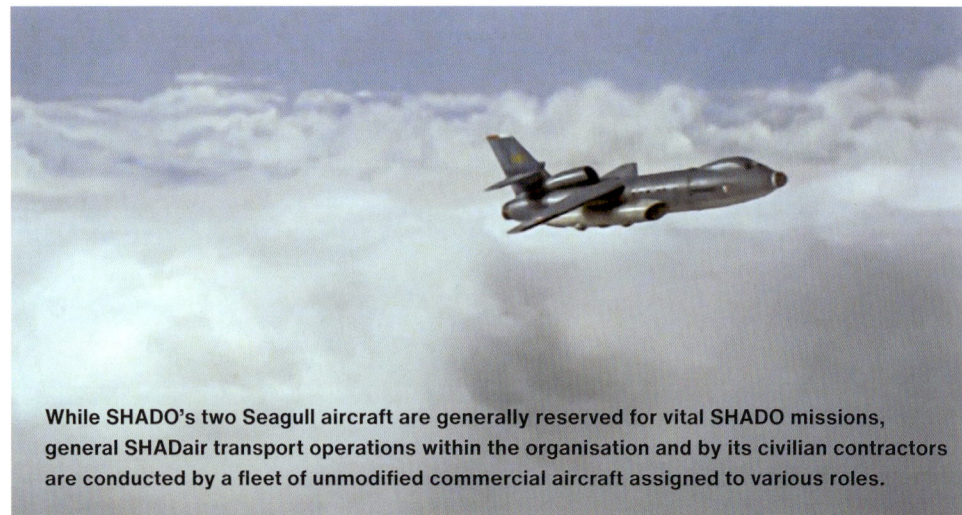

While SHADO's two Seagull aircraft are generally reserved for vital SHADO missions, general SHADair transport operations within the organisation and by its civilian contractors are conducted by a fleet of unmodified commercial aircraft assigned to various roles.

DESIGN

Smaller than most supersonic transports, the Seagull shares more characteristics with a jet fighter than a traditional commercial aircraft. Mounting the engines above the passenger compartment allows much of the airframe's internal space to be dedicated to the passengers and crew compartments. A cargo ramp to the back of the craft is used for the loading and unloading of luggage and heavier equipment, including a single SHADO car that can be carried in the hold.

COCKPIT

The Seagull is operated by a crew of four: a pilot, co-pilot, engineer and navigator. The flight deck has a layout similar to most commercial aircraft. Between the flight deck and the passenger compartment is a small galley which is operated by an attendant who sees to the well-being of the passengers throughout the flight.

PASSENGER CABIN

The aircraft's passenger compartment is conservative but relatively luxurious, providing a space where passengers can relax or work in comfort. A food dispensary, similar to what is found on Moonbase, is located on the forward wall along with a library of books, films and games. The entire compartment is soundproofed against the intense noise from the engines overhead.

SHADO's first defensive operation against the aliens occurred when a UFO was dispatched to destroy Seagull X-ray and the utronics team it was transporting. Prepared for such an eventuality, Colonel Freeman used the available cloud cover to elude the UFO while Sky 1 engaged.

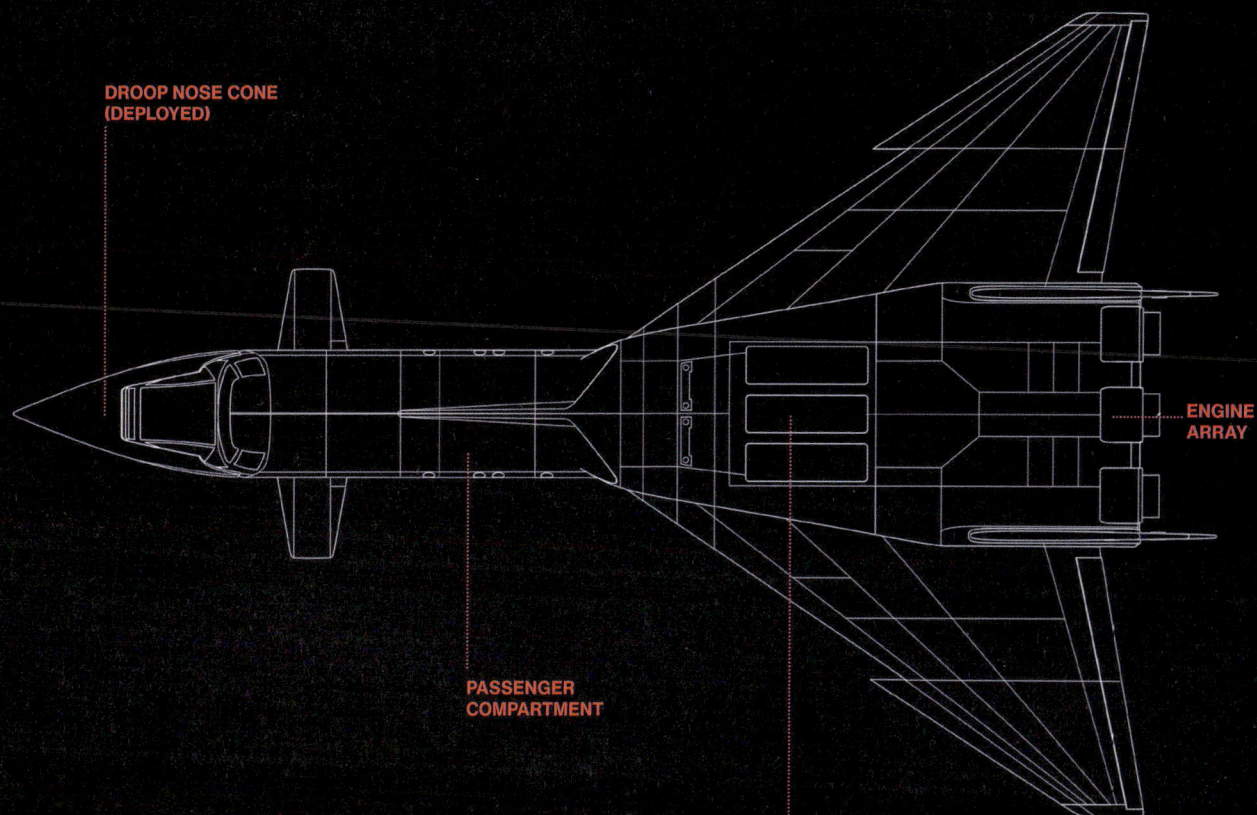

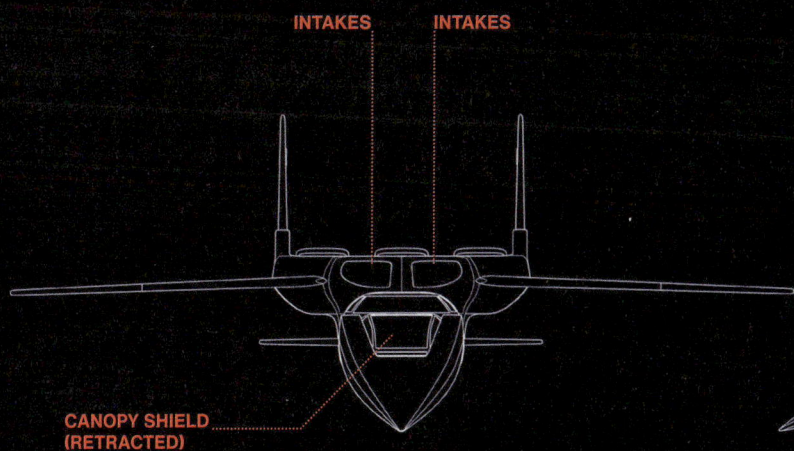

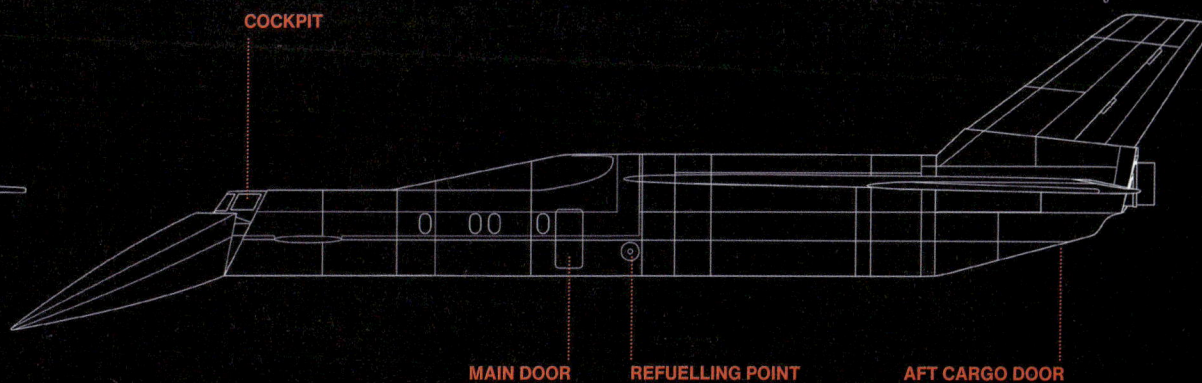

DROOP NOSE CONE (DEPLOYED)

ENGINE ARRAY

PASSENGER COMPARTMENT

HEAT DISSIPATION PANELS

INTAKES

INTAKES

COCKPIT

CANOPY SHIELD (RETRACTED)

MAIN DOOR

REFUELLING POINT

AFT CARGO DOOR

SHADO ALBATROSS

The SHADO Albatross, sometimes referred to as the SHADO Amphibian, is a modified commercial seaplane specifically obtained to service the Skydiver fleet. Operating from docks on the English coastline, these planes ferry operatives to and from Skydivers when out on patrol, as well as carrying out search and rescue duties.

The SHADO variant of the aircraft features a number of modifications to assist it with its various roles. The aft passenger section has been reconfigured, with half of its capacity dedicated to the carrying of diving and rescue equipment, while a concealed hatch in the ventral surface of the hull allows sonar buoys to be dropped as part of sub-smash operations. A small multi-sensor Airborne Warning and Control Systems (AWACS) pod has been fitted behind the cockpit to allow the crew to scan for air and surface contacts before a rendezvous with a Skydiver.

In the event of a sub-smash, the Albatross becomes the on-site command asset for the operation, tethering itself to the Skydiver's distress buoy then sending divers down to assess the situation, while simultaneously providing an aid station for any crew who have escaped to the surface.

While seaplanes have become increasingly out of fashion, SHADair has seen continued use of the aircraft type become a profitable side venture for the organisation. SHADair operates 10 of these aircraft, ferrying clients around remote polar and coastal regions, and inaccessible bodies of water.

PASSENGER CABIN

Most commonly, Albatrosses have become the primary method of recrewing Skydivers at sea, with its passenger compartment being able to take the full crew of six operatives. An inflatable dinghy is used to make the transfer. A number of the aircraft have been modified to carry and replenish fuel and munitions should a Skyfighter's stores be depleted while still on active duty. The operation usually requires calm seas, otherwise a landing can be risky.

TURBINE ENGINE

FLIGHT DECK

TURBINE ENGINE

SENSORS

AWACS POD

IN-FLIGHT AERIAL
REFUELLING PORT

ACCESS HATCH

COUNTERWEIGHT

HEADLIGHTS

COUNTERWEIGHT

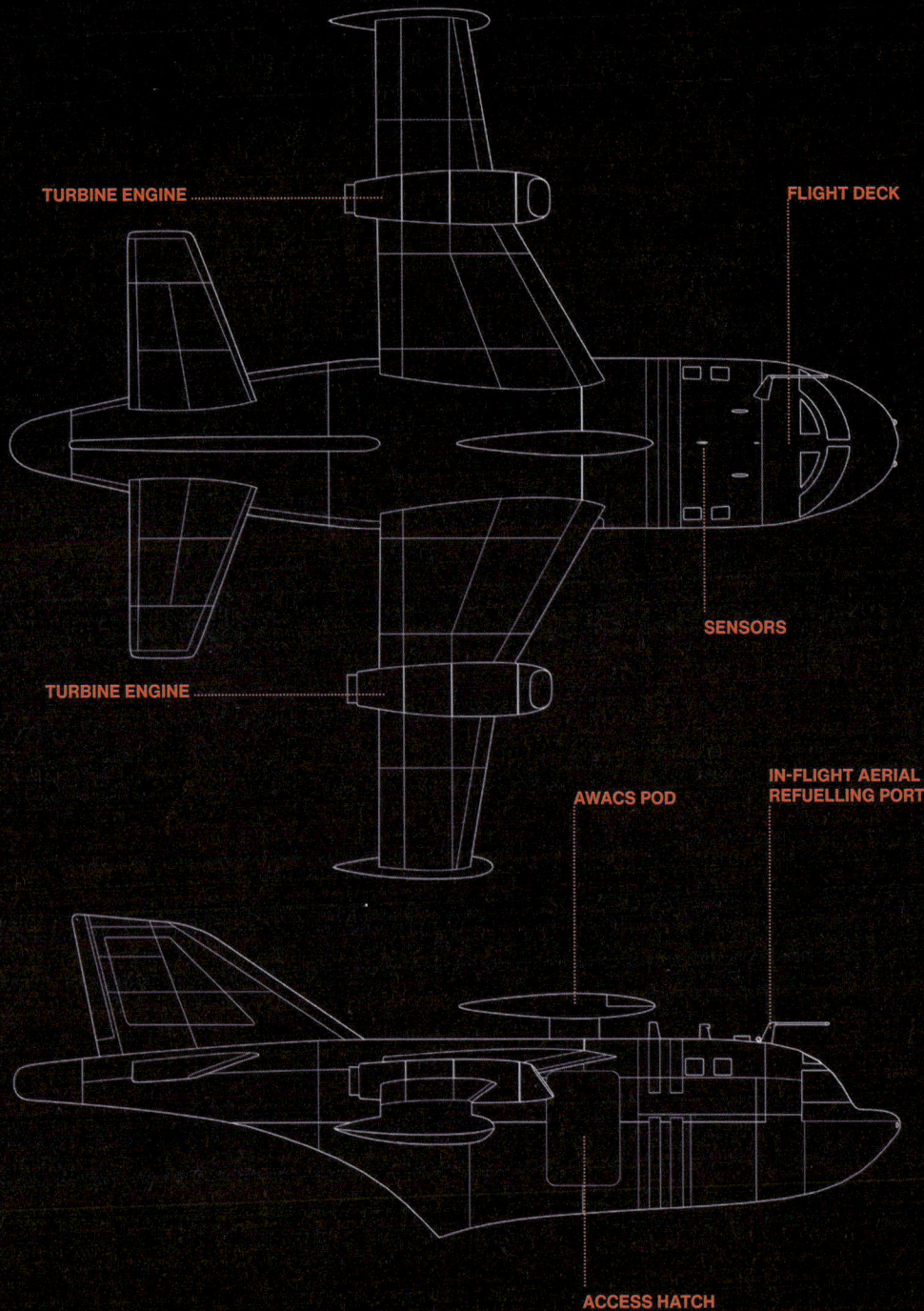

Should a UFO successfully penetrate SHADO's first lines of defence and manage to evade detection, SHADO's fleet of Albatrosses can be deployed, using their onboard sensor pods to detect the target and guide ground forces to it. Recent advances in SHADO technology have allowed the onboard radar to specifically recognise the unique signature created by the transparent components on a UFO's hull, allowing for an almost immediate positive identification.

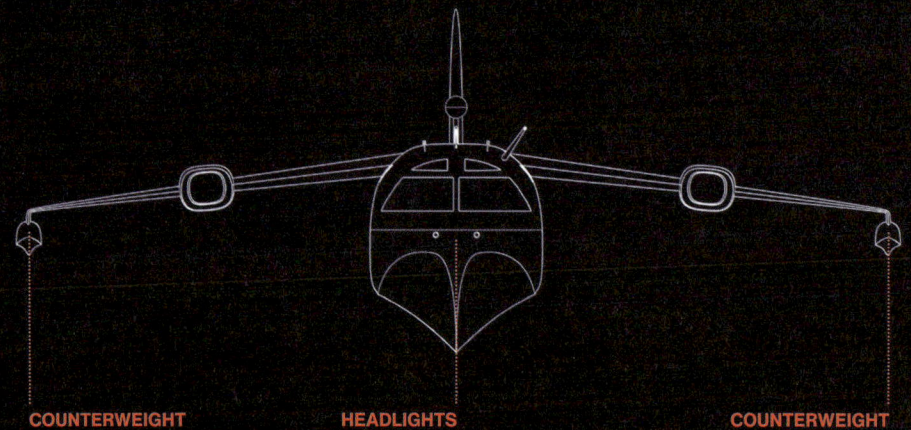

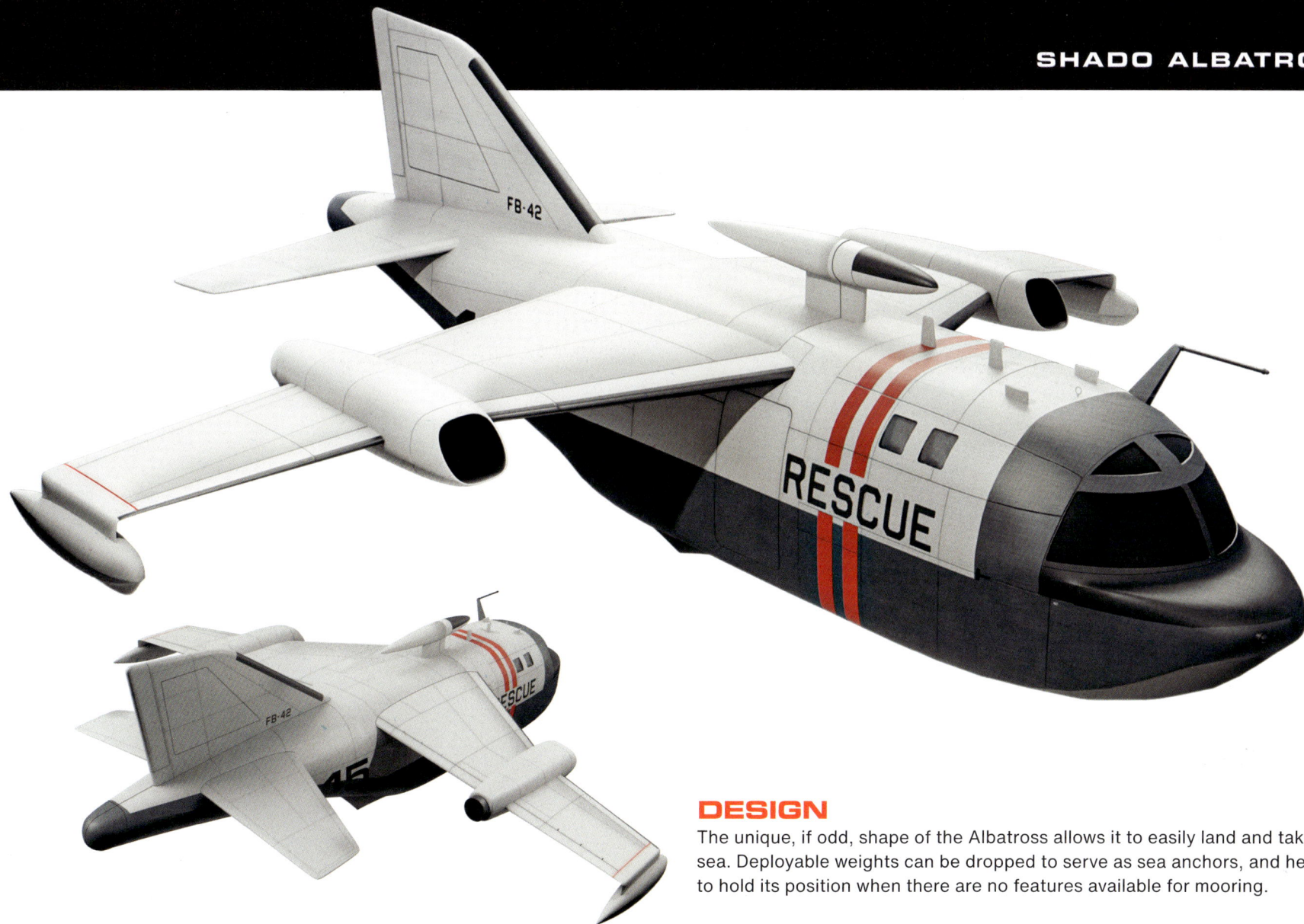

DESIGN

The unique, if odd, shape of the Albatross allows it to easily land and take off from the sea. Deployable weights can be dropped to serve as sea anchors, and help the aircraft to hold its position when there are no features available for mooring.

COCKPIT

The flight deck of the Albatross is designed for three operatives. The pilot and co-pilot sit forward, while a station behind them displays information from the aircraft's various sensor packages. When not in use, this station can be folded back to make room for additional passenger seating.

REAR COMPARTMENT

The rear compartment is split between passenger seating and storage for any emergency equipment the aircraft may be carrying. The main door is located on the starboard side of the craft and can be used as a small staging area to deploy and recover divers.

KINGFISHER VTOL AIRCRAFT

With the rest of the SHADair fleet managing SHADO's global logistics, it became evident that a smaller craft would be required in order to transport operatives quickly between SHADO installations or UFO landing sites.

Initially, helicopters were considered, but ultimately, several rotor-powered tiltrotor aircraft were bought and modified for this purpose. More commonly associated with ferrying around the super famous and the ultra-wealthy, the type, designated SHADO Kingfisher, has become a popular runabout for SHADO operatives, able to travel from the organisation's HQ to the furthest part of the UK within two hours, carrying a pilot and two VIPs.

The craft uses three main rotors to stay airborne. Two main engines mounted on the craft's wing can switch between vertical and horizontal flight and accelerate the craft to 385 mph, while a third vertically-mounted rotor system is only used to provide stability when hovering.

Given that the Kingfisher is used publicly, plus its small size, SHADO's modifications to the craft have been minimal, but include the fitting of hardpoints on the belly of the craft in order to allow it to carry sensor equipment, cargo winches or, in extreme situations, automatic cannons.

At present, Harlington-Straker Studios does not have its own heliport, as one was deemed too austentatious for what is meant to be a low-key film studio. Instead, when requested, the Kingfishers are called in from nearby Halton spaceport, usually landing within designated areas around the grounds of the studio. These flights can be easily passed off as the studio executives providing VIP travel services for executives and celebrities.

The Kingfisher has a range of approximately 430 miles without refuelling. For longer journeys, the craft can be dismantled and carried by Valkyrie transporter.

The craft's three-engine system gives it a high degree of control when landing, even in rough sites. Because of the protective shield around the rotors, Kingfishers can safely operate out of extremely tight spaces, making them an ideal advanced scout and reconnaissance type for SHADO operatives.

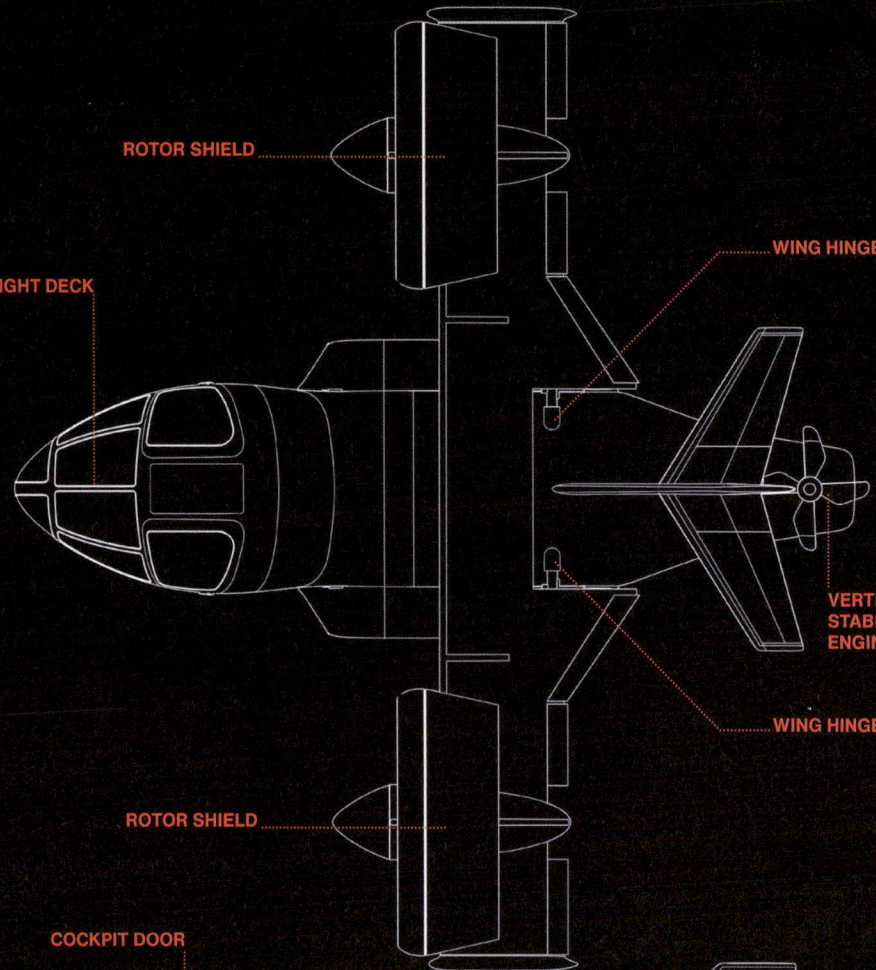

ROTOR SHIELD

WING HINGE

FLIGHT DECK

VERTICAL STABILISING ENGINE

WING HINGE

ROTOR SHIELD

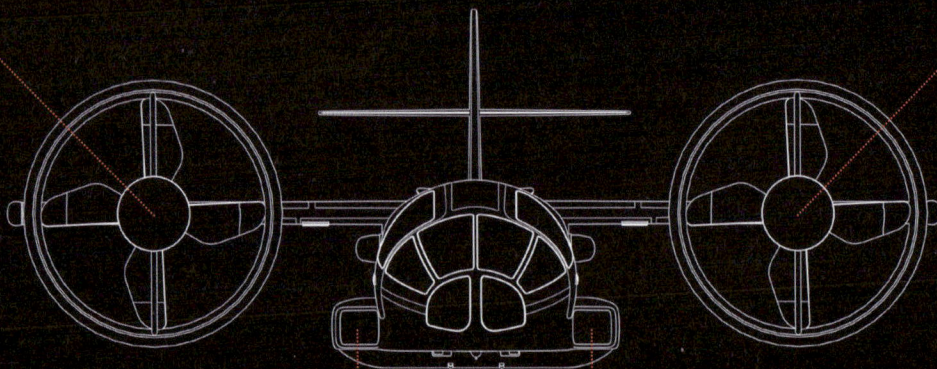

PRIMARY ENGINE

PRIMARY ENGINE

COCKPIT DOOR

TAIL FIN

INTAKE

INTAKE

SENSORS

EXHAUST

DESIGN

With its small size, the Kingfisher's operational role is limited, generally being restricted to the transport of high-ranking operatives to meetings and incident sites. However, the potential versatility of the craft has not gone unnoticed, and plans are currently in development to design a larger, longer-ranged and fully-armed variant of the craft that can supersede the SHADO Mobiles in remote or inaccessible areas around the globe.

INTERIOR

The interior of the Kingfisher features a small cockpit fitted with three seats. The pilot controls the craft from the centre position, while the other two seats are for passengers who can access the Kingfisher's communications system or, when necessary, other systems fitted to the craft, e.g. weapons. The cockpit is shielded from external noise to allow the crew to converse without the need for headsets.

GROUND FORCES

Once the other branches of SHADO have done their work, a network of ground vehicles is required to directly deal with the situation on the ground. Whether the alien spacecraft has landed, crashed or just departed, SHADO needs to be able to establish a perimeter on-site and deal with the threat.

SHADO ground vehicles can be split into two categories: those operating covertly and those operating in plain sight of the general public.

Of the former, the SHADO Mobiles are the primary combat element, an armoured attack force designed to directly engage alien UFOs within a contained perimeter. Transporting this force in secret represents a massive logistical challenge, so the ground and infantry have to coordinate closely with SHADair and specialised carriers in order to get these vehicles on station as fast as possible.

The priority of most ground-based engagements is the capture of an intact UFO. This will put active ground force operatives directly in harm's way from either alien weaponry or the destruct systems of the UFOs themselves. Should it become clear that a UFO cannot be captured without significant loss of life, it will be up to the Colonel on the scene to determine whether the situation is untenable.

SHADO 3

SHADO 2

THE SHADO MOBILE

Having found methods of combating the aliens in space and in the air, SHADO was also keen to develop a vehicle that could successfully engage them on the ground. The finished design would need to be versatile and adaptable, and fully capable of operating in a variety of environmental conditions while fulfilling a number of roles, including mobile command post, personnel carrier, armoured fighting vehicle or self-propelled artillery.

The SHADO Mobile was the final result of this design brief, a tracked, amphibious vehicle modelled after armoured personnel carriers used by most modern armies. Because a UFO could potentially land in any conceivable environment – from polar ice caps to thick jungle – all-terrain caterpillar tracks were fitted, which give a fairly consistent top speed of 40 mph over all but the roughest of terrain.

The boxy nature of the Mobile's design makes the vehicle easier to transport discreetly, fitting snugly into covert carrier vehicles such as the Markers Universal truck or the Valkyrie transport aircraft. The basic chassis of the vehicle can also be easily field-modified to carry additional sensors and equipment packages, resulting in subtle differences across the entire Mobile fleet.

The basic model, sometimes referred to as the Reconnaissance Mobile, is constructed from a heat-resistant, blast proof metal capable of stopping most conventional weapons. The vehicle has two main compartments, a driver's cabin that seats three, and a transport compartment that can hold eight passengers along with weapons and stores, medical supplies and specialised equipment for containing and preserving aliens and their craft. Two other variants, the Control Mobile and Assault Mobile, are currently operational.

AMPHIBIOUS CAPABILITIES

All of a SHADO Mobile's vital systems are completely sealed, while its air vents, radiator and exhaust are housed at the top of the vehicle. This allows it to traverse water courses while submerged, or use its hydrodynamic hull to travel on the water's surface. A small turbine system allows the craft to travel up to 18.5 mph when afloat.

During night operations, a remote-controlled, high-powered searchlight can be mounted above the cab. This is operated by the co-driver or navigator.

INTERIOR COMPARTMENTS

The Mobile's two interior compartments are kept separate to enhance survivability in the event of damage from enemy fire. Access to the rear compartment is through the double doors at the back of the vehicle, while access to the cabin is via the side window hatches.

ARMOUR

While the Mobile's advanced armour would give it near-total protection against conventional weaponry, a direct strike from a UFO's energy weapon is capable of completely destroying the vehicle. As such, when engaging UFOs, Mobile crews rely on speed and manoeuvrability to avoid alien fire.

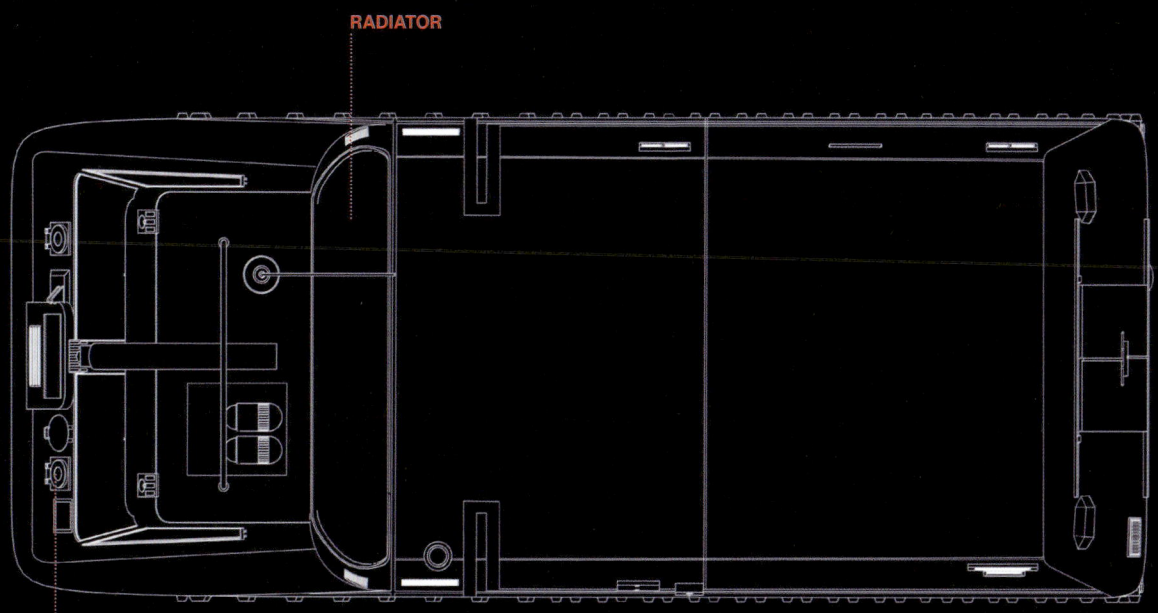

RADIATOR

AFT DOOR

SENSOR MODULE
HATCHES

EXHAUST

REFUELLING POINT

AIR CONDITIONING

CABIN HATCH

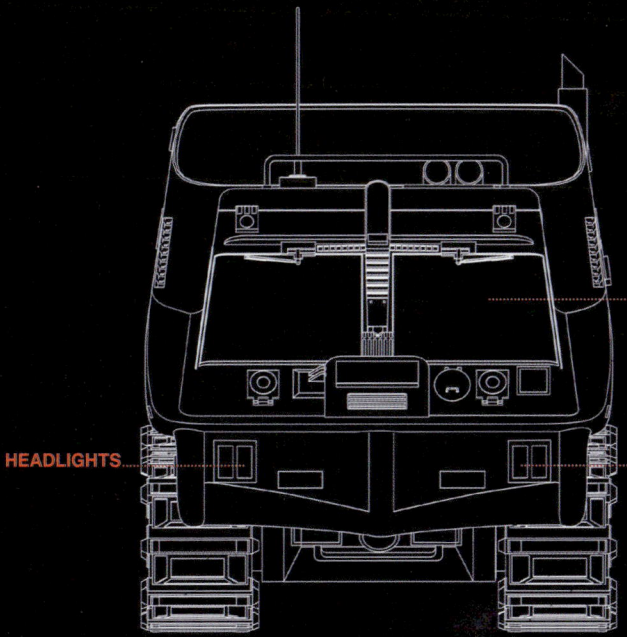

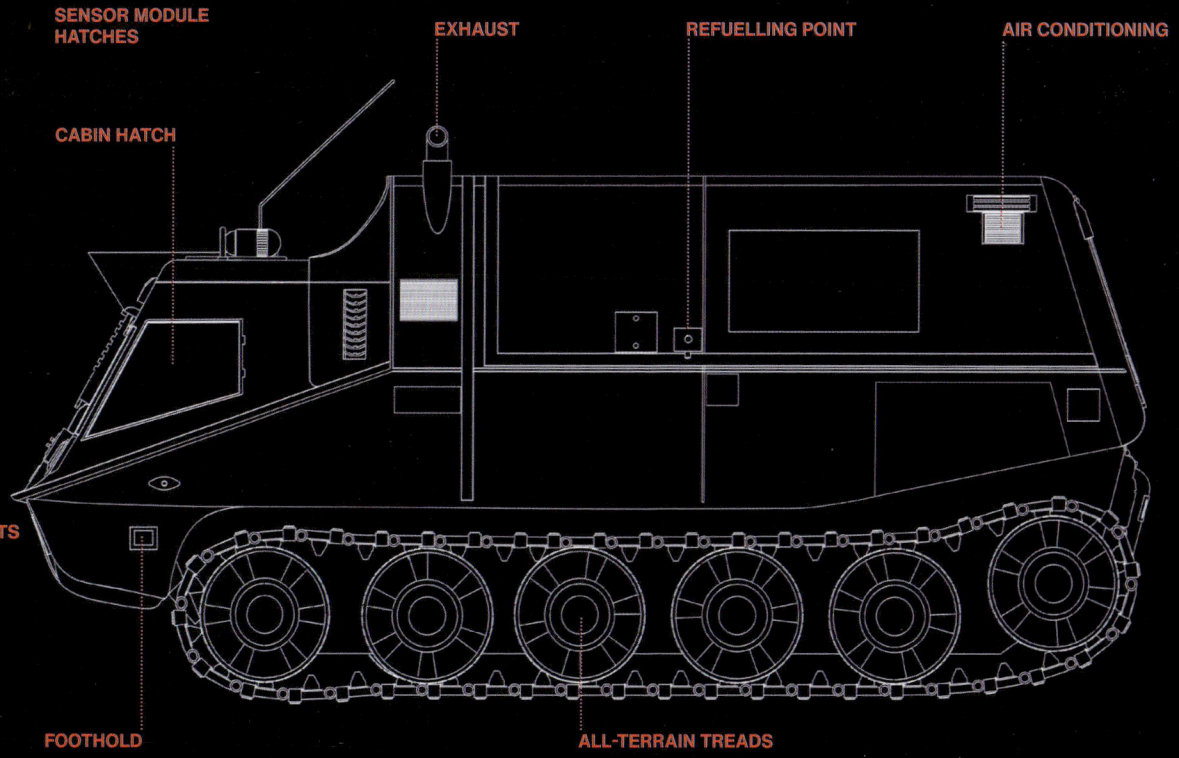

CABIN

HEADLIGHTS

HEADLIGHTS

FOOTHOLD

ALL-TERRAIN TREADS

VARIANTS

ASSAULT MOBILE

While their primary roles are those of personnel transport and reconnaissance, Mobiles are sometimes required to engage in combat if the on-site Commander deems the situation to be too dangerous to warrant trying to secure a living alien or its craft. In this instance, the Assault Mobiles can be deployed.

The Assault Mobile has two primary weapons, the hardware for which takes up much of the rear passenger compartment. A high-velocity automatic cannon is fitted in a turret capable of traversing 360 degrees and can fire 300 rounds a minute. The second, heavier weapon is an artillery turret, capable of firing depth charges and impact-triggered mortars from over half a mile away.

When not in use, these two turrets can retract into the chassis of the vehicle for ease of transport.

CONTROL MOBILE

Mobiles generally operate in squadrons of four vehicles, the fourth of which is almost always the Control Mobile, essentially a mobile command centre with an operations hub taking up the entire back compartment. The vehicle is usually commanded by a SHADO Colonel who oversees operations, providing information and intelligence to the other three Mobiles, who relay their own data back to the Control Mobile's onboard computer.

A large antenna is fitted to the top of the vehicle and acts as both an electronic detection system and a direct communications link to SHADO HQ. This antenna is disassembled for transport and quickly reattached once the Mobile is ready to begin operations.

INTERIOR

The driver's compartment on the SHADO Mobile is comparable in many ways to its lunar counterpart, with a similar layout of navigation and control instruments. Additional seating is located behind the drivers, replacing where the aft door would be on the lunar model. The primary visual difference between the two types is the wrap-around windows on the SHADO Mobile that offer the drivers and navigator a full, unrestricted 180-degree view of their surroundings. The windows also act as the main entry to the cabin, with the side windows hinging open to allow access.

The driver sits on the right side of the cabin and controls all of the vehicle's primary functions, while the navigator operates the mission-specific equipment, such as the searchlight or weapon systems.

AFT SECTION

The aft compartment is separated from the cabin and accessed through the double doors at the back of the vehicle. On most reconnaissance models, this section will contain space for operatives to be transported to a UFO incident and equipment for the capture, securing and sustaining of an alien and/or UFO debris.

COMMAND MOBILE

The aft compartment on the Command Mobile differs from the usual interior. It features a more open space, fitted with electronic systems and navigational materials that allow the Colonel in charge to oversee and control operations while being able to communicate directly with SHADO HQ. This section will generally carry two personnel – the Colonel and an operations specialist.

A Mobile location readout

B Sensor controls and readouts

C Spare charts

D Map-reading station

E Supply shelf

F Radar

G Communications station

H Ventilation

DRIVER'S VIEW

While the large windows on the front of the Mobile could be perceived as a potential weak point, the canopy is actually constructed from an experimental form of composite armoured glass that is strong enough to deflect shell splinters, shrapnel, small arms, automatic cannon fire and even tank shells from some angles. While being no match for the directed energy weapon used by the aliens, the canopy has proven successful in protecting Mobile crews from debris caused by the self-destruction of a UFO.

MOBILE CARRIER

Given the unmistakably military appearance of the Mobiles, a method of deploying them into the field without alerting the local populace needed to be developed. Another shell company run by SHADO, Markers Universal, had previously been used to transport small- and medium-sized loads for the organisation, but then the company purchased a number of high-capacity haulage trucks and modified them to be able to covertly carry Mobiles.

RMS 1932

Larger than traditional trucks, large-capacity haulers have started to become a more frequent sight on British and American roads, moving equipment between military bases, spaceports and film studios. Harlington-Straker Studios owns six of these vehicles, four of which have been modified to transport the Mobiles.

The truck itself has a single cab which offers a good panoramic view around and below the vehicle and is powerful enough to pull up to two fully-loaded trailers at once. The trailer houses the Mobile and can act as a resupply station in the field with additional fuel reserves and ammunition being stored at the front of the compartment.

Being able to reach a speed of 50 mph when fully loaded, the transporters are faster than the Mobiles and can quickly move them around the country without drawing public attention. A contingent of operatives usually travel discreetly with the hauler in cars or jeeps to help cordon off areas where their cargo can be offloaded in secret.

STAGING AREA

In some instances, a number of haulers will use a larger staging area, such as a woodland clearing, playing field or car park, to deploy their cargo all at once. If the incident site is surrounded by suitable roads, then it is deemed more tactically efficient to distribute the Mobiles individually around the perimeter, speeding up deployment time, especially if the UFO's position on the ground is already known.

The SHADO Control Mobile's onboard antenna is too large to be fitted on board the transport trailer intact. It is assembled after disembarkation, while the other three mobiles are moving to their assigned positions.

MOBILE ATTACK STRATEGY

Once deployed, Mobiles will engage in either a search/reconnaissance role, or if the target UFO's position has already been identified, an attack formation. A third procedure, designated *Operation Prometheus*, the capture of an intact UFO, will be instigated under specific circumstances detailed elsewhere.

RECONNAISSANCE

Generally, on arriving at a suspected incident site, SHADO operatives will establish a cordon that can be up to six miles square. With the aliens prioritising forested and woodland areas and with the UFOs able to land precisely within small clearings, an aerial search usually has little hope of finding the landing site, forcing SHADO's ground force to comb the area using visual devices (including the 'mark 1 eyeball') or thermal sensors. A standard search pattern, which can be modified to suit different terrains, is employed, with each Mobile being designated a square which it will then cover in a slowly decreasing quartering pattern. This method ensures the search area is covered efficiently while allowing Mobiles to remain close enough to each other that once the UFO is detected, they can move quickly to provide mutual support.

Often, UFOs will seek a body of water in order to conceal themselves for more protracted periods, away from the corrosive effects of Earth's atmosphere. To combat this, Assault Mobiles have been outfitted with depth charges in order to flush out or destroy concealed UFOs. Reconnaissance Mobiles have sonar equipment on board that can be lowered into the water to check for submerged alien craft.

ATTACK STRATEGY

Should a UFO be positively identified, located and a kill order issued, the Mobiles will envelop the area, positioning themselves as close as possible to the target while maximising the use of natural cover. Coordinating from the Control Mobile, the Colonel on site will direct the operation as the situation unfolds.

If crashed, then one or two Mobiles may be directed to move into harm's way to see if the UFO's energy weapon is still operational. This generally takes the form of the Mobile breaking cover in a quick, high-speed dash then returning to cover, keeping the craft's strong side armour towards the UFO.

Once the nature of the threat is confirmed, the three Mobiles (not the command vehicle) will begin assaulting from different directions. While the UFO's weapon has a 360-degree field of fire, it is believed that it can take a few seconds to redirect the weapon, presenting a window of vulnerability which SHADO's forces can exploit. The Mobiles will use their automatic cannons and mortars to destroy the craft, the kinetic nature of these weapons being extremely effective against the UFO's energy-based defences.

BATTLEFIELD OVERVIEW

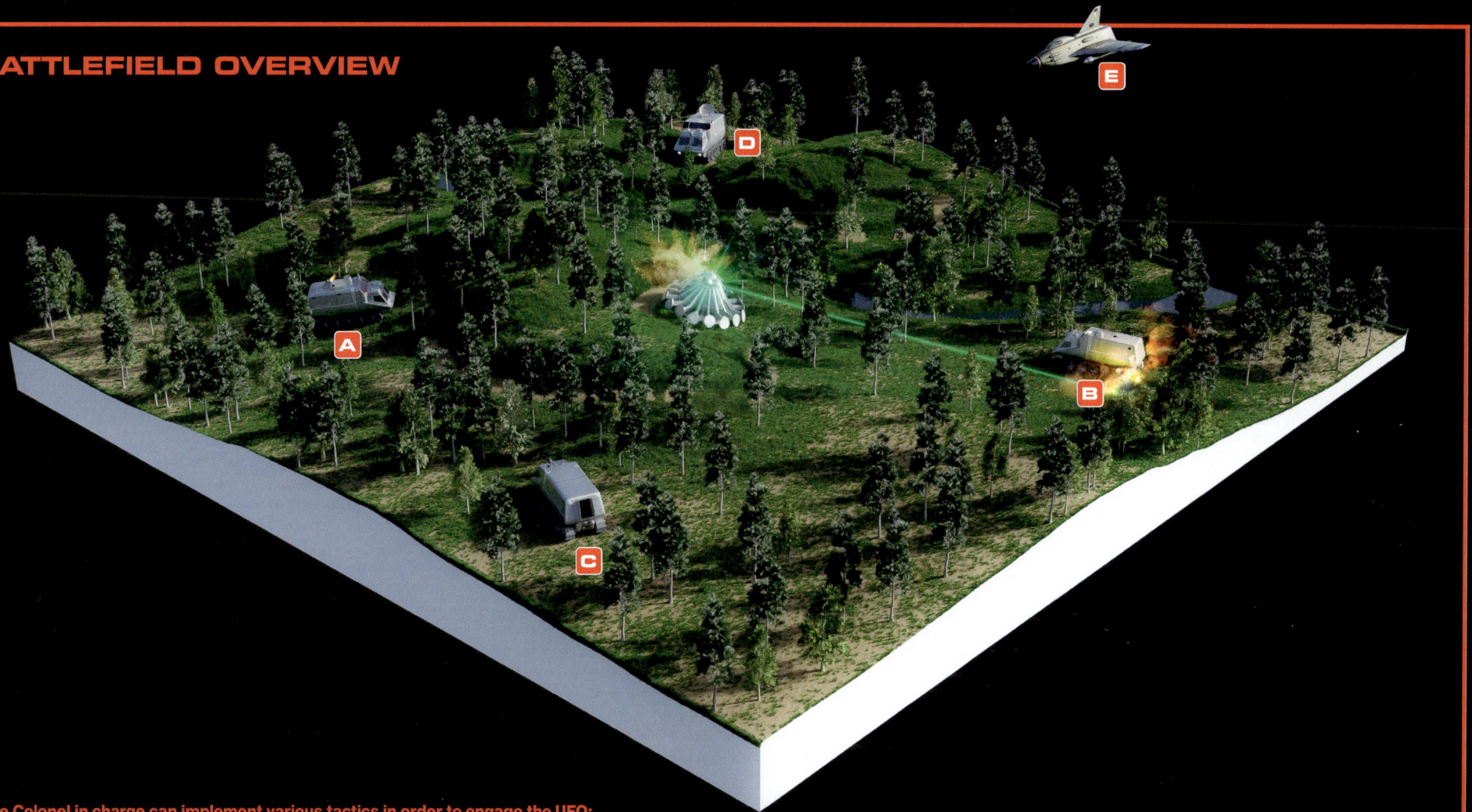

The Colonel in charge can implement various tactics in order to engage the UFO:

A The Assault Mobiles can use cover and indirectly fire their mortars at the UFO from a distance. While the safest option for the crew, this is only effective when combined with the element of surprise or if the UFO is immobilised.

B If a UFO is airborne, then Mobiles need to directly engage within line of sight. All three Mobiles will attack simultaneously in an effort to overwhelm the UFO's energy weapon. The mortar cannons can fire a specialised mix of pyrophoric flares and magnesium shards, which have proven to confuse a UFO's targeting sensors.

C The Reconnaissance Mobiles can deploy their contingent of operatives who can use small arms and rocket launchers to engage the UFO.

D The Control Mobile usually remains safely away from the battle area. However, in extraordinary situations, it can act as another Reconnaissance Mobile.

E With the potential for an airborne UFO to escape, a Skyfighter will generally be vectored either into the airspace close to the UFO site or en route (but will be held back so as to not alert the aliens to an impending attack). Should the UFO take to the air, the Skyfighter can engage.

SHADO EXECUTIVE CAR

While giving ranking SHADO operatives a comfortable vehicle for general travel, these personal cars were also provided with additional capabilities and protection that befitted the highly secretive – and dangerous – nature of their work. The attack on General Henderson had necessitated the need for additional security to be taken in the event that aliens decide to attack other ranking SHADO operatives directly.

For this purpose, SHADO turned to the Universal Secret Service, an international intelligence organisation that has a long history in converting commercially available cars and modifying it to suit clandestine operations.

The SHADO Executive car is a modified Ford Astro, a prestige vehicle often used by wealthy business executives. It was felt that this vehicle wouldn't look out of place in the car park of Harlington-Straker Studios. The entire chassis and engine assembly was stripped down and refitted with a significantly more powerful engine, while the bodywork was painstakingly cast and replicated with a lightweight armour that renders the vehicle immune to small arms or automatic cannon fire and shrapnel. The tires have been swapped out in favour of a puncture-resistant design unique to the USS, while the windows are the latest in bulletproof glass. Ultimately, the only parts of the original USS vehicle retained are several interior cosmetic pieces. To the untrained eye, the vehicle is identical to its commercial counterpart.

While most of the vehicle's new capabilities focus on passenger safety in extreme circumstances, SHADO was also very keen to incorporate a large suite of electronic equipment. Many surveillance and recording devices are stored within the vehicle's bodywork, allowing the driver to covertly follow other vehicles or carry out surveillance on locations of interest, while an onboard radar system provides the driver with a warning system for possible airborne attack.

STATEMENT PIECE

Chosen by Commander Straker himself, the Executive car has become an iconic sight at Harlington-Straker Studios. The luxurious if understated nature of the vehicle made it the perfect choice for his cover as a film executive.

CONCEALED EQUIPMENT

The rear of the car reflects the streamlined nature of the vehicle. A standard set of brake lights and indicators hides additional sensors as well as rear-view cameras that remove the need for a rear-view mirror or wing mirrors. The boot ('trunk' to American readers) is spacious, with an additional compartment containing emergency equipment.

INTERIOR

The interior of the vehicle follows the understated but stylish design of the exterior, with leather upholstery and a straightforward, ergonomically designed dashboard. Much of the car's specialist equipment can be accessed via a central console that runs between the passenger and driver seats, which gives the occupants shared access.

CAR PHONE

Located on the central console is the vehicle's in-built car phone. Able to function as a regular phone or in conjunction with SHADO's communication satellite network, this device allows Commander Straker to remain in command, receive intelligence, and be briefed on developing situations whilst on the road.

GULL WING DOORS

The vehicle retains the iconic gull wing doors of the original design. Reflecting the 'luxury' status of the Astro, the doors are button-operated. A telescopic stand can be added to hold the doors open and prevent undue wear on the door motors, should the doors need to be held for extended periods. A beeper on the key fob allows the driver to open them externally.

SECURITY SYSTEM

As part of the vehicle's on-board security systems, a small two-button panel is located on the driver's door. The red button activates a camera built into the passenger-side sun shield that can covertly photograph whoever is sitting in the passenger seat.

The green button is a panic button that immediately activates an alarm on the lead controller's desk in SHADO Control, and activates a homing signal that broadcasts the car's location.

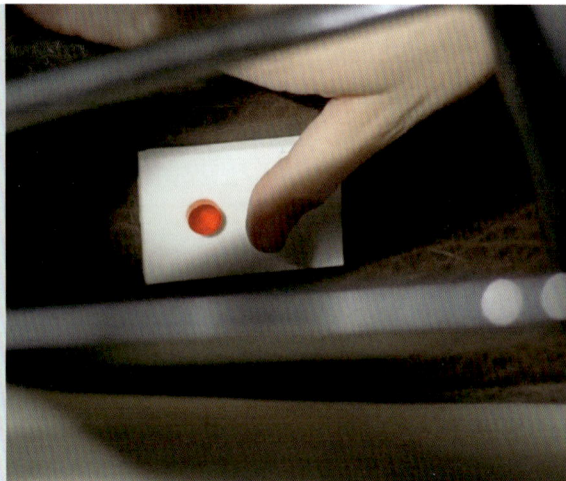

HEADLIGHTS

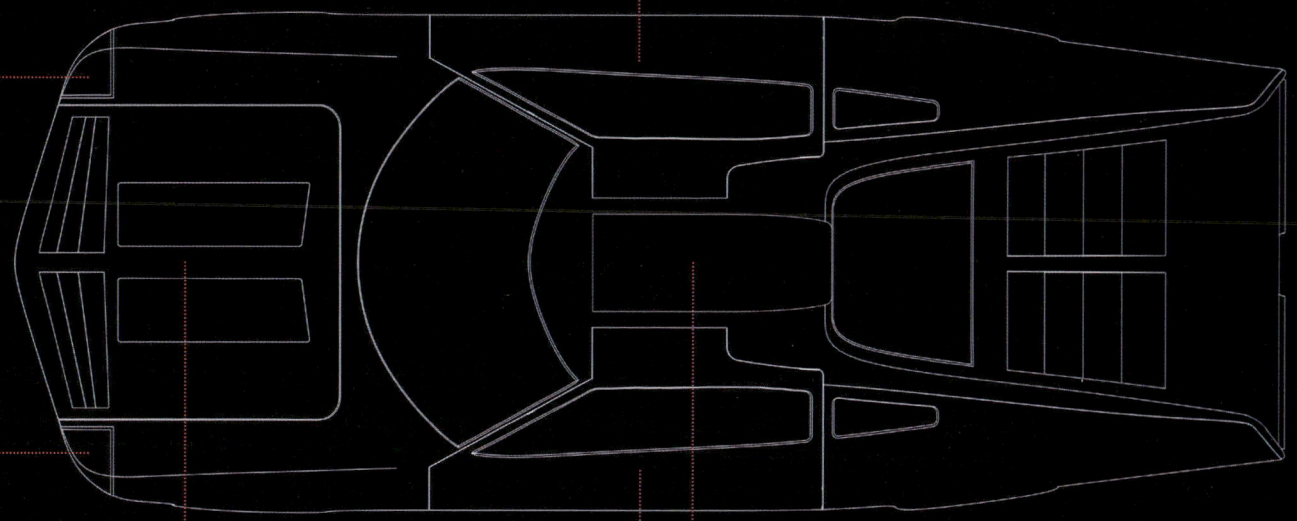

PASSENGER SIDE DOOR

HEADLIGHTS

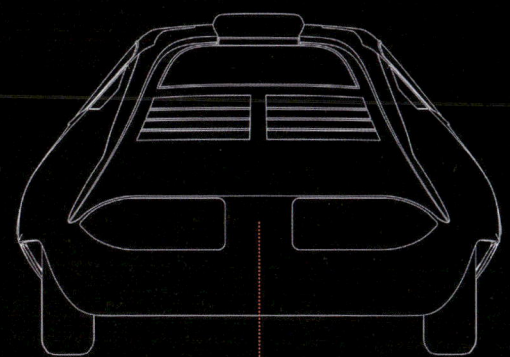

BRAKE LIGHTS AND INDICATORS
WITH HIDDEN REAR VIEW CAMERAS

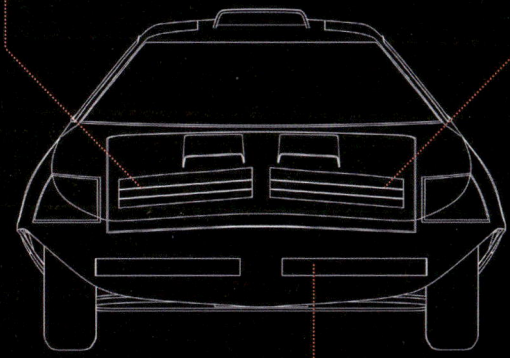

MAIN INTAKE

MAIN INTAKE

BONNET

DRIVER SIDE DOOR

RADAR AND COMMUNICATIONS SYSTEM
(DISGUISED AS AIR CONDITIONING VENTS)

BOOT

FORWARD SENSORS AND CAMERAS
(DISGUISED AS INTAKES)

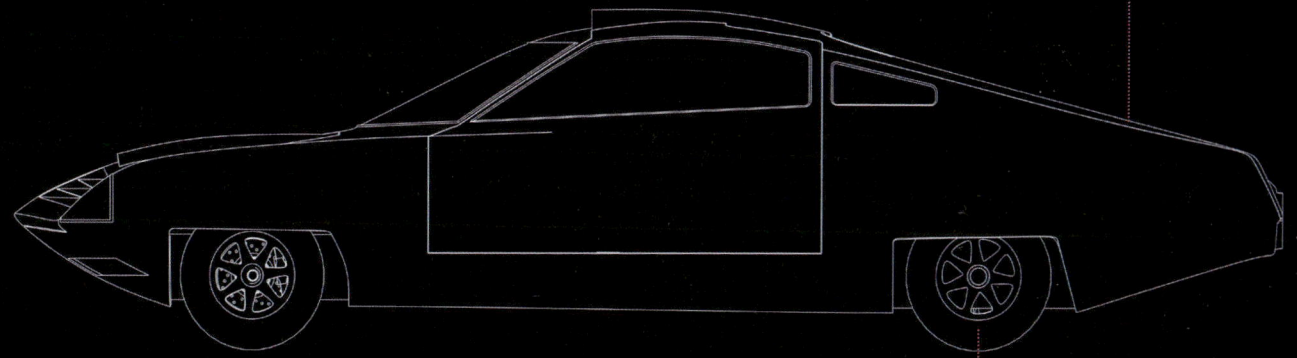

PUNCTURE-PROOF WHEELS

While the car is unarmed (beyond any weapons carried by the occupants), its armoured chassis and speed provide very effective indirect defence measures in the event of direct attack. When a UFO was sent to assassinate technician Paul Roper, the car was able to keep him alive while itself sustaining heavy damage.

JAVELIN CAR

While the Executive car focuses on passenger safety and surveillance, the Javelin is a much more aggressive class of vehicle. A modified variant of a car developed by the Universal Secret Service, the Javelin was originally designed as quite literally an 'attack car', with a powerful engine and concealed weapons.

Paul Foster's public perception as an easy-going young producer, coupled with his experience as a test pilot for the Royal Air Force, made the Javelin car the perfect choice for his personal vehicle. More recently, Colonel Lake has started using the Javelin as well, reflecting her expanded role in field operations.

The first models were used for assasination and asset escort missions, and came in a variety of shapes and sizes but generally took on the appearance of a custom sports car. Additional intakes and fins hid various weapon systems, while the aerodynamic frame allowed the car to achieve speeds of almost 220 mph.

While an attack car wasn't necessarily useful to SHADO, a few Javelin cars were ordered as it had slowly become apparent that the aliens were running their own clandestine operations against SHADO, using local populations as cover. Faced with the possibility of the organisation becoming involved in a more traditional Cold War style of espionage, it was decided that SHADO should invest in hardware suitable for such an eventuality; this included the Javelin.

The SHADO variant of the vehicle is extrapolated from a Ford Experia. As with the Executive car, almost all of the vehicle's chassis was replaced with lightweight armoured panelling and glass, while the addition of a new, more powerful engine enhanced the Experia's maximum road speed. SHADO also took the decision to install the engine of its Javelins in the rear of the car. The vacant space is now fitted with surveillance equipment and the concealed weapons installed within the intakes on the sides of the gull wing doors.

While lacking the heavier ordnance arming the USS version of the car, the Javelin still retains two automatic cannons set at tire level, where they can be used to cripple other vehicles and force them off the road. Smoke can also be deployed from the vehicle to confuse any pursuing vehicles.

The unmodified Ford Experia is slightly more streamlined than the USS version and is a common sight on British and American roads. The reputation it has garnered as a recreational vehicle for younger, more reckless drivers made it an ideal choice for modification.

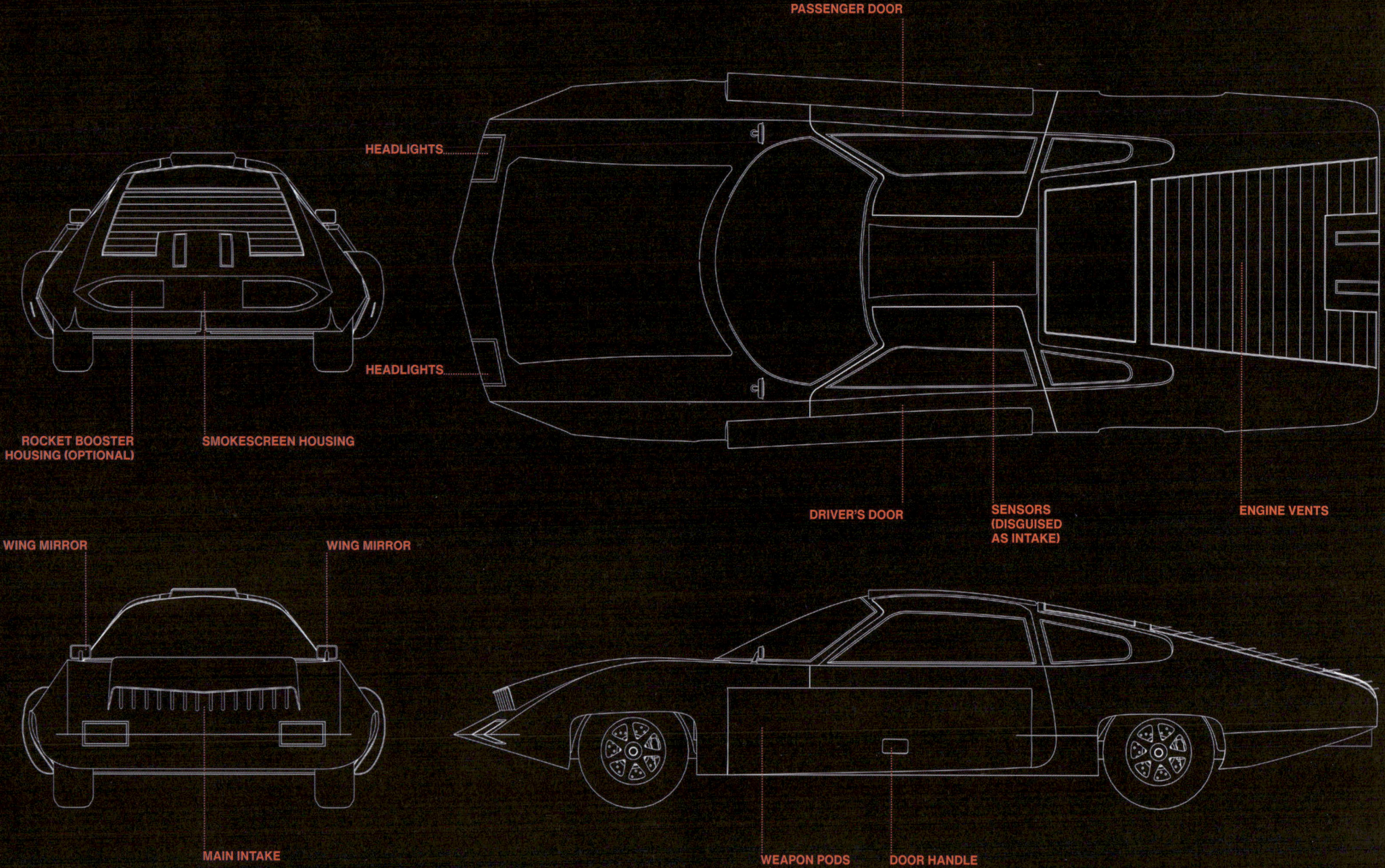

PASSENGER DOOR

HEADLIGHTS

HEADLIGHTS

ROCKET BOOSTER
HOUSING (OPTIONAL)

SMOKESCREEN HOUSING

DRIVER'S DOOR

SENSORS
(DISGUISED
AS INTAKE)

ENGINE VENTS

WING MIRROR

WING MIRROR

MAIN INTAKE

WEAPON PODS

DOOR HANDLE

INTERIOR

The interior of the Javelin features white leather upholstery and a dashboard similar in arrangement to that of the Executive car, while the car's special equipment can be operated from the central console. Given the sportier nature of the vehicle, the seats are tilted back to help deal with Javelin's rapid acceleration. When the weapons are employed, a projector can display a targeting reticule, along with target and firing information to the windscreen.

WING MIRROR

Unlike the Executive car, which exclusively uses video cameras to provide the driver with an all-round view of the car, the Javelin uses a single camera mounted at the rear, in conjunction with two traditional wing mirrors just in front of the gull wing doors.

REAR

The layout of the Javelin's rear differs from the Executive, while following the same basic shape. The vents for the engine are more pronounced and the brake lights are mounted in the centre. What appear to be exhaust vents towards the very back actually house smoke generators, while rocket boosters can be fitted to provide a little extra acceleration.

CHALLENGER JEEP

A common sight around large-scale civilian and military facilities is the British Motor Corporation Challenger utility vehicle, informally referred to as the 'jeep'. An adaptable design allows the Challenger to be modified to fulfil numerous roles, including the transport of personnel, cargo or equipment.

One of the first electrically powered vehicles on the civilian market, the Challenger can travel at up to 74.5 mph for two hours. As such, BMC marketed the jeep as a short-range runabout, ideal for servicing airports and stations, military bases, industrial sites and office complexes – including film studios.

Harlington-Straker Studios utilises a small fleet of these vehicles, most of which can be easily requisitioned for SHADO operations at a moment's notice. Primary modifications made by SHADO include additional batteries to significantly extend the vehicle's range; hardpoints on the top of the vehicle to house search lights or machine guns; and a concealed compartment underneath the back seats which can house stores, restraints, firearms and other equipment.

HS STUDIOS

The Challengers used by Harlington-Straker Studios are painted with the iconic HS blue branding and can be often seen parked by the main reception. In this context they are used to transport VIPs around the studio or move heavy equipment between sound stages.

SUPPORT ROLE

When requisitioned by SHADO personnel, the Challengers are used in a support role, creating roadblocks around incident sites, covert convoy escort, or transporting witnesses back to SHADO HQ for debriefing. The jeeps and their crews usually operate under the guise of a film crew working on a night shoot.

CONVOY

The exact size of a supporting force varies, usually dictated by information and intelligence garnered on the UFO landing site and the nature of the incident. Usually, at least four Challengers will be deployed to shadow the Mobile Transporters, with four operatives per vehicle.

EQUIPMENT HARDPOINT

PASSENGER DOORS (REMOVEABLE)

A2 221

REAR INDICATORS, BREAK
AND REVERSE LIGHTS

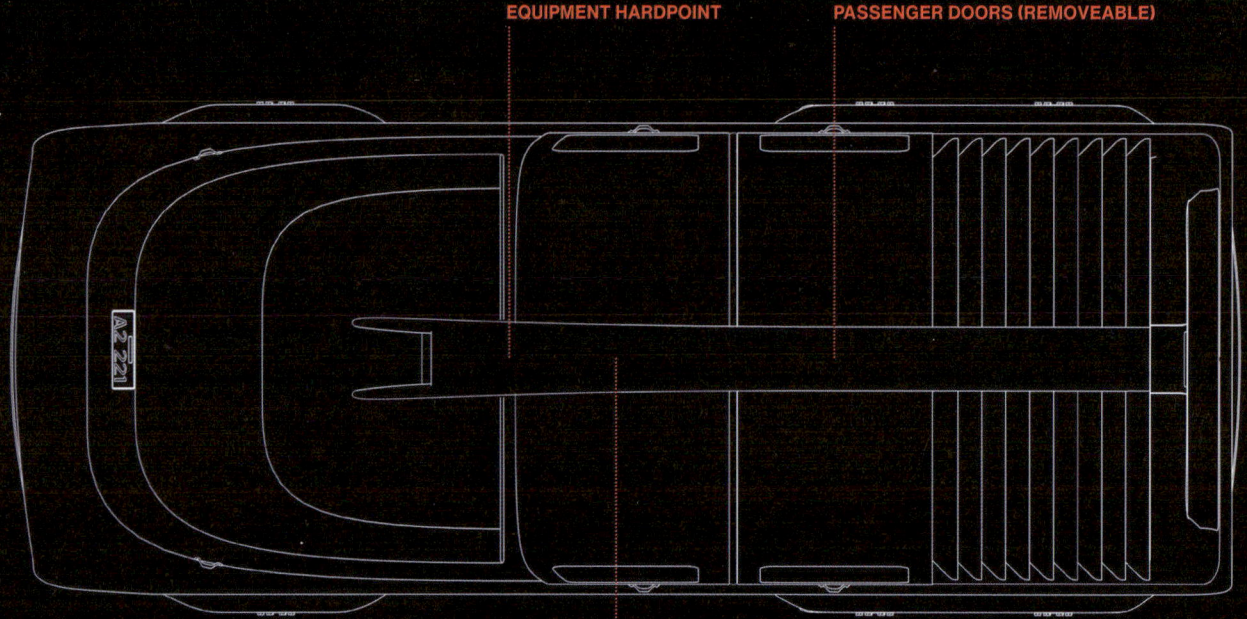

FORWARD DOOR FRAME
(REMOVEABLE)

CARGO SECTION
(REMOVEABLE)

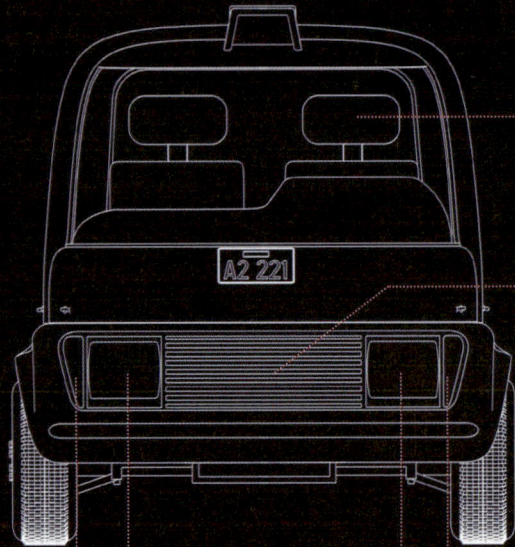

DRIVER'S SEAT

INTAKE

A2 221

DRIVER'S DOOR

HEADLIGHT

HEADLIGHT

FORWARD
INDICATOR

FORWARD
INDICATOR

VARIANTS

The Challenger's top chassis can be removed or interchanged with other commercially available parts, while the doors, back section and seats are all removable and allow the jeep to be quickly modified into, amongst others, an ambulance, fire appliance, flatbed truck or security vehicle.

EASE OF USE

The controls on the jeep are very straightforward. The electrical nature of the vehicle has removed the need for a traditional clutch. As such, the Challenger can be operated with little to no training (training can be conducted within the grounds of HS Studios). Given the enhanced nature of the SHADO variants, additional security is provided in the form of a combination code that is used to start up the vehicle and provide access to the secret compartment.

EQUIPMENT

UNIFORMS & EQUIPMENT

The unprecedented nature of SHADO's mission statement makes it imperative that its operatives are equipped with the latest technology and hardware in order to protect themselves while engaging the alien threat. To this end, the organisation can requisition whatever it needs from military and/or commercial suppliers.

A large part of SHADO HQ is dedicated to the 'Resources and Development' department, which is mandated to create and streamline technology across the organisation. Once fully operational, much of this department will be relocated to the new SHADO Los Angeles facility in America.

As a new operative, you will be provided with extensive briefings on the uniforms and equipment detailed in this section. You will be regularly tested in order to demonstrate and develop your knowledge and ensure you remain fully conversant in all aspects of this department.

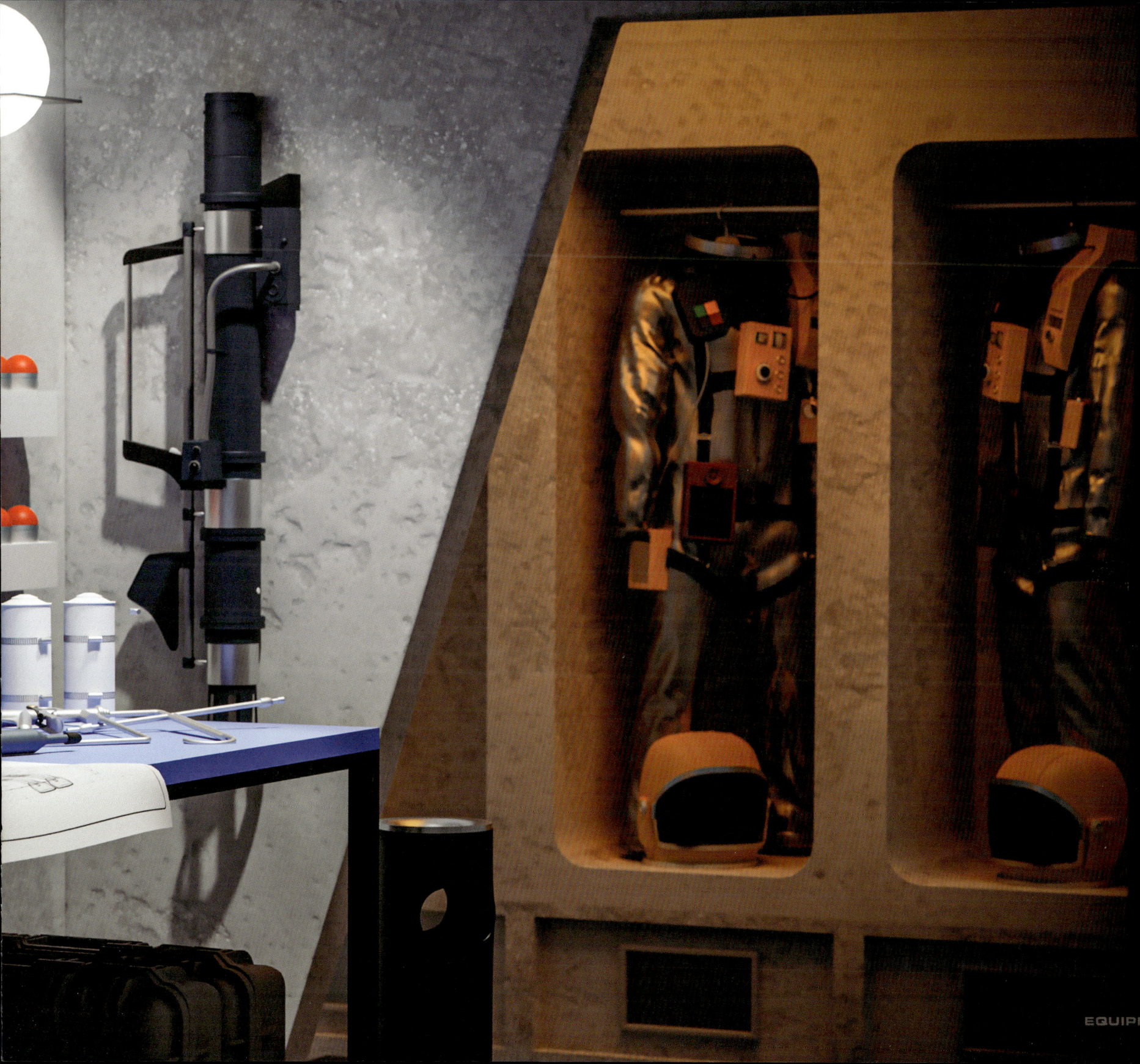

UNIFORMS

Each service branch of SHADO is indicated by its own distinctive uniform that is designed to complement the environment in which it is worn. Upon officially joining SHADO, you can requisition a new uniform from the quartermaster for each deployment.

HIGH RANKING OFFICERS

More often than not, the Commander and Colonels will retain their civilian clothes as they will more frequently be expected to leave the base for meetings and briefings. SHADO still requires a smart, business-style dress code and, as such, officers are generally expected to dress according to the status of their rank.

SHADO HQ

Operatives working in SHADO HQ are issued with utilitarian off-white uniforms with yellow accents. The basic nature of this uniform is to provide an additional security measure by making it difficult for devices or documents to be smuggled in and out of the facility. Operatives can expect their uniform and belongings to be scanned and inventoried when going through security.

Tracking operators and operations controllers in SHADO HQ and Moonbase will sometimes be issued with a shortwave radio in order to assist them with quickly contacting other internal departments. A mirror and make-up kit is also included in the device.

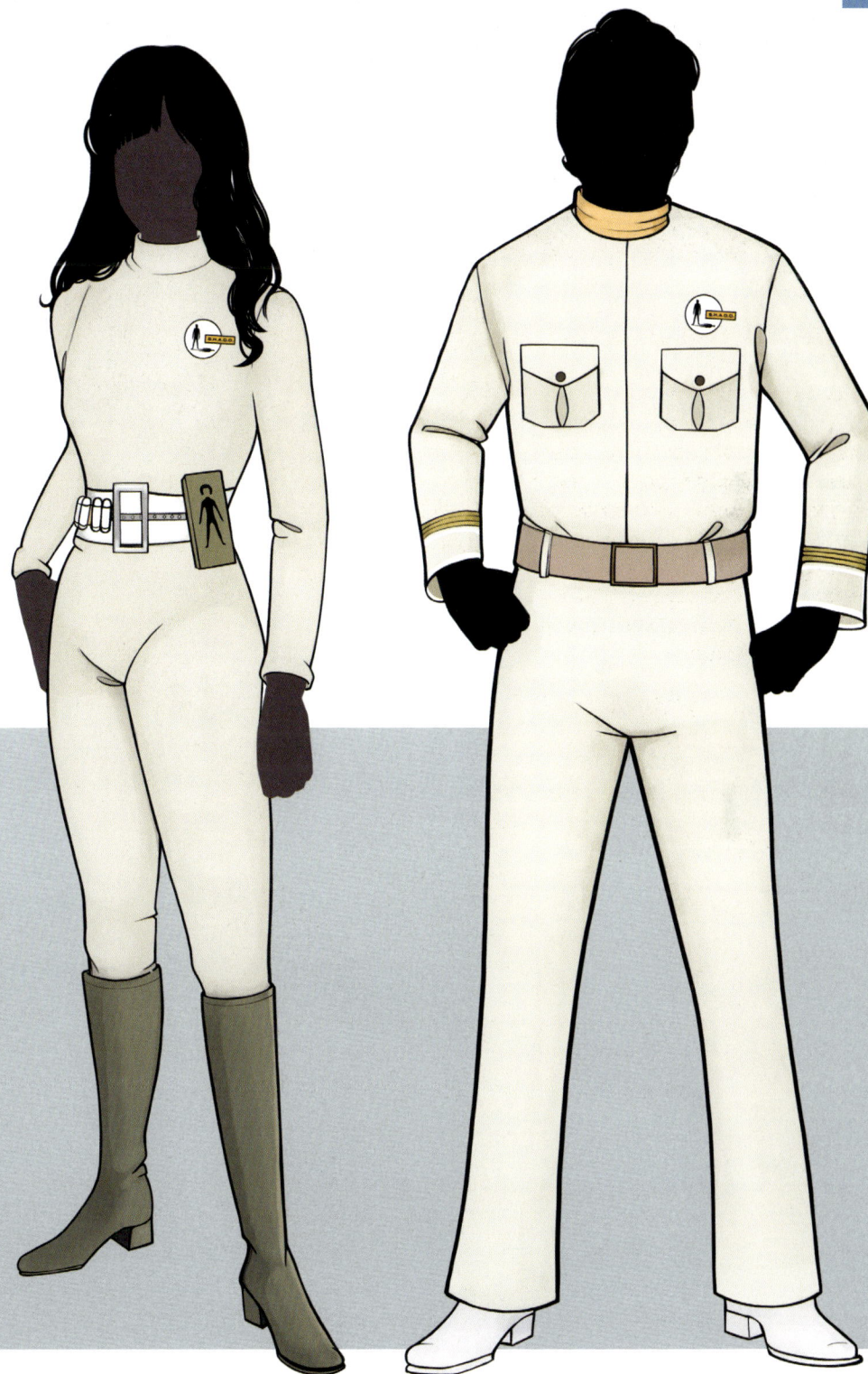

MOONBASE

Moonbase personnel are issued with a silver alternative to the uniforms worn in SHADO HQ, with overalls for men and women. These uniforms are designed to be worn both on and off-duty. The female variant has removable sleeves and leggings, and can be paired with a skirt for a quick transition to a much more casual outfit.

The purple wigs worn by female operatives are primarily an aesthetic choice, though they have proved useful in keeping longer hair under control and free of static in the somewhat unreliable artificial gravity on Moonbase.

SKYDIVER

Due to the relatively small size of the Skydiver vessels, the interior temperature can become rather hot due to the proximity of the crew to the main reactor. For this reason, Skydiver crews are issued with a lightweight fishnet vest and matching trousers. The Captain and XOs are denoted by a lighter colour.

When going topside or piloting Sky One, a leather jacket can be worn, as the base uniform offers little protection against colder environments.

INTERCEPTOR PILOT

The Interceptor pilots on Moonbase wear thermal overalls that can be linked to the cockpit of the Interceptor, providing a live feed of their bio signs. A small control unit on the cuffs allows for temperature regulation during flight. Given the quick response time required for launch, it was deemed that spacesuits would be too cumbersome, so these, coupled with a pressurised compartment, were considered to be the best alternative.

SECURITY

SHADO's installation security forces wear a semi-official navy uniform designed to look in keeping with other security contractors. This way, they can be seen in public without raising too many questions. Obviously, in these instances, the SHADO security tags are removed.

A slight variantion on these uniforms is used by the SHADair branch of SHADO, with epaulettes added for chief pilots.

More uncommon variations can be found across the organisation, serving specific purposes. Ultimately, they will simply be a stylised design with a removable SHADO badge (worn for quick identification by personnel).

SPACE SUIT

As it became apparent that SHADO would have to conduct extensive operations in space and on the Moon, a bespoke spacesuit needed to be developed that would allow astronauts to safely operate in this new environment. Funding was provided to civilian contractors, and their research resulted in the Arc-1 environment suit.

Rather than securing most of the components in a backpack, as commonly done in other environment suits, the Arc-1 distributes most of its components across the front of the suit, making for a slightly more cumbersome design but also allowing for easy access, repair and modification in the field. The user can easily change their own air and water tanks, meaning theoretically that EVA in the Arc-1 is limited only by the needs and fatigue of the suit user.

As the Arc-1 was developed through civilian contractors, it has become a common sight across multiple space programmes such as Dalotek and Eurosec.

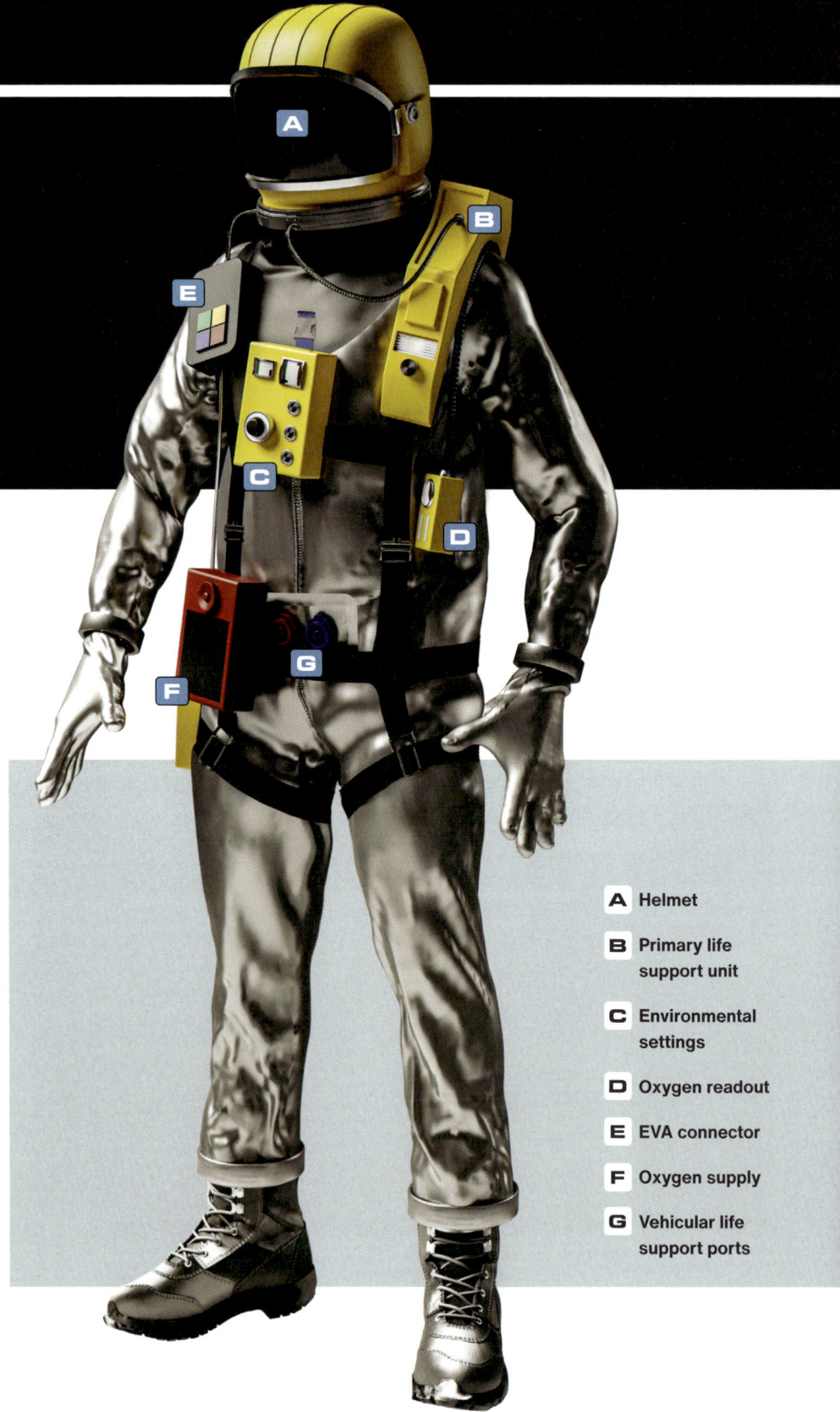

A   Helmet

B   Primary life support unit

C   Environmental settings

D   Oxygen readout

E   EVA connector

F   Oxygen supply

G   Vehicular life support ports

EVA PROPULSION UNIT

While navigating in zero gravity, a handheld propulsion unit can be used to help astronauts travel while untethered. Compressed air is fired evenly out of the two nozzles on either side of the unit, allowing the user to move in whatever direction they point it.

An additional equipment pack can be added to greatly increase the duration of an EVA while in open space. This not only extends the duration of the EVA but, should the user find themselves untethered from their home craft, it also provides increased time for a successful rescue.

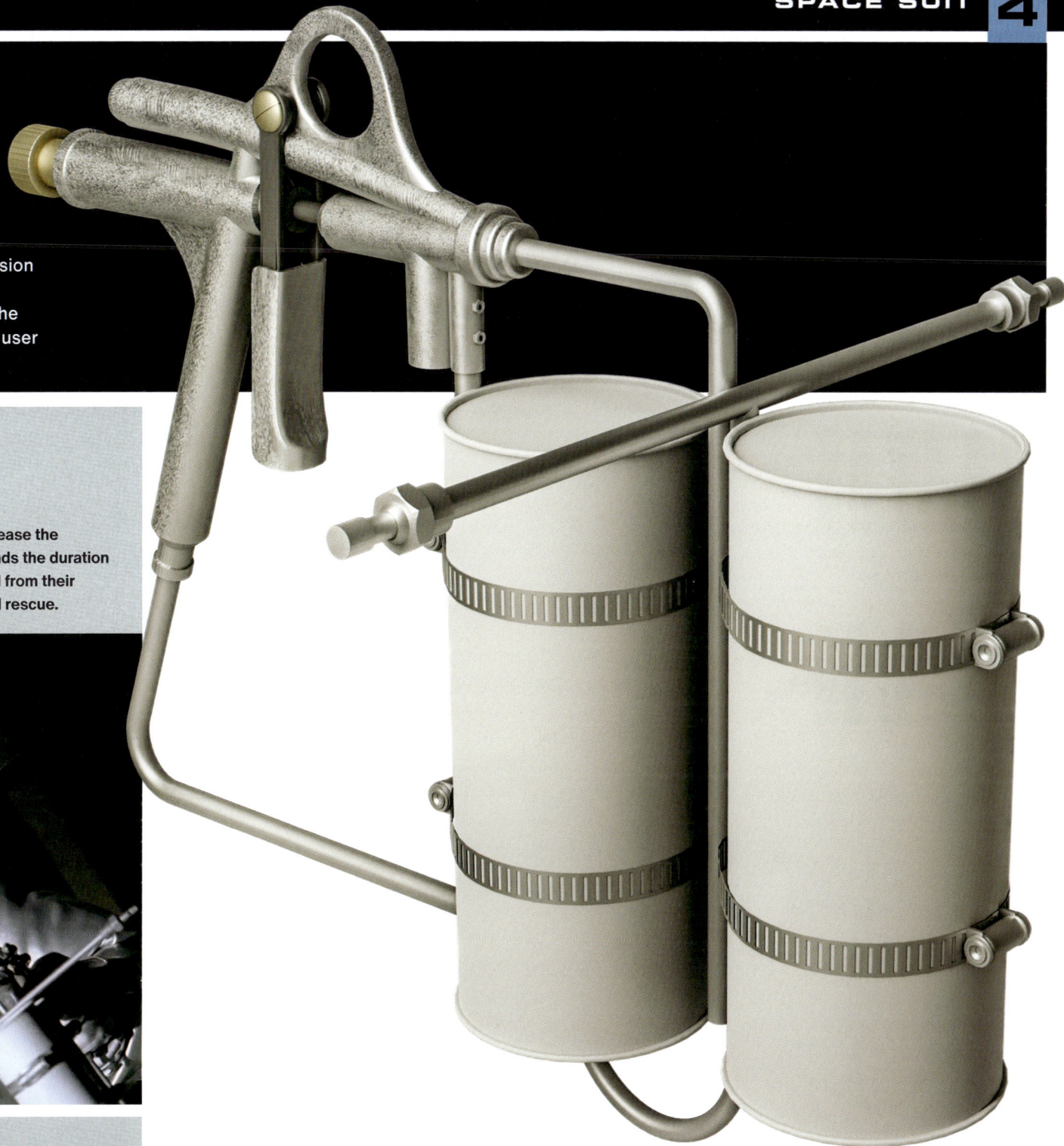

WEAPONARY

Currently available in SHADO's arsenal are five types of personal defence weapons. These will be stored within secure locations across all SHADO facilities and vehicles, and can be signed out for practice at SHADO HQ's firing range.

SHADO SIDEARM

The primary sidearm used within SHADO and a common sight amongst regular military and security firms, the standard pistol is a personal defence weapon that is issued to operatives across all installations. The pistol is a refined version of the traditional automatic pistol design, with a clip that holds 12 rounds and an extended barrel that functions as a suppressor and helps prevent the barrel from flooding if immersed in water.

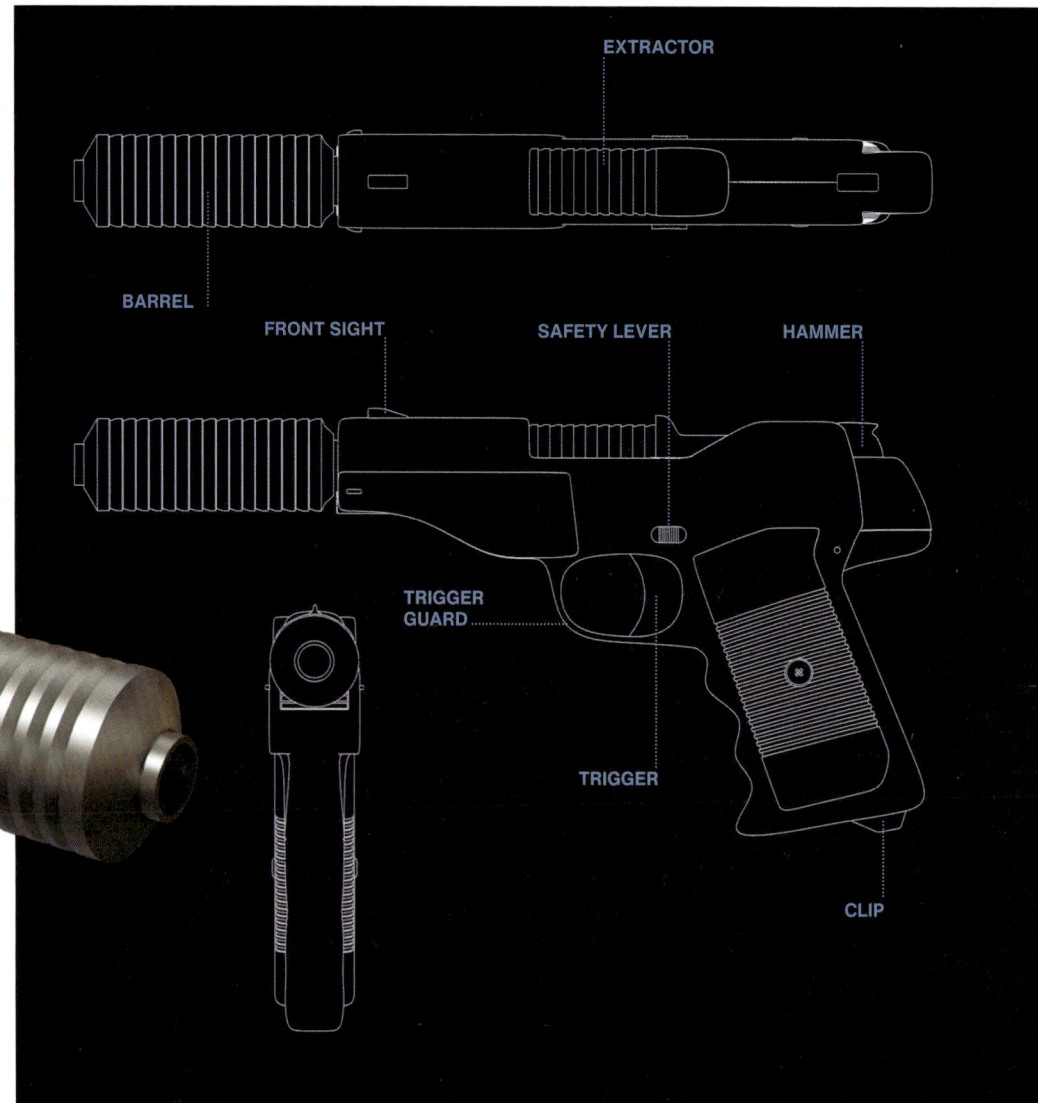

EXTRACTOR

BARREL

FRONT SIGHT   SAFETY LEVER   HAMMER

TRIGGER
GUARD

TRIGGER

CLIP

SUBMACHINE GUN

The many and varied theatres of operation that SHADO work in necessitates the development of weapons that can function in the most difficult of environments. The SHADO submachine gun (SMG) was the first of these to be developed. Designed to be relatively small so it can be easily stowed as part of the inventory on a

Moonmobile or Mobile, the SMG's primary innovation is an isolated combustion chamber slung under the weapon, allowing uninterrupted functionality in and out of a vacuum. The downside of this design means that less space can be allocated to the clip, which holds 35 rounds. An optical sight can be attached when necessary.

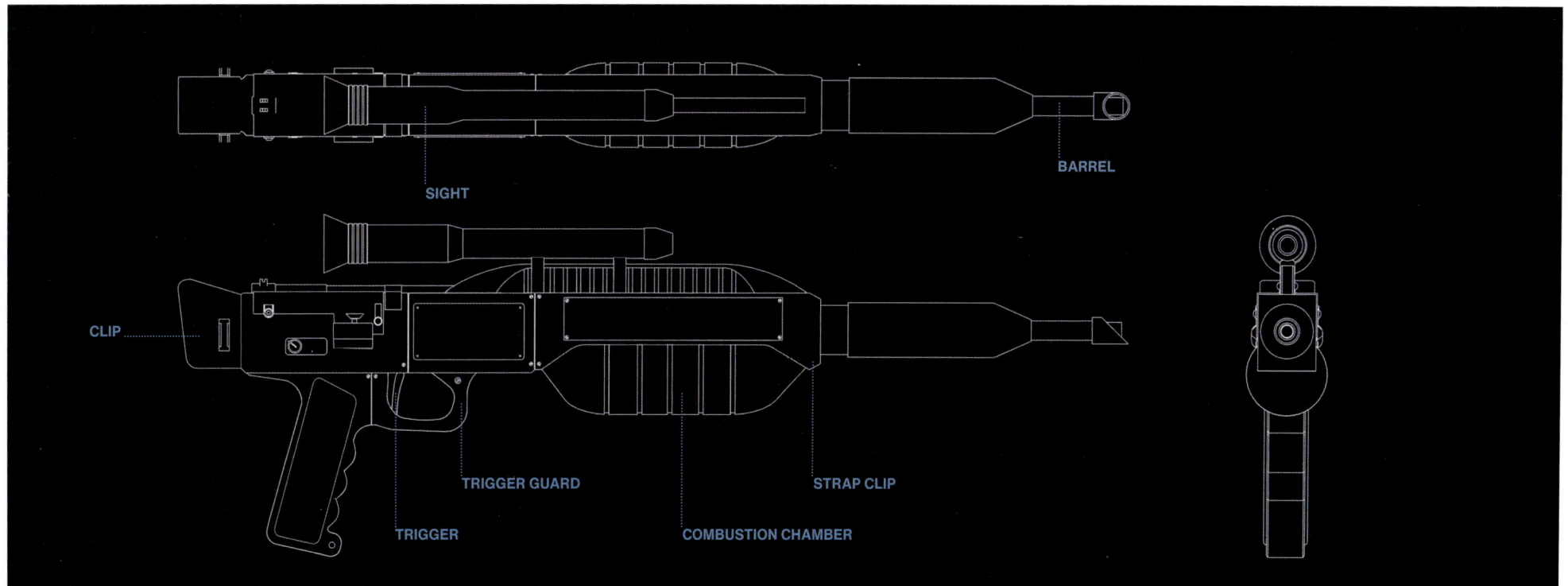

SIGHT

BARREL

CLIP

TRIGGER GUARD

STRAP CLIP

TRIGGER

COMBUSTION CHAMBER

ASSAULT RIFLE

Developed in the second year of
SHADO's operation, the assault rifle was
designed around various shortcomings
of the SMG, while also taking advantage
of the intelligence gained from captured
alien weaponry. Incorporating many
elements of the SMG, the assault rifle
is a larger weapon featuring a stock,
enlarged clip and more durable sight.

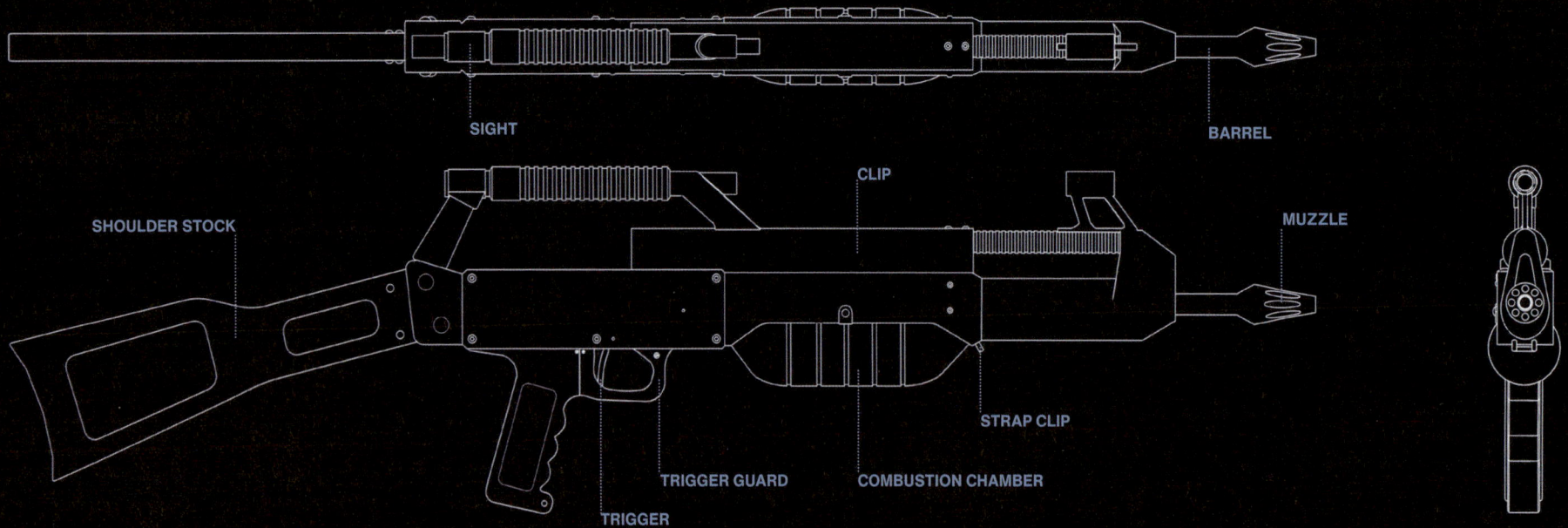

SIGHT

BARREL

CLIP

SHOULDER STOCK

MUZZLE

STRAP CLIP

TRIGGER GUARD

COMBUSTION CHAMBER

TRIGGER

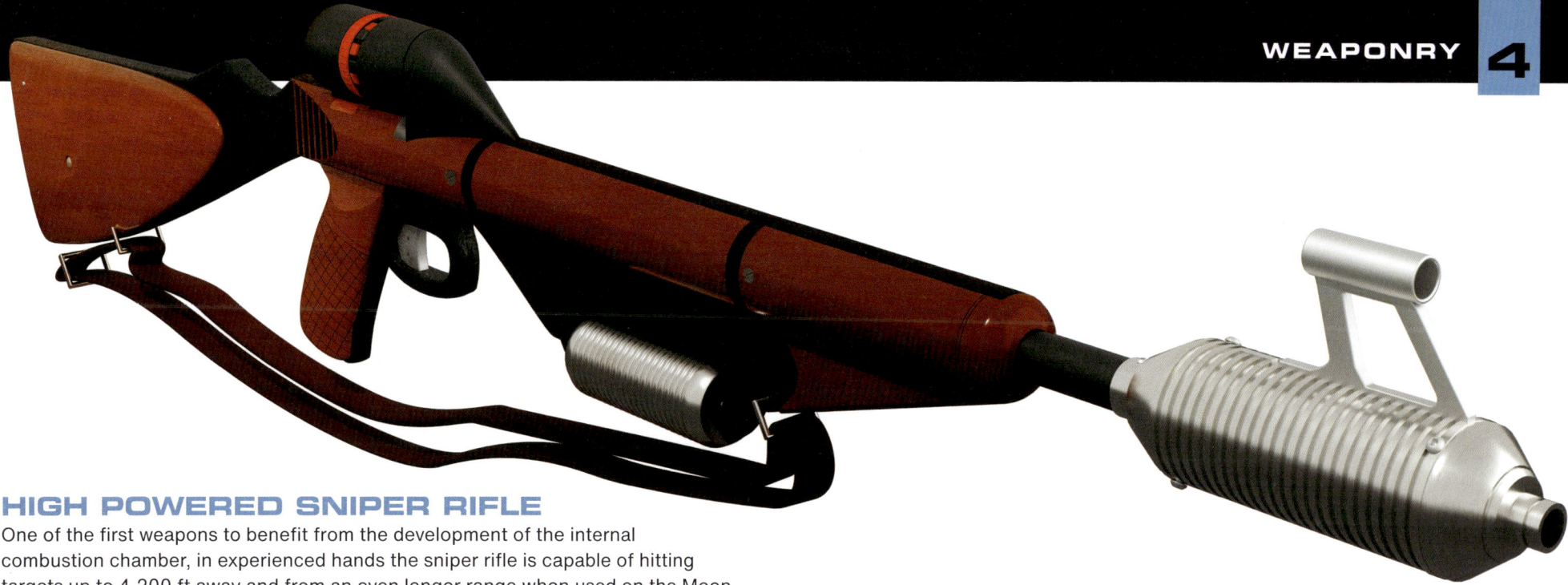

HIGH POWERED SNIPER RIFLE

One of the first weapons to benefit from the development of the internal combustion chamber, in experienced hands the sniper rifle is capable of hitting targets up to 4,200 ft away and from an even longer range when used on the Moon or in space. An electronic sight can be calibrated for various factors, including wind speed, gravity (or lack thereof) and air pressure.

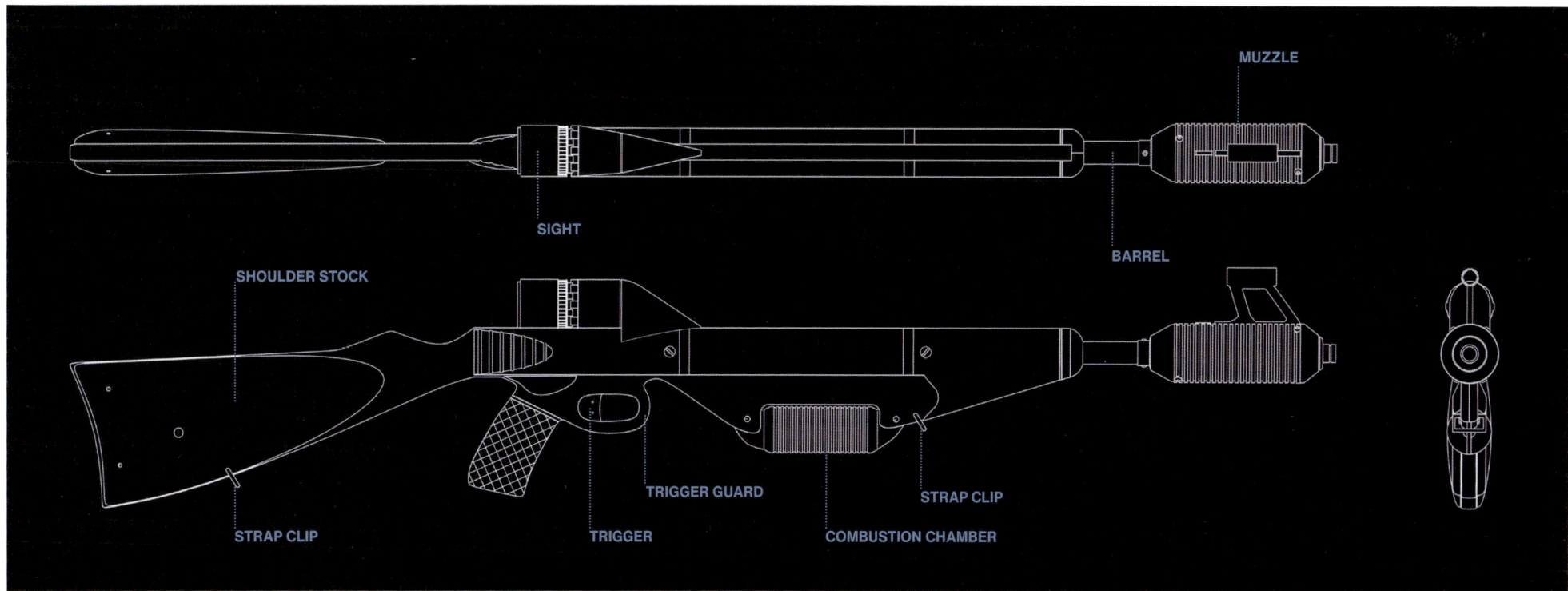

MUZZLE

SIGHT

BARREL

SHOULDER STOCK

TRIGGER GUARD

STRAP CLIP

STRAP CLIP

TRIGGER

COMBUSTION CHAMBER

SURFACE TO AIR MISSILE SYSTEM

With little information available about alien weaponry, it was deemed that static ground defence systems would make an easy target for the agile and hyper-accurate UFOs that they would be going up against. For this reason, man-portable rocket launchers were chosen to provide tactical flexibility; it was also appreciated that an operative with a launcher was harder to detect than a vehicle or ground installation.

The launcher is a five feet-long firing tube capable of firing a variety of projectiles, ranging from flares to laser-guided missiles and cluster munitions. An advanced electronic sight allows the user to see targets and lock onto incoming threats up to 2.5 miles away, though experience has shown that, when engaging UFOs, it is preferable to wait until the target is within minimum range. This maximises the effectiveness of the weapon, while also minimising the response time of any retaliation.

MOONBASE DEFENCES

Until the armoured Moonbase defence vehicles became operational in SHADO's second year, stationing armed astronauts on the base perimeter during high alerts was considered to be Moonbase's second line of defence.

ARMOURY LIFTS

Given the low-key nature of SHADO HQ's operation, traditional defences are not an option. In an instance where there is a direct attack on Harlington-Straker Studios, four armoury lifts containing missile launchers and spare ordnance are sent to easily defendable points on the surface.

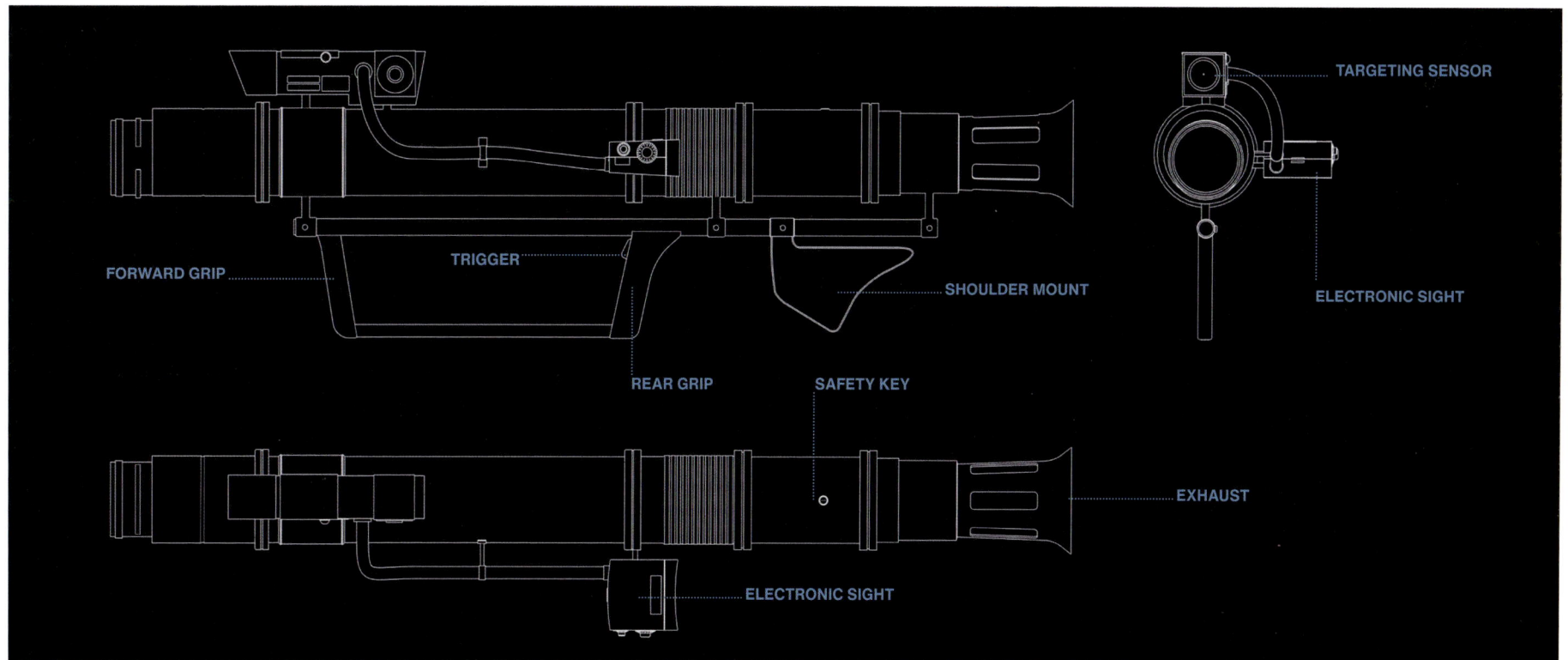

TARGETING SENSOR

FORWARD GRIP

TRIGGER

SHOULDER MOUNT

ELECTRONIC SIGHT

REAR GRIP

SAFETY KEY

EXHAUST

ELECTRONIC SIGHT

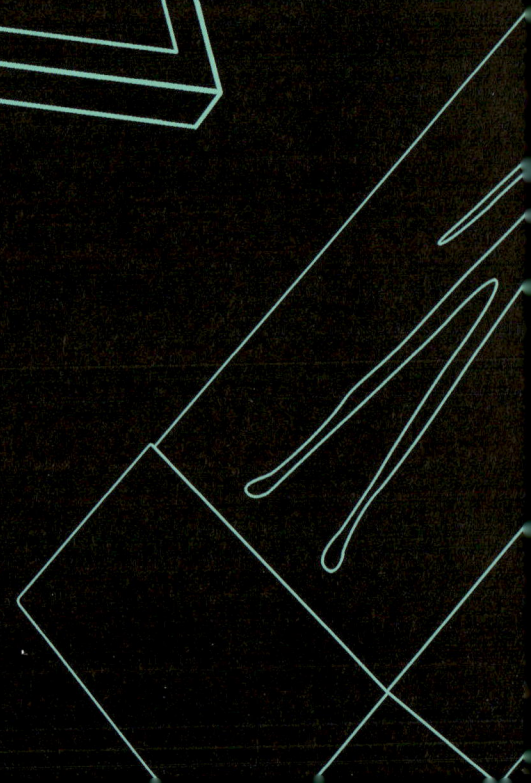

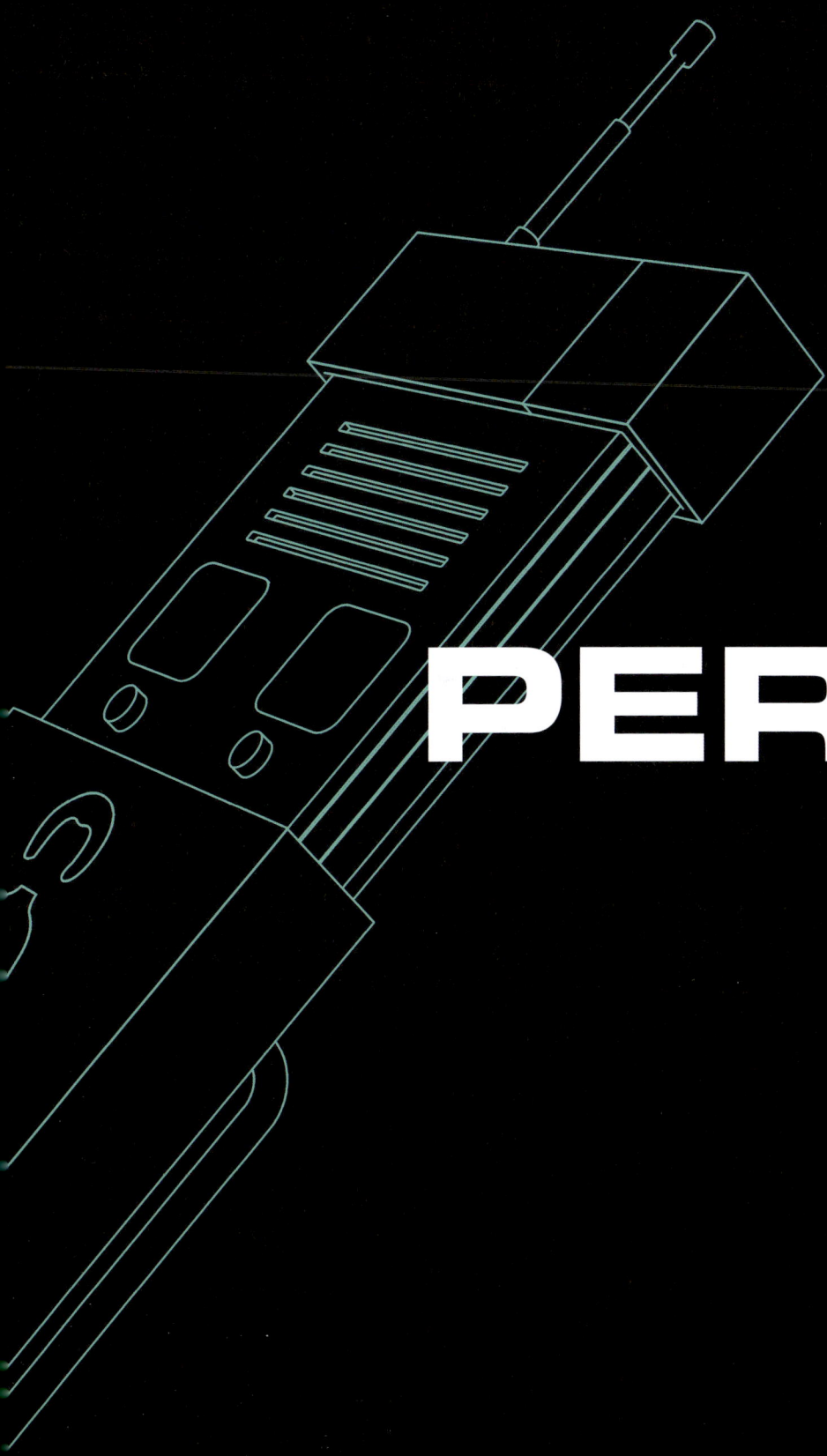

DEPARTMENT:

PERSONNEL

PERSONNEL

For all its technological prowess, the key to SHADO's continued successful operation lies with the highly skilled personnel that comprise its ranks.

Initially, it was decided that SHADO operatives would be drawn from strictly military backgrounds, but as time went on and the organisation began to take shape, the selection process was altered, removing the requirement for military service, provided that certain other criteria were met.

SELECTION

SHADO's international scope allows for the recruitment of operatives from a wide variety of countries and backgrounds. The strict selection process and rigorous testing of potential personnel ensures that any operative inducted into SHADO's ranks will be ideally suited to their role.

From astronauts to technicians, submarine commanders to medical staff and a host of other key positions, the personnel are selected, trained and sworn to secrecy. Many of them end up with dual roles, both as SHADO operatives and with a cover role as a member of the Harlington-Straker Studios team. Often, the second role can be just as vital in preventing breaches in security.

SHADO operates as a military organisation, albeit a top secret one, and the rules and regulations governing its operatives are just as stringent, with the penalties for failing to abide by these regulations equally severe.

RANKS

The ranks within SHADO's command structure follow a military-inspired hierarchy, but the ranks used are not always analogous to their regular military counterparts. The highest rank within SHADO's infrastructure is that of Commander. The ranks then proceed from highest to lowest through Colonel, Captain, Lieutenant and Non-Commissioned Operative.

TRAINING

SHADO has an extensive cross-training programme for its operatives, providing the opportunity for far more varied assignments than would otherwise be possible. Over the course of a standard tour of duty, an operative may find themselves stationed on Moonbase, aboard a Skydiver submarine, based at a ground station, or serving at SHADO HQ. Personnel who have completed their cross-training can then be placed on the rotating duty roster for reassignment to another section.

SECURITY

Security remains of paramount importance, and every SHADO operative is charged with ensuring that everything they do is carried out under conditions of strictest secrecy. The highly secretive (and dangerous) nature of the work, plus the fact they are forbidden to discuss it with even their closest and most trustworthy friends and relations, is often enough to dissuade potential candidates from accepting a position with SHADO.

While a career with SHADO may mean making considerable sacrifices in an operative's personal life, to date it appears to be a cost that SHADO's dedicated personnel are willing to pay in the fight to protect humanity from the ongoing threat of UFO attacks.

NAME:

STRAKER, EDWARD

BORN:
JUNE 11, 1942

PLACE OF BIRTH:
BOSTON, MASSACHUSETTS, USA

RANK:
COMMANDER

Edward (Ed) Straker is the Commander-in-Chief of SHADO operations. He was appointed to the position with overwhelming committee support at SHADO's inception and took charge of the set-up of the organisation over the ten-year development period, commencing in spring 1970.

A decorated ex-US Air Force Colonel, Straker's no-nonsense attitude and reliance on cold logic and facts makes him perfectly suited to such a demanding position. The responsibility for every major decision taken by SHADO rests on his shoulders, and he is accountable only to General James Henderson of the International Astrophysical Commission.

Straker sacrificed everything for SHADO, including his marriage, which began to break down from the moment he took over as Commander. Tragically, Straker's only son, John, was critically injured years later, and the Commander was forced to choose between saving John's life or dealing with a potentially deadly UFO. Putting the greater good ahead of personal considerations, Straker had to deal with the death of his son, an event that shook him profoundly.

According to his medical records, Straker suffered with severe claustrophobia for many years until a sub-smash incident on Skydiver One forced him to face his fears and overcome them. SHADO medical records no relapses and consider the condition cured.

Commander Straker has an unusually high degree of self-control. He smokes, but not to excess, and he never consumes alcohol – though it has been noted that in rare special circumstances, he will permit himself one drink to honour the occasion.

Within SHADO HQ, Straker has few friends. He regards the majority of his subordinates as just that, with the exception of Alec Freeman, whom he knew for years before SHADO was formed, and the two continue to remain close.

While he does not consider true friendships, either within SHADO or in his personal life, a luxury that he can afford, he nevertheless maintains a leadership style that is fair and open, and he is not averse to occasionally letting the personnel under his command enjoy themselves.

He welcomes ideas that can further SHADO's aims, regardless of who they come from, but does not suffer fools gladly, nor does he tolerate any action that could potentially put the lives of the general public at risk.

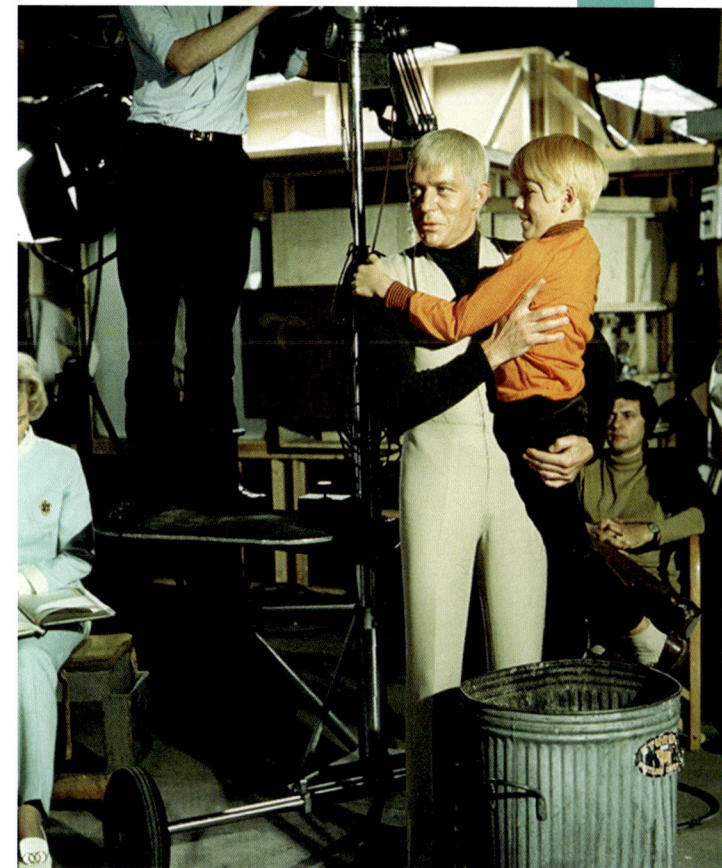

NAME:

FREEMAN, ALEC EUGENE

BORN:
AUGUST 31, 1934

PLACE OF BIRTH:
IVER HEATH, BUCKINGHAMSHIRE, ENGLAND

RANK:
COLONEL

Alec Freeman was the first new recruit selected to join SHADO and he was personally chosen by Commander Straker. The pair shared a close friendship prior to the formation of SHADO, with Freeman having been the best man at Straker's wedding.

A veteran combat pilot and Royal Air Force intelligence operative, Freeman was known for fast reflexes and a cool head under pressure, and his experiences during active service made him the perfect candidate to fill the role of SHADO's second-in-command.

Freeman's duties include planning the recruitment of SHADO personnel, seeing to the welfare of existing operatives, and keeping a watchful eye on the efficiency of the organisation.

Colonel Freeman's loyalty to SHADO is total. While he may not always agree with the morals of Commander Straker's decisions, he nonetheless abides by his superior's orders, knowing that these actions are for the greater good.

While naturally ambitious, it took Colonel Freeman some time to adjust to the burden of command. On the first occasion on which he assumed temporary control of SHADO HQ, Freeman was uncomfortable making command decisions and showed reluctance to act on information provided by subordinates.

However, in time he came to accept his responsibilities. When SHADO's Los Angeles division became operational, Freeman accepted Commander Straker's offer to head up anti-UFO operations in the United States, and he relocated to that facility. His successor at SHADO HQ is Colonel Virginia Lake.

Freeman's cheerful and easy demeanour has won him many friends throughout SHADO. His colleagues generally find him very approachable, while he in turn is quick to defend those whose performance or conduct Freeman feels has been unfairly questioned.

As part of SHADO's cover operation, Freeman played the role of an actor in Harlington-Straker Studios' repertory company, albeit one who is rarely hired and more often than not fails to make the finished cut of the film.

NAME:

FOSTER, PAUL

BORN:
DECEMBER 24, 1951

PLACE OF BIRTH:
BLACKBURN, LANCASHIRE, ENGLAND

RANK:
COLONEL

Foster drew the attention of SHADO when a UFO incident occurred in the vicinity of a high-altitude test flight that Foster was conducting. The incident resulted in the death of his co-pilot and, despite an elaborate cover-up attempted by SHADO, Foster's investigations led him to discover the truth about the organisation.

Commander Straker was suitably impressed by Foster's determination, fearlessness and refusal to take the 'truth' at face value, and awarded Foster the rank of a Colonel in SHADO as a result.

Foster's early service with SHADO saw him garnering experience during a major spike in UFO incidents. In the space of just a few months he was assigned to Moonbase's duty roster, serving as Moonbase Commander.

During his time on Moonbase, Foster unexpectedly formed an alliance of necessity with an alien attacker when the two were stranded on the lunar surface. Unfortunately, due to a radio fault, Foster was unable to alert his SHADO rescuers to the existence of the informal truce and the alien was killed before Foster could save him.

Colonel Foster also served aboard Skydiver One shortly after Captain Waterman was given command of the vessel. He rated the crew's performance highly and provided a very positive performance review to SHADO on his return.

Foster is known for his hotheadedness and impulsive behaviour on occasion; these have at times been cause for concern. Nevertheless, his actions are usually warranted and have saved lives more than once.

When Foster was put on trial for allegedly transmitting classified information to the press, Commander Straker and Colonel Freeman did everything in their power to prove his innocence. They eventually succeeded and all charges were dropped.

Foster pursued a brief relationship with his colleague, Colonel Virginia Lake, but it did not last long. The pair parted amicably and have remained close.

Like Commander Straker and Colonel Freeman, Colonel Foster plays a double role in the interests of maintaining SHADO security. He can often be spotted on the studio lot above SHADO HQ, posing as a film executive.

Virginia Lake commenced her association with SHADO while working as head of the Utronix project, designed to track UFOs in deep space, even while travelling at super-light speeds. She was formally asked to join the ranks of SHADO as a full Colonel, replacing Alec Freeman as second-in-command, following his assignment to SHADO's Los Angeles facility.

Lake's background in electronics and research provided an ideal basis for her work with SHADO, and she has shown great adaptability in a variety of roles throughout the organisation. She has been assigned to the position of Moonbase Commander on a semi-regular basis, a role which she excels at.

During one particular UFO incident, Colonel Lake and Commander Straker became trapped within an area affected by time distortion. They only managed to survive and escape thanks to the use of the X-50 serum.

As well as her expertise in electronics, Colonel Lake also specialises in the field of interrogation, always knowing how best to draw out details from those claiming to have encountered UFOs.

NAME:

LAKE, VIRGINIA

BORN:
AUGUST 5, 1945

PLACE OF BIRTH:
BRIGHTON, SUSSEX, ENGLAND

RANK:
COLONEL

NAME:
ELLIS, GAY

BORN:
MARCH 30, 1954

PLACE OF BIRTH:
LAHORE, PUNJAB, PAKISTAN

RANK:
LIEUTENANT

Lieutenant Gay Ellis holds the distinction of being the first person selected to command SHADO's Moonbase. Although she was recruited to SHADO later than those who became her fellow Moonbase operatives, Ellis' aptitude and qualifications made her the prime candidate for the position.

Lieutenant Ellis is a dedicated member of SHADO, and her service record speaks for itself. She was instrumental in the development, design and installation of key Moonbase systems and lunar facilities.

After an Interceptor pilot was killed in a UFO attack, Lieutenant Ellis and the surviving Interceptor pilots were transferred to Earth for evaluation. Computer analysis subsequently suggested a potential romantic attachment between Ellis and one of the astronauts, Mark Bradley. However, the assessment found that Lieutenant Ellis' actions during the UFO attack were unaffected by her personal feelings and were the correct and only choices made in order to save the other astronauts. She was cleared to return to duty.

When SHADO's Los Angeles facility became operational, Colonel Freeman personally requested that Lieutenant Ellis be assigned to the base as his second-in-command. Knowing that Moonbase would be in safe hands with Lieutenant Barry, Ellis accepted the transfer.

NAME:

JACKSON, DOUGLAS

BORN:
MARCH 12, 1933

PLACE OF BIRTH:
ZGIERZ, POLAND

RANK:
CHIEF MEDICAL OFFICER

Doctor Douglas Jackson is SHADO's incumbent Chief Medical Officer.

Originally something of a mystery to his colleagues, Jackson served the interests of the International Astrophysical Commission under the watchful eye of General Henderson.

When then-civilian Paul Foster accidentally encountered a UFO during a test flight, Jackson was tasked with Foster's supposed psychological evaluation, though this was later revealed to be nothing more than a ploy to test how far Foster would go in maintaining his version of the incident.

On another occasion, Jackson acted as prosecutor during Foster's Court Martial when the latter was accused of espionage and treason against SHADO. However, contrary to Commander Straker's opinions about Jackson's motives and intentions, Foster was apprehended using non-lethal force, at Jackson's suggestion. Jackson later admitted that he suspected Foster's innocence, but could not prove it himself.

Doctor Jackson has had the opportunity to examine a number of aliens recovered from UFO incident sites and has formulated fascinating theories about them as a result. He was the first to posit the notion that the aliens themselves may not be humanoid at all, but rather they transmit their will and knowledge into humanoid hosts and use them for their own ends.

Jackson is recognised as secretive by nature, often playing his cards close to his chest. He prefers to have all the facts at hand before making an assumption, and will rarely reveal his true thoughts on a matter before he deems it prudent to do so.

His expertise, meanwhile, is recognised as invaluable, and his powers of deduction are extremely impressive. His theories about the nature of the aliens have provided some potential answers to questions SHADO has been asking since it was founded.

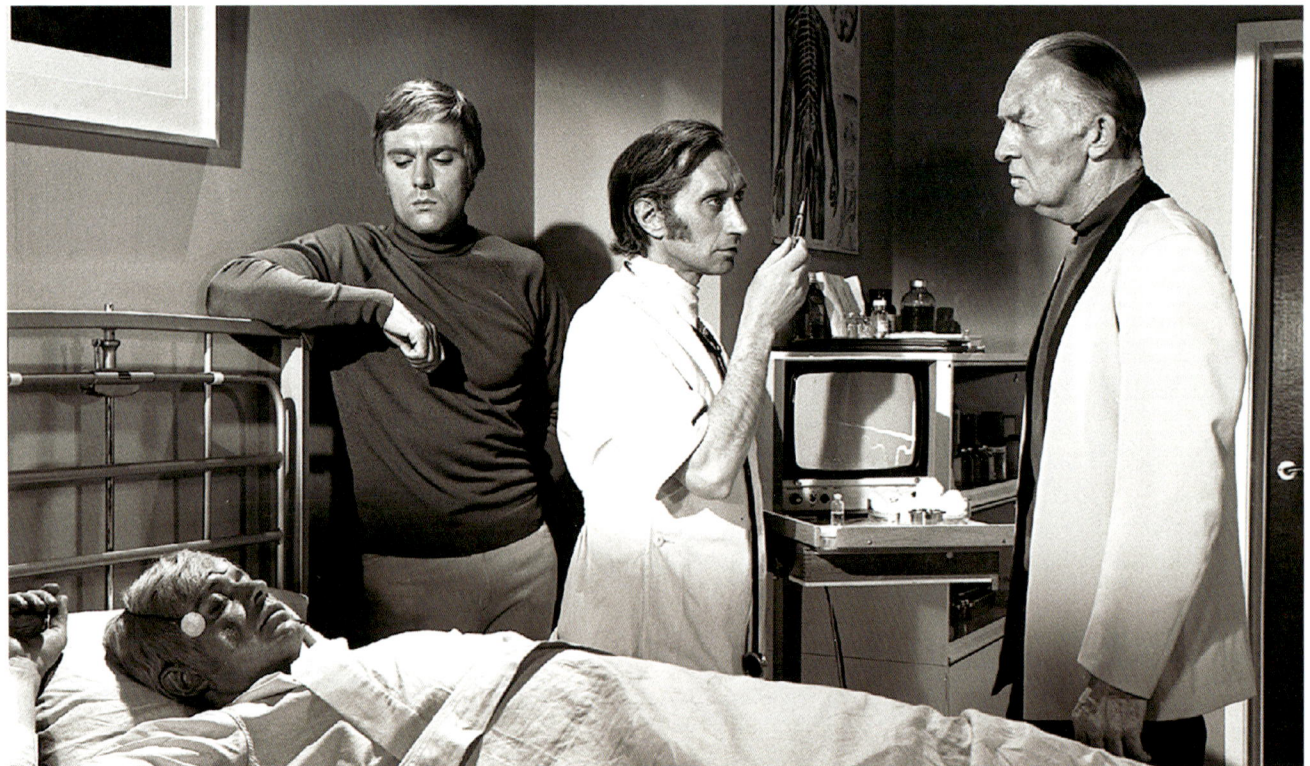

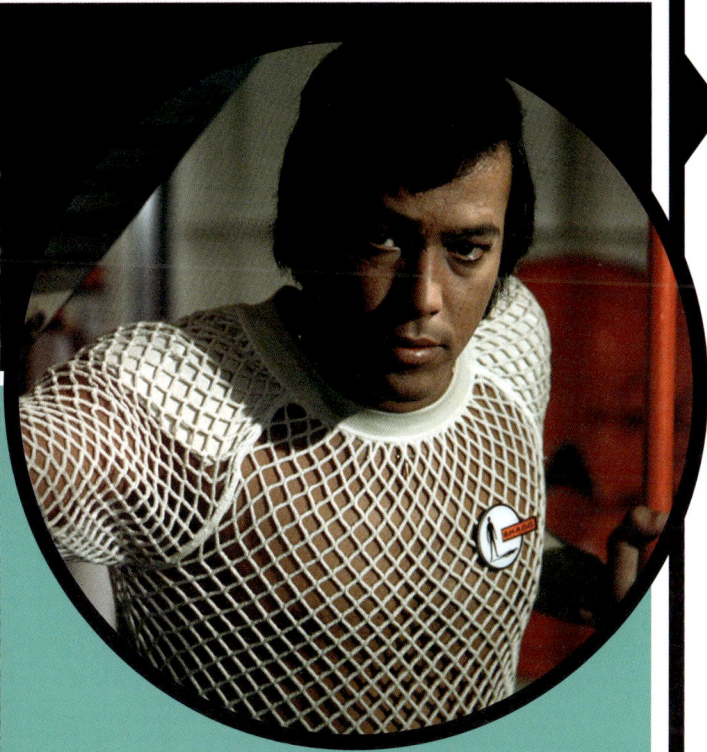

NAME:
CARLIN, PETER

BORN:
JUNE 20, 1949

PLACE OF BIRTH:
RANGOON, BURMA

RANK:
CAPTAIN

Captain Peter Carlin is one of the few members of SHADO to have had direct contact with the aliens. Along with his sister Leila and their friend Jean, he stumbled upon a UFO in a forest clearing in 1970 (prior to the formation of SHADO). Carlin managed to capture some footage of the craft on his camera, but the trio were fired on and Jean was killed instantly.

Carlin and Leila escaped, splitting up to try and avoid their alien pursuers. Carlin was shot and collapsed from his injuries, awakening sometime later in hospital with no sign of Leila.

The film was found still undeveloped in the camera and was brought to the attention of General Henderson and then-Colonel Straker. They used frames of the footage to help prove the existence and very real threat of UFOs, necessitating the formation of SHADO as a countermeasure.

Carlin was recruited and trained as the Captain of Skydiver One, then known simply as Skydiver. He was instrumental in shooting down a UFO that had evaded the Moonbase Interceptor squadron, resulting in the alien craft crashing into the ocean.

Reconnoitring the floating debris, Carlin confirmed the sighting of a body which was promptly recovered and taken to SHADO HQ for analysis. The alien's body showed signs of transplant surgery, including, in a distressing twist of fate, a human heart that had been harvested from Carlin's sister Leila.

After the completion of Skydiver Two, Captain Carlin was transferred to that vessel as commanding officer, and Captain Lew Waterman succeeded him as Skydiver One's Commander. Carlin oversaw the training of the primary crew of the new ship, and he continues to contribute his valuable knowledge to the development of SHADO's fleet.

NAME:

BARRY, NINA

BORN:
OCTOBER 17, 1946

PLACE OF BIRTH:
LIVERPOOL, ENGLAND

RANK:
LIEUTENANT

Lieutenant Nina Barry was one of the earliest recruits to SHADO. During the formation of the organisation, she was one of the key members of the small team tasked with setting up vital SHADO systems.

Once SHADO began operating, Barry was transferred to Moonbase as a space tracker and given responsibility for the monitoring and confirmation of UFO incursions. She was also given rotational shifts as Moonbase Commander, sharing the role with Lieutenant Gay Ellis.

During this time, Lieutenant Barry was assigned to Skydiver One when, during the hunt for a hidden UFO, the enemy craft was able to launch a strike on the submarine. However, Barry survived the attack and was later rescued by the SHADO recovery team. She received a commendation for her actions during the incident.

When Ellis accepted a transfer to SHADO's Los Angeles facility, Barry accepted the role of Moonbase Commander on a full-time basis.

NAME:

JOHNSON, AYSHEA

BORN:
NOVEMBER 12, 1958

PLACE OF BIRTH:
HIGHGATE, LONDON, ENGLAND

RANK:
LIEUTENANT

Lieutenant Ayshea Johnson was recruited to SHADO as an auxiliary Moonbase space tracker, but was reassigned to SHADO HQ before commencing her role.

Johnson's duties include drawing up refuelling schedules for the Skydiver fleet, authorising flight plans for transport aircraft and ensuring that security clearances are kept up to date.

Always approachable, willing to help, and known for her sense of humour, Lieutenant Johnson is very popular with her fellow operatives, many of whom she maintains friendships with during her leisure time.

When Lieutenant Joan Harrington requested an exceptional leave of absence, Johnson was assigned to Moonbase as relief space tracker, taking up the position that she was originally recruited for.

NAME:
FORD, KEITH

BORN:
JULY 8, 1947

PLACE OF BIRTH:
BRISBANE, QUEENSLAND, AUSTRALIA

RANK:
LIEUTENANT

Lieutenant Keith Ford was recruited by Colonel Alec Freeman during SHADO's formation. An expert in electronic communication and data analysis, Ford's talents were put to good use during the initial establishment of SHADO HQ and the development of the communications network used throughout the organisation.

In the late 1960s, Ford conducted a series of interviews with noted members of the scientific community, such as Doctor Frank E. Stranges, regarding UFOs. These interviews, which were viewed by high-ranking SHADO operatives, later provided the key to unlocking the mystery of the sudden communication blackouts during the so-called 'Dalotek affair'.

While his colleagues continued to assist in the day-to-day formation of SHADO, Ford had his hands full fine-tuning the electronic communications systems, devising encryption systems and working on the development of SID's tracking capabilities. As a result, he returned to his intended post at SHADO two years before the arrival of the vital Utronix tracking equipment.

Despite the constant pressures of the job, Ford has acquitted himself admirably, whether providing tracking status and landing coordinates of UFOs, or giving fellow SHADO operatives the benefit of his technical expertise.

NAME:
BRADLEY, MARK

BORN:
MAY 12, 1941

PLACE OF BIRTH:
GEORGETOWN, GUYANA

RANK:
INTERCEPTOR SQUADRON LEADER

Originally a career astronaut for EUROSEC, Lieutenant Mark Bradley was recruited to SHADO in its early days as part of the Moonbase construction team. Currently, he serves as Squadron Leader on Moonbase, piloting the lead Interceptor, running launch drills and training new pilots.

On occasion, he will be transferred out to lead SHADO's ground force or do tours of duty on Skydiver.

In 1980, he was briefly reassigned when it became apparent that he and Lieutenant Gay Ellis had developed romantic feelings for one another. Following further evaluations, it was determined that their ongoing relationship was not compromising their decisions in the field and they both returned to Moonbase.

He was briefly promoted to Moonbase Commander when Colonel Paul Foster was presumed dead on the lunar surface, and he continues to step in during the absence of ranking officers.

DEPARTMENT:
ALIENS

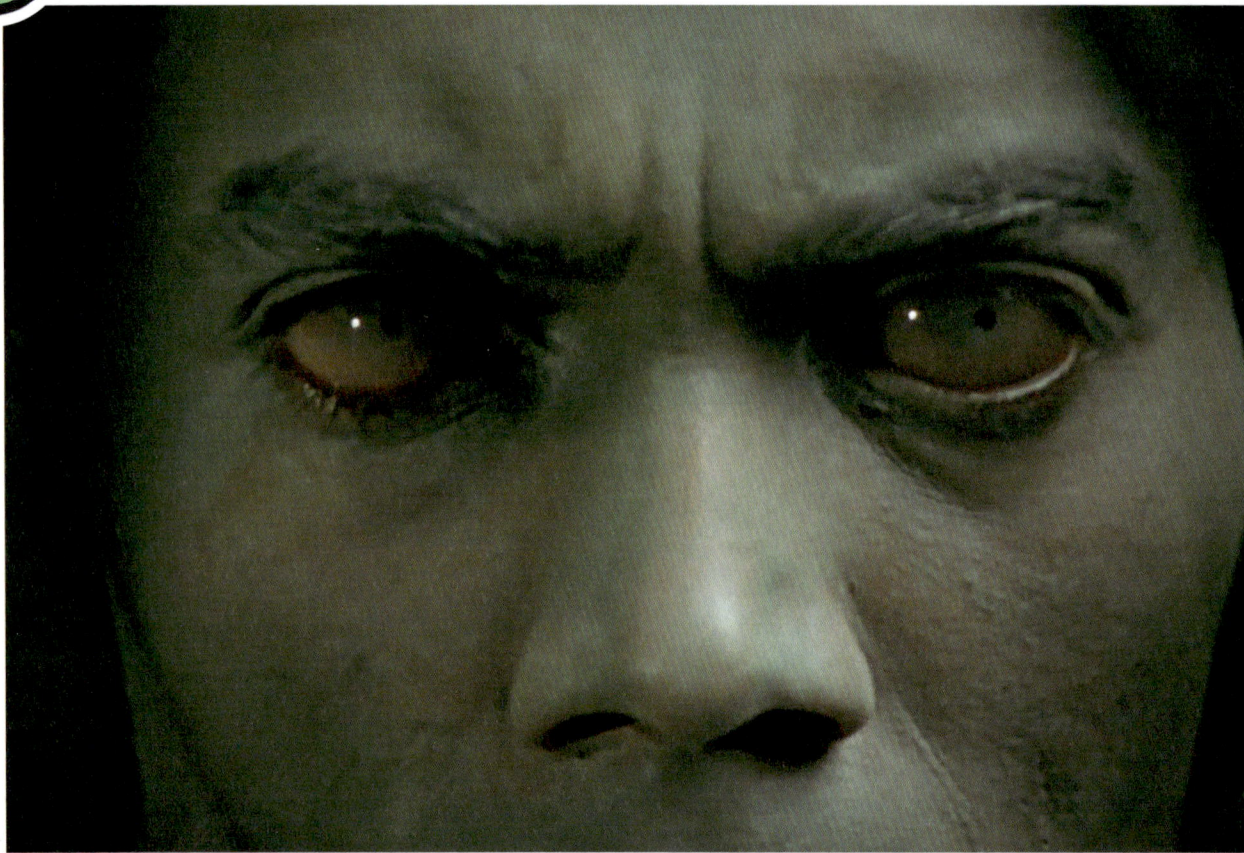

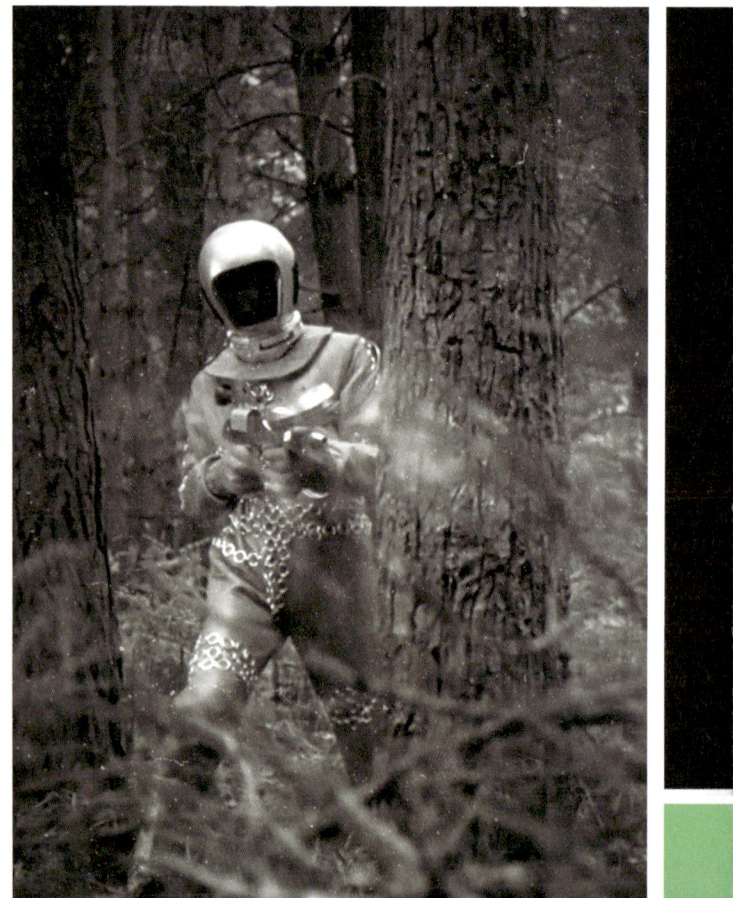

THE ALIENS

SHADO was created to defend the Earth from the threat of hostile alien attacks, but to be as effective as possible in combating these extra-terrestrial forces, three vital questions needed to be answered: Where do the aliens come from? Who are they? What do they want?

In the decade leading up to SHADO's first official operation, there were numerous alien encounters, sightings and traces of UFOs. At that time, it was not possible to track the alien craft, which were travelling beyond the speed of light on their approach to Earth, nor were any effective defensive countermeasures available.

Knowing that the development of such capabilities was only a matter of time, the decision was taken to permit the aliens to arrive and leave without being directly engaged. While such a decision may on the surface seem odd, even reckless, it allowed vital strategic data to be gathered about typical UFO flight corridors and operations.

During this period, abductions were relatively common around UFO incident sites, especially those located in remote areas or at sea. These disappearances were officially covered up – a standard procedure designed to avoid mass panic.

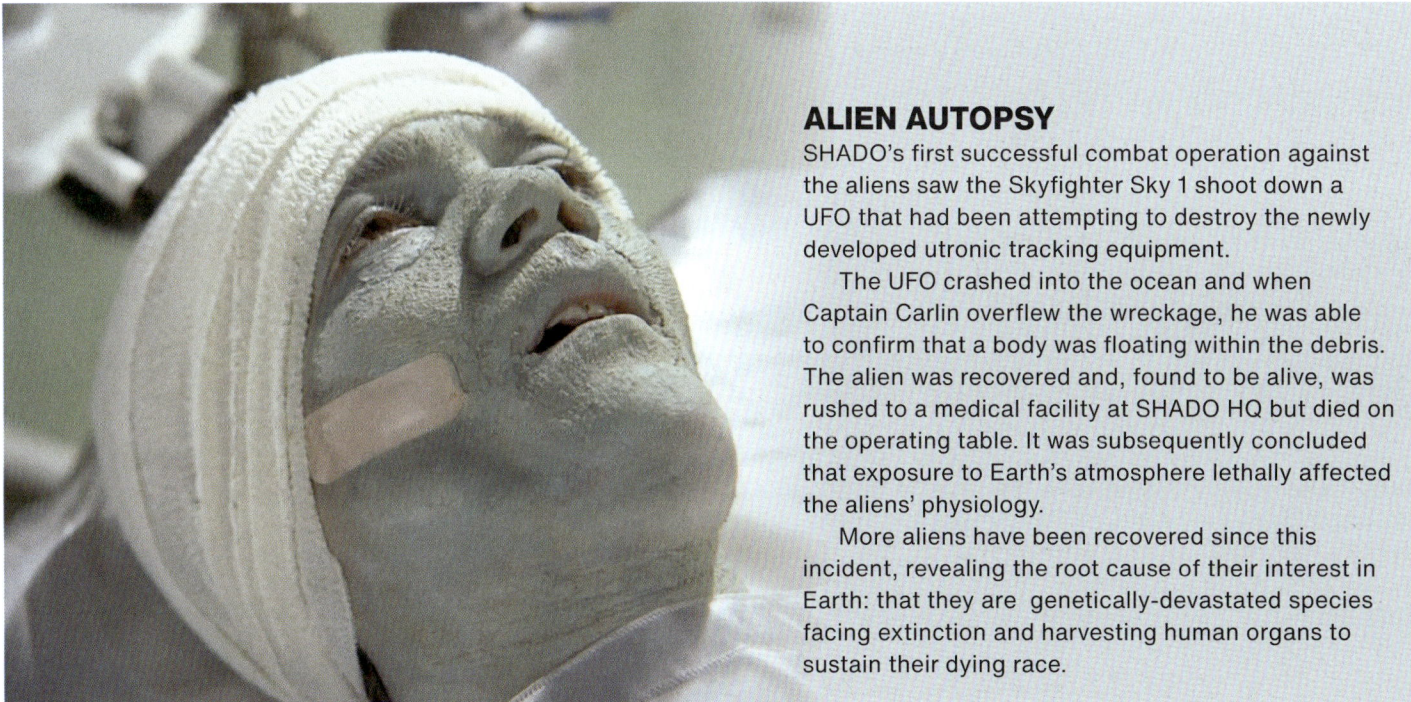

ALIEN AUTOPSY

SHADO's first successful combat operation against the aliens saw the Skyfighter Sky 1 shoot down a UFO that had been attempting to destroy the newly developed utronic tracking equipment.

The UFO crashed into the ocean and when Captain Carlin overflew the wreckage, he was able to confirm that a body was floating within the debris. The alien was recovered and, found to be alive, was rushed to a medical facility at SHADO HQ but died on the operating table. It was subsequently concluded that exposure to Earth's atmosphere lethally affected the aliens' physiology.

More aliens have been recovered since this incident, revealing the root cause of their interest in Earth: that they are genetically-devastated species facing extinction and harvesting human organs to sustain their dying race.

THE ALIEN PLANET

The alien home world was located early in the second year of SHADO's operation. A B142 space probe was reprogrammed to track a UFO on its return trip to its home planet. After almost a year in space, it was able to transmit back the first pictures of the alien world located just beyond the solar system's oort cloud. While a fault in the camera meant it was impossible to assign scale to the images (rendering them strategically useless), the pictures of a barren, desolate world confirmed once and for all the perilous situation the aliens were in. With the location of the alien planet confirmed, a second mission is underway.

As SHADO became more proficient at combating UFO attacks and preventing aliens from reaching Earth, the tempo of the aliens' raids increased. Each new attack became more daring, apparently borne of desperation due to SHADO's increasingly successful efforts at stopping them.

It is estimated that by the end of SHADO's second year in operation, the aliens were failing in about 80–85% of their incursions.

ALIEN WEAPON

The aliens' weapon of choice is comparable in size to a semi-automatic rifle and has the same function. The whole piece is manufactured from highly-polished metal, similar to the composite material found in the helmet of their spacesuits.

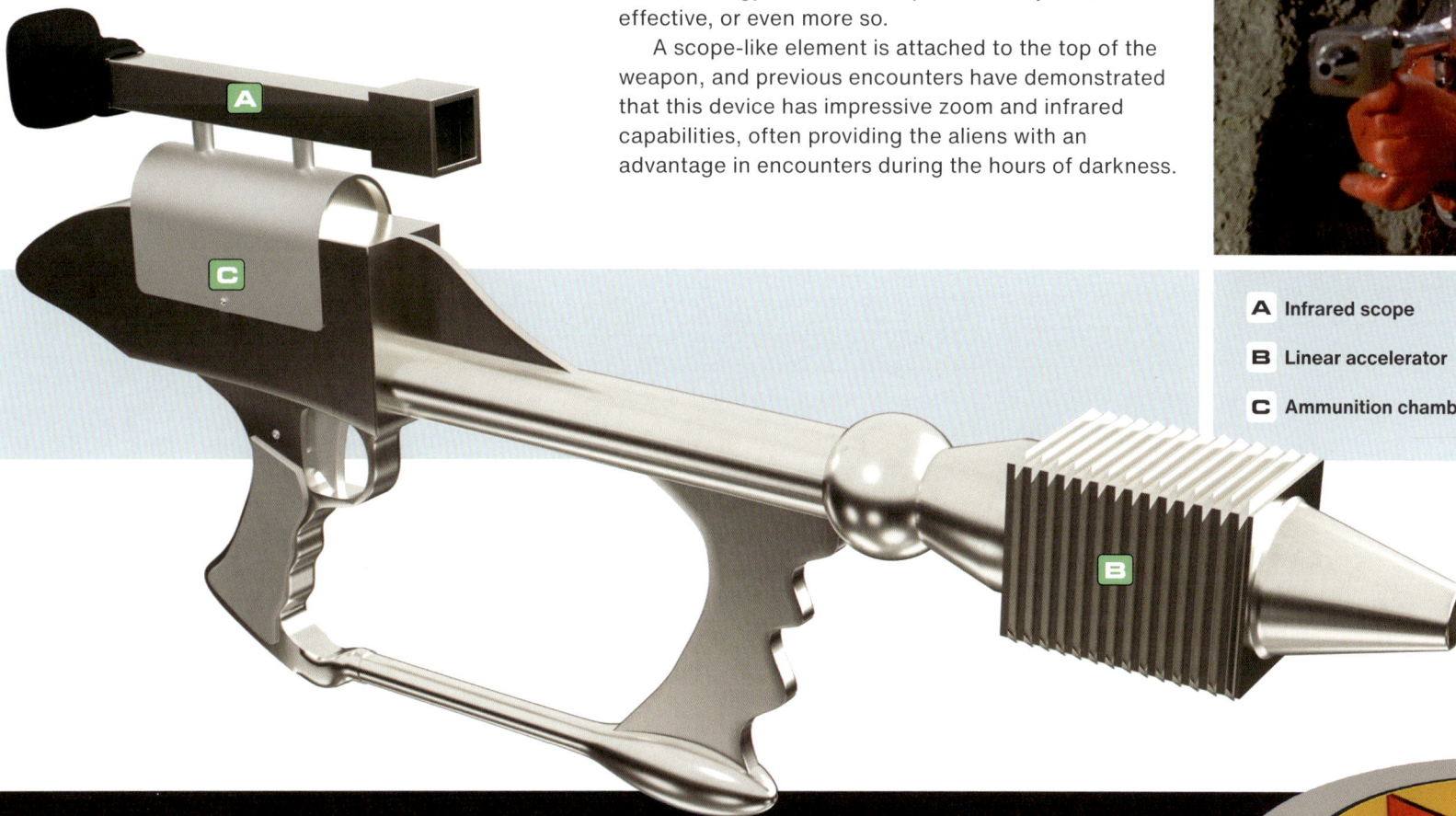

Unlike their spacecraft, the aliens' handheld weapons do not use projected energy beams, but a more conventional form of ammunition. Each round is fired at extremely high velocity, using linear motors and electromagnetic force. This effectively negates the need for explosive projectiles, as the resulting kinetic energy transfer on impact can be just as effective, or even more so.

A scope-like element is attached to the top of the weapon, and previous encounters have demonstrated that this device has impressive zoom and infrared capabilities, often providing the aliens with an advantage in encounters during the hours of darkness.

A Infrared scope

B Linear accelerator

C Ammunition chamber

ADVANCED WEAPONRY

In addition to their standard weaponry, the aliens have employed more advanced technology against SHADO. For example, a large-scale explosive device was recovered in England that could have theoretically devastated the entire country. On other occasions, the aliens have demonstrated an ability to directly control humans and animals through extra-sensory perception and even alter their victims' molecular structure, creating walking psycho-bombs. In one instance, a UFO was able to 'freeze' time around SHADO Control, opening up the facility to a direct attack from the aliens. It is believed that these technologies consume phenomenal amounts of power and resources, requiring the aliens to use them sparingly. This is fortunate as widespread employment would have seen SHADO – and the Earth – very quickly overwhelmed.

SPACE SUIT

The spacesuits worn by the aliens bear superficial similarities to those worn by SHADO personnel in that they are completely sealed from the vacuum of space and – equally vital for the aliens – from contact with Earth's atmosphere. However, that is where the similarities end.

The primary feature of the spacesuit is the life-support system that it contains. The main components of the life-support system are the helmet, the cardiopulmonary unit on the chest section, and the fluid regulator unit on the back portion.

The helmet is made from a composite metal, some elements of which cannot be identified, and features a toughened transparent visor. A green-coloured liquid is pumped into the helmet from the fluid regulator unit on the rear of the suit, while the cardiopulmonary unit helps regulate heart and respiratory functions. It is our hypothesis that the fluid regulator was introduced to help combat the theorised stresses caused by super-light travel. The aliens' physiology is clearly adapted to allow them to use such a method for an extended period of faster-than-light travel, perhaps months at a time or longer. Prolonged exposure to the liquid inside the helmet gives the aliens' skin a characteristic green hue. It has been noted that they wear protective coverings over their eyes possibly to protect them from similar side effects.

A Helmet

B Cardiopulmonary unit

C Fluid regulator

D Protective covering

E Equipment harness

To date, SHADO has identified two notable variants of the spacesuit during encounters with the aliens. The first version has a chainmail-like material covering parts of the arms, torso and legs. The second version replaces this with a flat silver-coloured material that covers the torso and waist. It is unknown whether this material serves a practical purpose, or is purely used to differentiate functions such as mission type or rank.

UFO

UFO is the designation given to a craft of non-terrestrial origin used by aliens to make the long journey across space from their home planet to Earth.

Without having direct access to a functional UFO, much of what is known about the craft has been pieced together from wreckage, debris and a careful study of the aliens themselves. Information has also been gleaned from tracking the interstellar movements of the UFOs, including the location of the alien homeworld.

While the majority of these craft are outwardly identical, they vary in size depending on the number of occupants they carry. To date, SHADO has recorded UFOs ranging in diameter from approximately 20 to 50 feet.

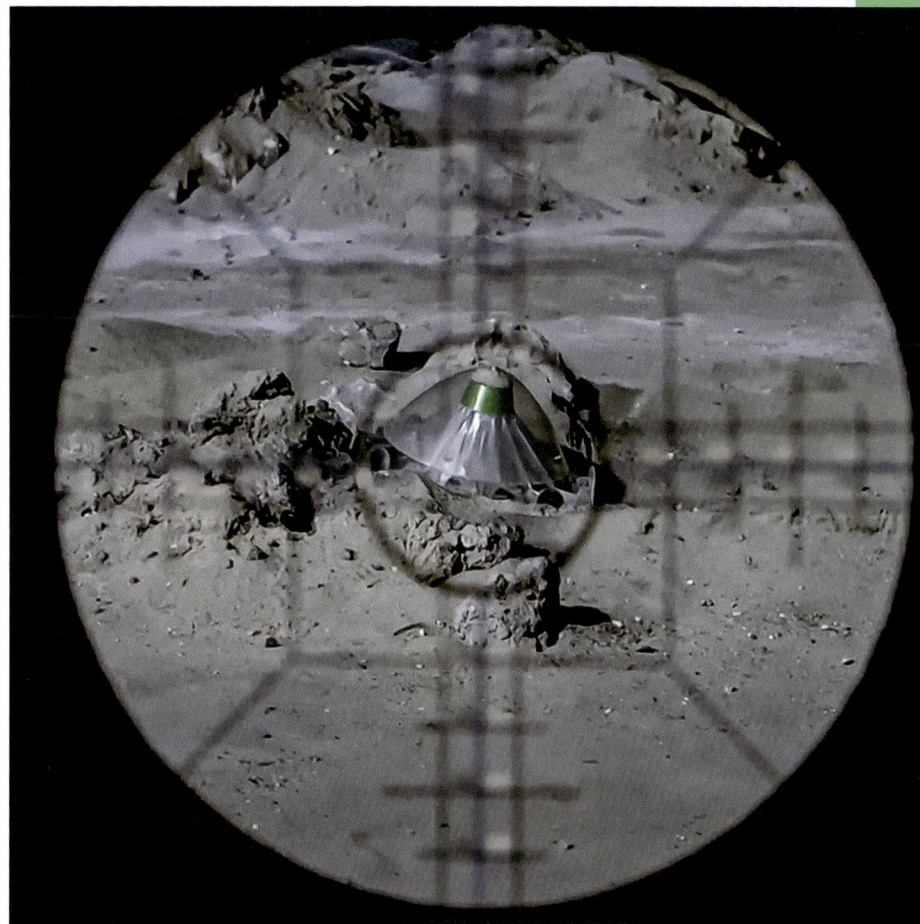

WEAKNESSES

The transparent material covering the majority of the UFO's surface provides an effective screen against direct attack. However, the section of the hull around the rotating paddle assembly is unshielded and is the vessel's only true weak spot. It has been noted that a projectile strike in this region can be enough to cripple or even destroy a UFO.

The UFO has one other distinct vulnerability: its velocity is severely limited in Earth's atmosphere, bringing it within the engagement envelope of the Skydiver fleet and SHADO ground forces.

Furthermore, prolonged exposure to the Earth's atmosphere has a critical destabilising effect on a UFO, causing the craft to disintegrate or explode violently. This side effect of contact with our air makes it virtually impossible to capture an intact UFO for closer examination. It is possible that this reaction is intentional, designed by the aliens as a self-destruct failsafe to prevent their technology from falling into enemy hands.

TRANSMITTER ARRAY

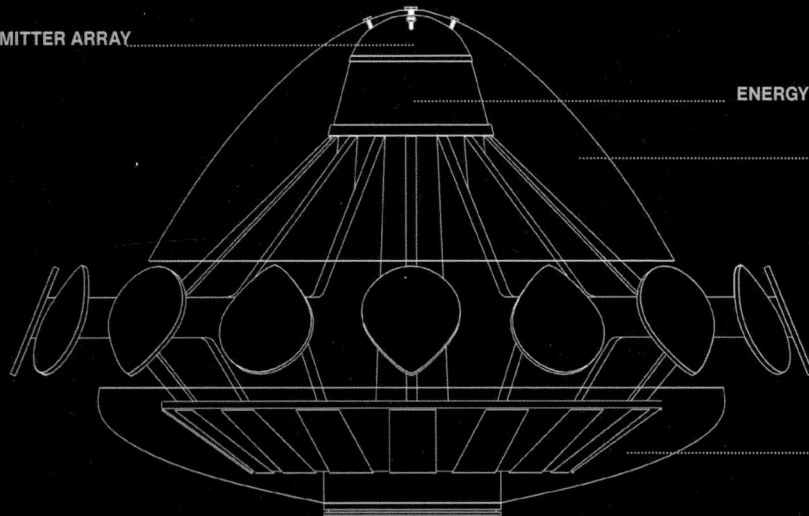

ENERGY WEAPON PROJECTOR

DORSAL PROTECTIVE DOME

VENTRAL PROTECTIVE DOME

ROTATING PADDLE
ASSEMBLY

TEARDROP-SHAPED PADDLE

ESCAPE UNIT

RAMP ACCESS

ENERGY WEAPON

Although UFOs have no visible weapons array, each craft is capable of firing devastatingly powerful energy blasts. These energy generators are far beyond our level of weapons technology and carry a greater destructive power than any experimental laser system currently in development.

The energy required for such attacks is most likely generated as a by-product of the propulsion system, syphoning off excess energy to the craft's weapon projector. Even with additional and reinforced ablative armour, SHADO craft and vehicles don't usually survive a direct hit from a UFO's fully charged energy weapon.

THE DOME

The dorsal portion of the hull is encased in a transparent dome of unknown composition. It is resistant to cutting tools and almost impervious to direct impact by missiles and other weapons. SHADO has designated this transparent material as UCX-01 and has collected fragments of it for analysis from several UFO incident scenes.

Inside the dome, and attached to its underside, is a cylindrical component, which tapers slightly towards the top. This is the transmitter array, an advanced piece of technology with multiple functions.

PROPULSION

Directly below the transmitter array is a conical structure with 16 thin struts attached. Each of the struts is connected to a single teardrop-shaped paddle. The entire assembly rotates at high speed while the UFO is in flight, and therefore the logical assumption is that the assembly is a vital component of the craft's propulsion system.

While travelling in space, UFOs reach relativistic velocities far in excess of the speed of light. The craft are obviously adapted to traverse the vast and empty regions of space in this manner. It is theoretically possible that the shape of the craft, combined with the rotating assembly, may somehow create a slipstream bubble in space, allowing the craft to reach such incredible speeds.

The ventral section of a UFO is encased in a transparent saucer, similar to the dome on the dorsal side. The saucer encloses a platform at the base of the rotating paddle assembly. This platform houses the ramp that provides access to a UFO's interior via a concealed hatch in the side of the craft.

While we are still yet to document the interior of a UFO in detail, Commander Straker and Colonel Foster were able to infiltrate an alien facility on the Atlantic seabed in late 1982. The walls had an almost biomechanical quality and allowed the two operatives to pass through them with little effort. This could account for why we have as yet been unable to identify an entry point on a UFO.

UFO INTERIOR

To date, SHADO has been unable to capture a UFO for study and analysis. As a result, details about the craft's interior are virtually non-existent. However, based on what is already known about the UFOs and the aliens themselves, it is possible to speculate on what the interior of a UFO may contain.

Operative James Regan was debriefed upon his safe return to SHADO following his abduction by aliens in a UFO. He recalled glimpses of a boarding ramp reaching ground level and a darkened room with a glowing green light source. The light source moved over him as if performing a scan. It would appear that the boarding ramp and scanning chamber are located on the lower level of the UFO.

The main cabin is apparently located above the scanning chamber, and it is from here that the aliens must control the UFO and reside during their extended space voyages.

SHADO has encountered UFOs in a variety of sizes and, while outwardly almost identical, the number of occupants within must vary accordingly. Of all the UFO incident scenes SHADO has attended, the largest UFO recorded had a crew of 10, while the majority of others typically hold between one and three aliens.

Propulsion, weapons and life support systems are no doubt monitored and controlled from the main cabin, which is shielded from outside attack by the dome-shaped transparent cover.

Above the main cabin is the transmitter array. This specialised piece of equipment seems to have a variety of functions, including, but not limited to: signalling/communication, defence screen enhancement, sensor jamming, time manipulation within a limited area, and remote control of human subjects via auto-suggestion or advanced hypnosis.

A Transmitter array

B Main control chamber

C Ladder

D Scanning chamber

E Escape pod

F Abductee containment pods

VARIANTS

While the standard UFO is by far the aliens' most frequently deployed craft, other types have been observed in operation, most likely designed to counter SHADO's specialised craft.

ALIEN ESCAPE CRAFT

The Alien Escape Craft (AEC) is a small single-seat type carried aboard some conventional UFOs, providing a means of escape for the occupant in the event of their main ship becoming critically damaged. This small craft is spherical in shape, with the main structure being enclosed in 15 smaller spheres approximately two-thirds of the way down its hull. These small spheres are similar to those found on the subaquatic USO craft and it is reasonable to assume they serve a similar purpose. Several nozzles are positioned on the underside of the craft and are most likely braking and/or landing thrusters for use when the escape craft is in the final stage of its descent.

Use of AEC has been infrequent, seemingly due in part to the outright destruction of UFOs usually inflicted by SHADO forces and the Earth's atmosphere before the escape craft can be deployed. On the rare instances in which SHADO has managed to observe the AEC in operation, it has been noted that it only ever operates in a descent trajectory, never trying to gain altitude. It is theorised that the craft has no ascent capability, therefore making its use an option of last resort.

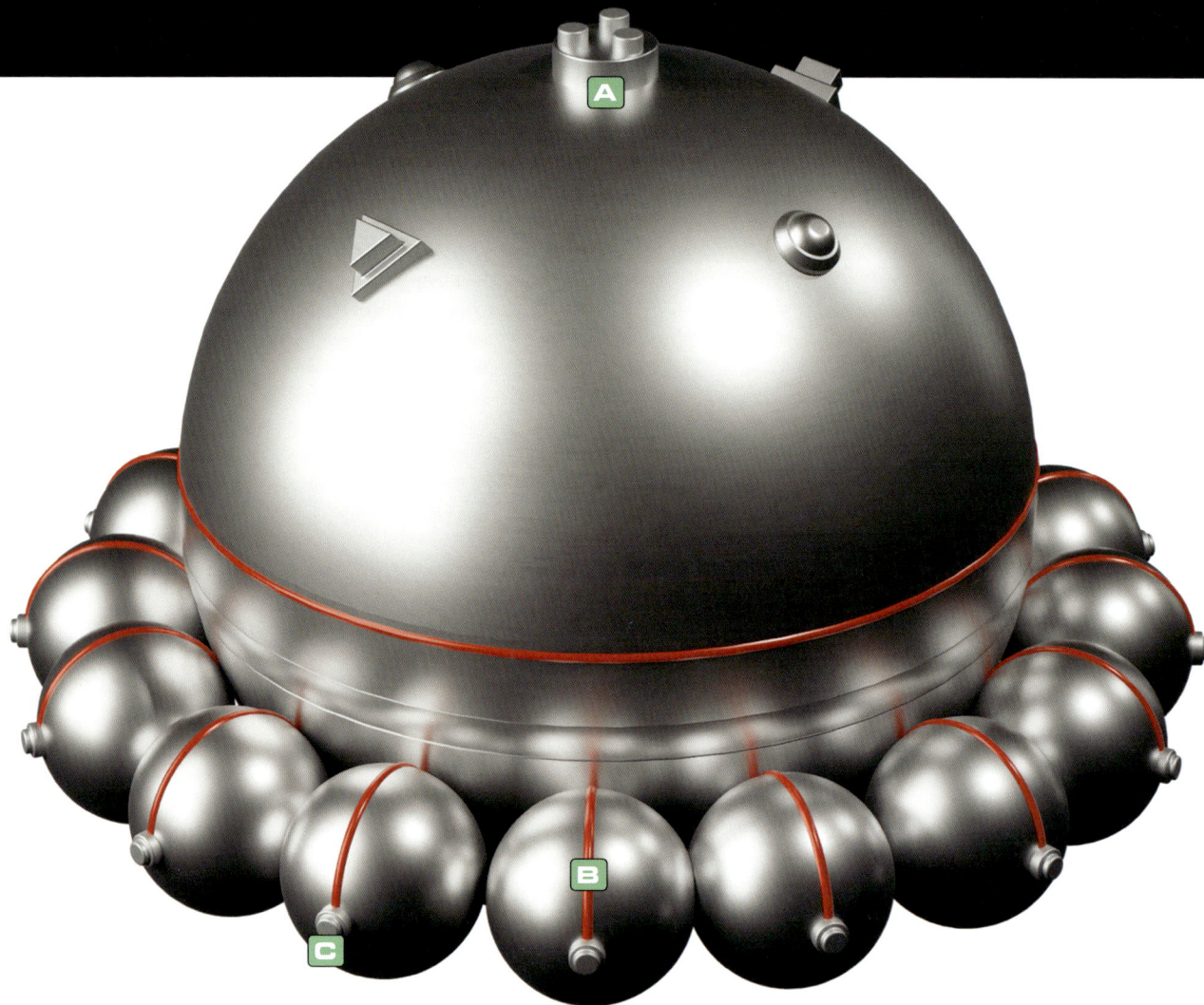

A   Entry hatch

B   Propulsion system

C   Landing motors

UNIDENTIFIED SUBMERGED OBJECT

The Unidentified Submerged Object (USO) is an infrequently-seen subaquatic variant of the typical alien spacecraft. Its design differs considerably from that of a conventional UFO.

It is roughly cylindrical in shape and incorporates a number of small spherical objects around its circumference. These may serve a similar purpose to the rotating paddle assembly on the other UFO craft.

The tapered end of the craft has four fin-like structures surrounding the main energy weapon. Like the weapons found on more commonly seen UFOs, the destructive capability of the USO is considerable. During one encounter, a single strike from a USO was enough to critically damage a Skydiver. Although clearly designed for subsurface operations, the USO can also travel in space and has atmospheric flight capabilities.

To date, there have been no encounters with this type of craft that suggest alien crew on board, so it is remains unknown whether USOs are manned or operated remotely from conventional UFOs.

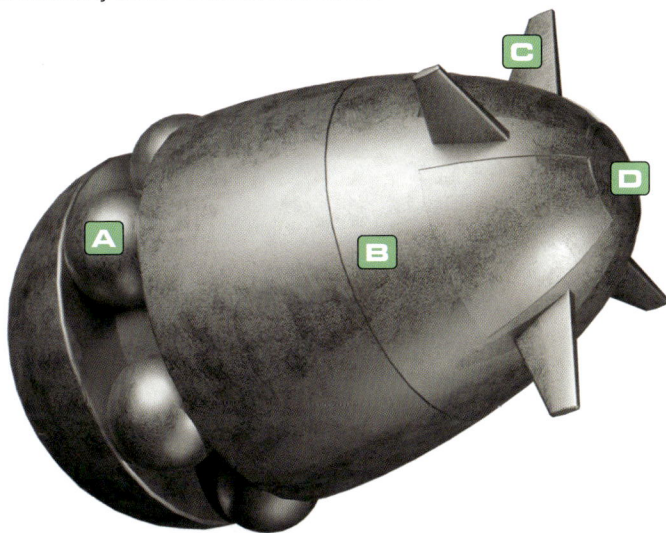

A Propulsion system

B Streamlined hull

C Control fins

D Energy weapon projector

LIMPET UFO

The Limpet UFO is a small and presumably automated alien craft used in infiltration/sabotage operations. The Limpet's small size gives it a major advantage over larger UFOs in that it is exceptionally difficult for SHADO systems to track.

The whole craft is designed around its sole weapon – an artificial gravity generator. While it can't compare with the destructive power of the standard alien energy weapon, the gravity generator can be equally devastating in the right circumstances.

This type of UFO was first encountered when one attached itself to a SHADO Lunar Module returning to Earth. The gravity generator was activated and the Lunar Module was drawn into a much steeper re-entry angle, which the pilot could not compensate for. The Module was destroyed as a result. At the time, it was not certain what had caused the loss of the Module and its crew, but an investigation revealed a Limpet UFO using space junk as a cover from SHADO tracking systems and the UFO was subsequently destroyed.

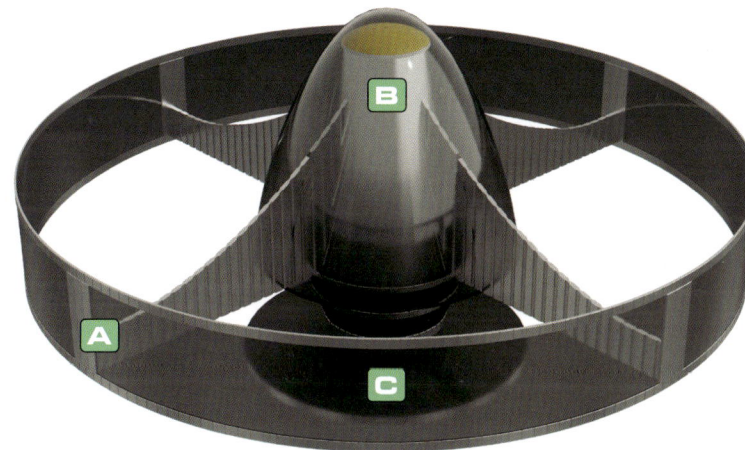

A Gravity generator

B Propulsion system

C Magnetic clamp

COUNTER-ALIEN OPERATIONS

OPERATION PROMETHEUS

Ever since the aliens were first discovered, it has been clear that there was a huge disparity between their technology and ours. Recognising this, it is clear that the aliens themselves have taken measures to ensure that key parts of their technology do not fall into human hands, substituting many of their systems and equipment to a level in parity with their antagonists on Earth. They have also ensured that their UFOs have self-destruct mechanisms that activate when tampered with or when the craft's hull naturally degrades in Earth's atmosphere.

From the very beginning, one of SHADO's key priorities has been to circumvent the aliens' efforts and gather as much information on the UFOs through observation and the recovery of wreckage from crash sites.

At present, SHADO has been able to amass debris from 18 separate UFOs. While the detonation of a UFO's power source is usually enough to completely vaporise much of the craft, it has been possible to recover parts of the outer shell and fins, some preserved on the lunar surface, others within bodies of water which seems to slow down or halt the corrosive effects of Earth's atmosphere. These fragments are housed at SHADO HQ and have given the organisation vital knowledge of the exotic materials that constitute a UFO.

While some familiar materials have been identified, such as steel, aluminium and plastic, unknown elements with extraterrestrial origins have been discovered. The clear material encasing the craft has been designated UCX-01. while components of the body panels have been isolated and catalogued as UMX-01 and UMX-02. These elements have been treated with a type of chemical which causes them to corrode when reacting with the mix of gases in Earth's atmosphere. This can be halted by immersion in liquid or vacuum.

With this knowledge, SHADO has been constructing a facility, built into the outer grounds of Harlington-Straker Studios, that will be able to receive and store an intact UFO. A large temperature-controlled tank containing a formaldehyde/water solution can store a UFO indefinitely, while being able to contain an explosion in the event that the UFO self-destructs.

A smaller, mobile version of this facility has been developed that can assemble itself around a UFO and encase it within a tank that can then be flooded. Given the unusual design of the vehicle, its design and construction used the cover of being an experimental transport for carrying damaged nuclear reactors.

With a facility to receive the delicate spacecraft now complete, SHADO was faced with the much more complex problem of capturing an intact UFO and transporting it from the field to the containment facility. The solution to this problem was designated Operation Prometheus.

RECOVERY VEHICLE

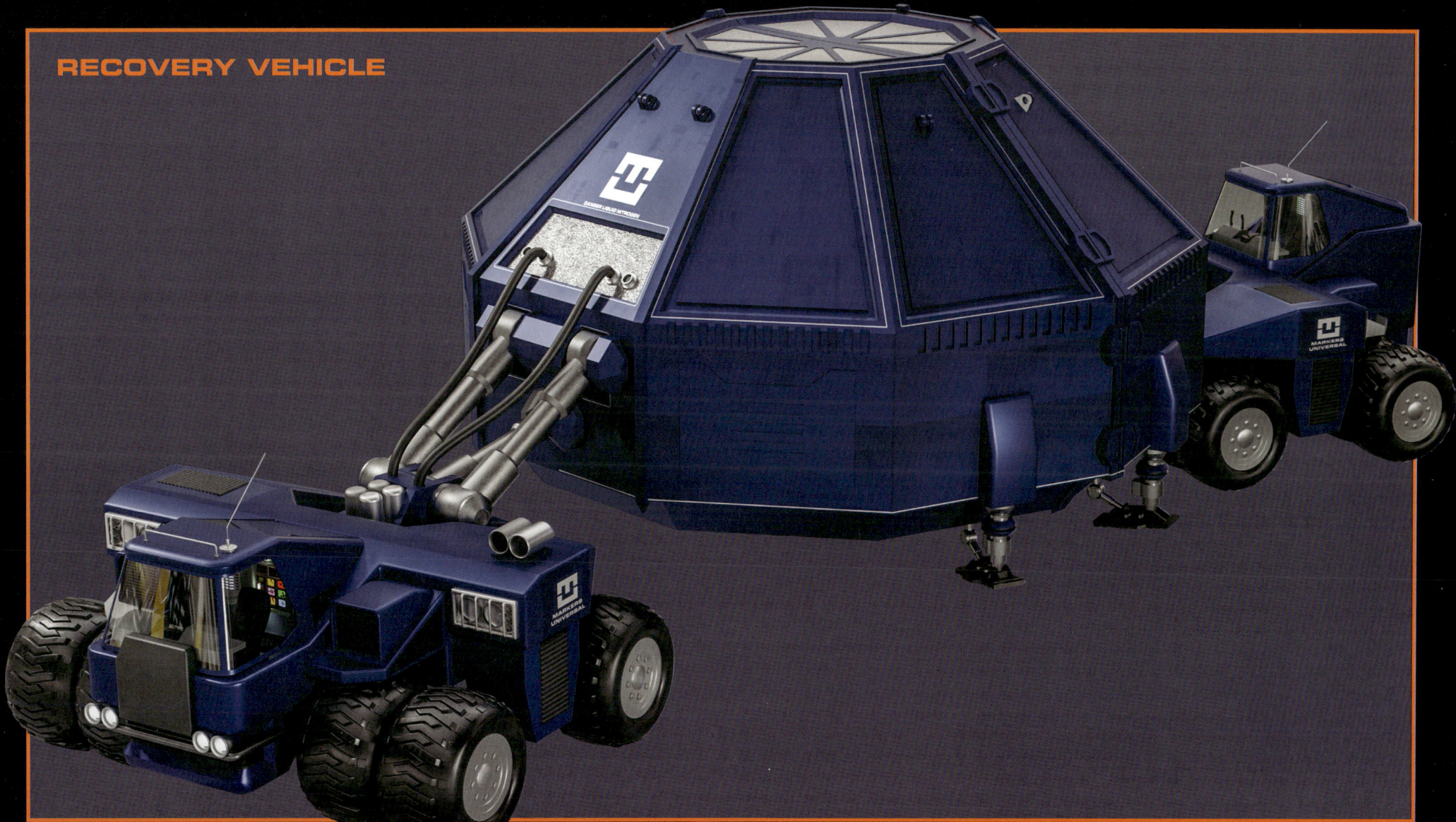

In order for Operation Prometheus to be activated, an approaching UFO needs to meet certain conditions:

SIZE: The UFO must be of dimensions small enough to be accommodated by the Recovery Vehicle.

TRAJECTORY: The UFO must be on a course to a location near enough to an airport capable of receiving SHADair transports. Ideally, the UFO landing site should also be within range of SHADO facilities whose ground forces can quickly secure the area.

COLLATERAL: The landing site must be in an area that can be easily evacuated by SHADO forces.

Once activated, Operation Prometheus proceeds through a number of phases.

PHASE 1

Once arriving on site, SHADO forces need to quickly assess the scene, determine the location of the UFO and ascertain whether the alien crew has disembarked. If available, Mobiles can then create a perimeter while also making every effort to conceal their presence.

PHASE 2

SHADO forces then separate the alien crew from their craft by any means necessary. The capture of a live alien is a priority, but secondary to the capture of the craft itself. Phase 2 is deemed successful if all alien contact and control with the craft has been severed, leaving the UFO inert.

PHASE 3

A safety perimeter is established around the craft, while local fire appliances can be requisitioned in order to keep the craft saturated with water and slow the atmosphere's corrosive effects while operatives wait for the Recovery Vehicle to arrive.

PHASE 4

The Recovery Vehicle is deployed. This vehicle splits in two to encompass the UFO, then lifts the craft using its interior grabs and seals it within the tank into which the formaldehyde/water solution is then pumped to halt corrosion. If successful, the UFO is now prepared for transit.

PHASE 5

The Recovery Vehicle is shipped back to SHADO HQ where it can lower its cargo tank into the containment facility. Once in the tank and submerged in liquid, the UFO is considered safe for study.

OPERATION CHIMAERA

Operation Chimaera is the codename given to a planned strike on the alien homeworld utilising a deadly virus developed by SHADO scientists.

While SHADO was initially created to act as a defensive organisation, as time went on and the alien attacks became more frequent and desperate, it became clear that alternative courses of action needed to be explored.

Doctor Jackson submitted the radical proposal known as Operation Chimaera to Commander Straker for his approval. At the time, this move was met with strong opposition from Colonels Alec Freeman and Paul Foster and, ultimately, Operation Chimaera was designated a plan of last resort.

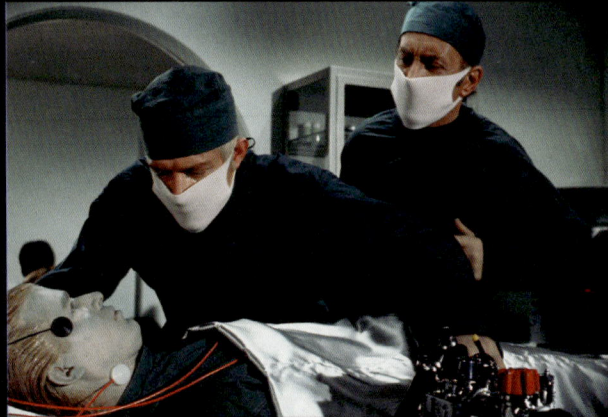

During the examination of one alien subject, SHADO doctors discovered that in addition to the advanced ageing typical of exposure to Earth's atmosphere, the alien also showed signs of extreme viral infection that could only have been contracted by exposure to an infected human. It was therefore theorised that the aliens themselves have a low resistance to viral infections and the theory was later proven to be true under laboratory conditions using samples of alien DNA. This discovery led to the fast-track creation of a genetically engineered virus, VK-50, as a potential weapon against the aliens.

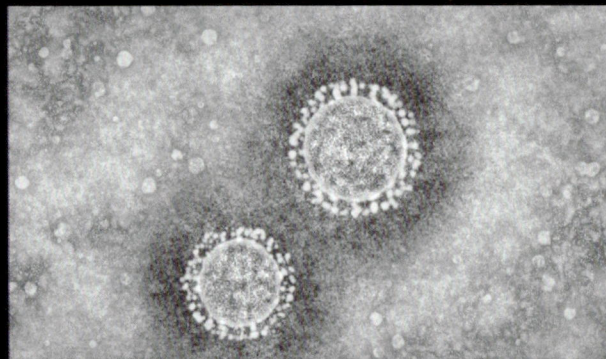

In order for VK-50 to be contracted by an alien, it would be necessary for them to have exposure to a human carrier. The idea of deliberately introducing the virus into a human host raised a number of moral questions when the proposal was first recommended. Doctor Jackson suggested that the selection of suitable human carriers should be limited to those currently serving life sentences for violent crimes.

The first stage of the operation requires a UFO with an estimated trajectory that terminates in close proximity to one of the chosen prison facilities. Once this has been confirmed by SID, the Moonbase Interceptors will attack the UFO, firing close enough to convince the aliens that the attack is real, while ensuring the UFO makes it through to Earth.

At the same time, the chosen prisoner, or group of prisoners, will be given a supposed inoculation (in reality, a carefully calculated dose of VK-50), before being loaded aboard a SHADO transport with the cover story that they are being transferred to another secure facility to serve the rest of their sentence. En route to the fictitious destination, the SHADO vehicle will be forced to stop at the site of a staged road traffic accident and in the confusion, the prisoners will be allowed to 'escape' in the vicinity of the UFO.

Given the aliens' previous modus operandi, the most likely scenario will be that they will capture at least one of the target humans for transport back to their planet. Once there, any exposure with the infected human will result in the aliens contracting the highly contagious virus and passing it on throughout their population at an exponential rate. Doctor Jackson's best estimates give a projected infection count in the region of half a billion individuals in the space of three to four weeks.

While Operation Chimaera is a weapon of last resort, the aforementioned moral questions raised should be weighed carefully before the plan is carried out.

It is a foregone conclusion that anyone captured by a UFO during the operation would be killed. Additionally, the inherent danger of allowing a UFO to land is not insignificant, nor is the threat of allowing violent criminals to be released, even if they unknowingly remain inside a wide SHADO cordon.

It should be noted that VK-50 is eventually lethal to humans, although the effects of the disease manifest more slowly. As a result, any prisoners not abducted by the aliens will be recaptured by SHADO forces and quarantined until their demise.

If successfully put into effect, Operation Chimaera would mean almost certain annihilation of the entire population of the alien planet. However, for a race already threatened by total sterility and on the threshold of extinction, such an action, taken to save countless human lives, could be considered merciful.

OPERATIONAL AREA MAP SITE ALPHA

As part of the testing phase for Operation Chimaera, a mock version of the operation was undertaken in a remote part of the Scottish Highlands, with paid actors filling in for the role of the convicts. From these tests SHADO has been able to ensure a reasonable degree of success should the criteria to enact the plan be met.

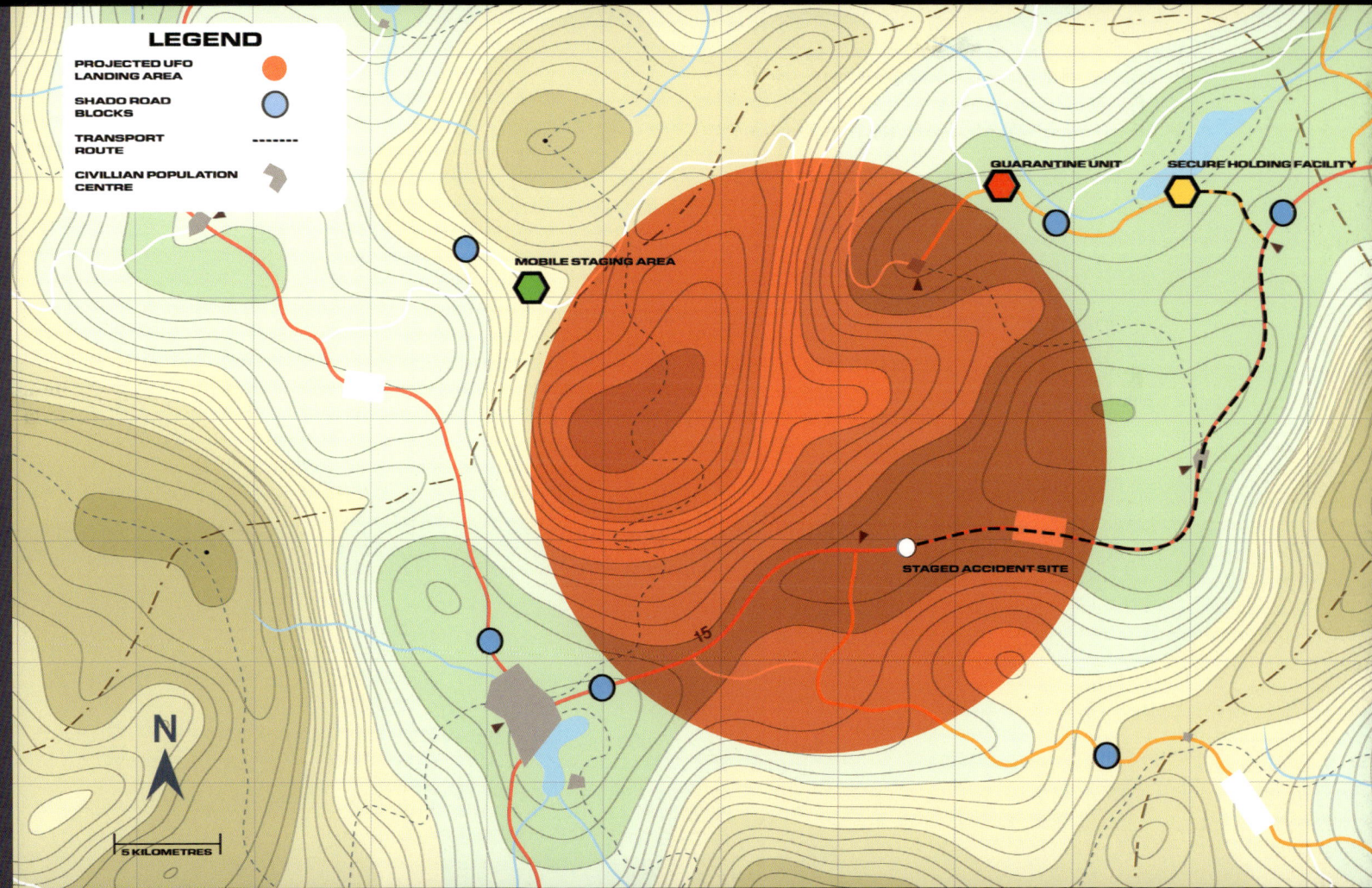

LEGEND

- PROJECTED UFO LANDING AREA
- SHADO ROAD BLOCKS
- TRANSPORT ROUTE
- CIVILLIAN POPULATION CENTRE

QUARANTINE UNIT

SECURE HOLDING FACILITY

MOBILE STAGING AREA

STAGED ACCIDENT SITE

15

N

5 KILOMETRES

As I write these words, SHADO has been operating for three years, two months and twelve days. In that time, we have successfully destroyed 142 UFOs, gained meaningful intelligence about the aliens and the planet they come from, and saved countless lives. We have an actionable plan to potentially purloin and 'back-engineer' their technology for weapons and craft of our own, and maybe, just maybe, a possibility of ending the threat they pose once and for all.

This has not come without cost. The 7,000 people who run SHADO's day-to-day operations have, for the moment, given up any hope of a normal life. They are unable to tell their loved ones what they really do, what is really happening, and the unspoken sacrifices they are making for the Greater Good. And lest we forget, 103 operatives have given their lives in the line of duty and to protect our homes. They go unhonoured in the wider world, but we won't forget them.

I spent 13 years of my life developing SHADO and I look forward to the day I give the final order for it to stand down. To evacuate Moonbase, send the people under my command home to their families, close the installation and fill it in with concrete and gravel, and stand under the sky, knowing that there's no longer anything to fear from it. Sadly that day is still a long way off.

SHADO
SUPREME HEADQUARTERS ......
ALIEN DEFENCE ORGANISATION...

SECRET LOCATION .... BENEATH FILM STUDIO

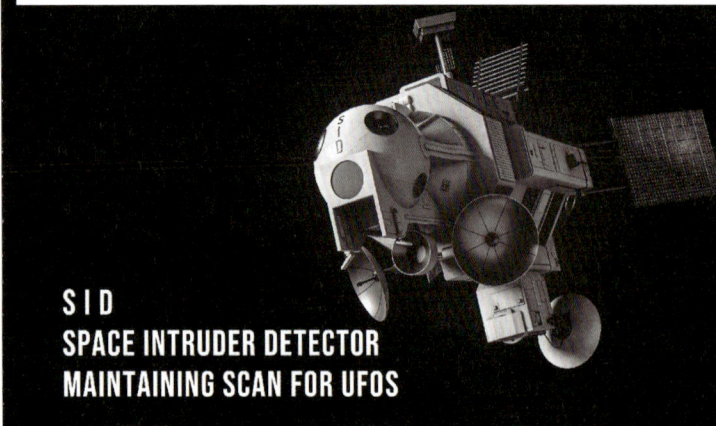

SID
SPACE INTRUDER DETECTOR
MAINTAINING SCAN FOR UFOS

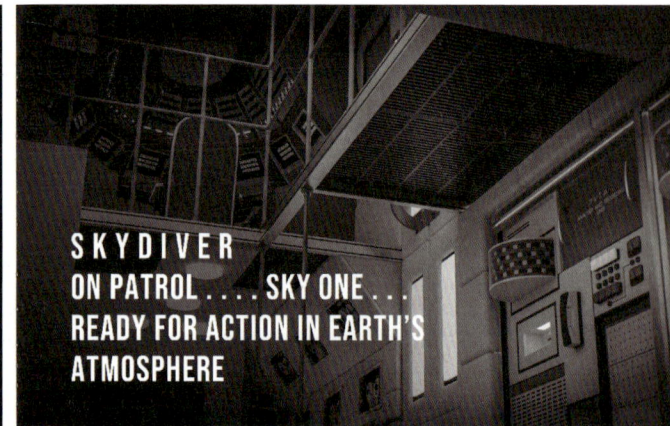

SKYDIVER
ON PATROL ..... SKY ONE ...
READY FOR ACTION IN EARTH'S ATMOSPHERE

Our analytics department has noticed an upward trend in UFO attacks and projects that, if the rate continues to rise, SHADO forces will find themselves stretched to their operational limits. In addition, the aliens have been using increasingly advanced techniques to disrupt our organisation. Could this be the start of a desperate gambit as they fear their own extinction looms, or have the aliens finally decided to see us as the true threat we really are?

I do not know what form the next phase of this war will take, but ultimately it will be you, standing alongside your colleagues and as a vital part of SHADO, who will safeguard the future of this planet.

GOOD LUCK, OPERATIVE.

COMMANDER EDWARD STRAKER......

MOBILES.....
ALL OPERATIONAL

MOONBASE
TRACKER SYSTEMS AND SPACE
INTERCEPTORS OPERATIONAL

![S.H.A.D.O.]

TECHNICAL OPERATIONS MANUAL

Written and Illustrated by
CHRIS THOMPSON

Sections 5 and 6 Written by
ANDREW CLEMENTS

Edited by
STEVE WHITE

Sub-Edited by
MARTIN EDEN

Project Management
and Book Design by
AMAZING15

Vehicle Painting by
GRAHAM BLEATHMAN

Uniform Illustrations by
CHRISTINA LOGAN

Produced by
JAMIE ANDERSON

**UFO created by
Gerry and Sylvia
Anderson**

WITH THANKS TO:
Ralph Edenbag, David Hirsch, Alannah
McDaid, Steph Briggs and Tim Collins

UFO

UFO ™ and © ITC Entertainment Group 1969 and 2022. Licensed by ITV Studios Limited. All Rights Reserved.

First published in the UK in 2022 by Anderson Entertainment.

Hardback 978-1-914522-40-6

Printed at Interak Printing House, Poland

itv STUDIOS
GLOBAL ENTERTAINMENT

ANDERSON ENTERTAINMENT

GERRYANDERSON.COM